# KRATU

SAMARPAN is a Hindu monk, teacher, and writer of several books, articles, memoirs, among other publications. His articles, under his monastic name, have appeared in various journals. His talks on scriptures are available online. Presently, he teaches ancient and modern scriptures at the deemed university of the organization to which he belongs.

## BOOKS BY THE AUTHOR

### Philosophical Fiction

*Tiya: A Parrot's Journey Home*
*Param*
*Junglezen Sheru*
*Carving a Sky: A Perspective on Life*

### Non-fiction

*Living Hinduism: Scriptures, Philosophy, Practices*
*The World of Religions*
*The Hindu Way*

### Hindi Poetry

*Pathik*

# KRATU

**SAMARPAN**

PAN

First published 2021 by Pan
an imprint of Pan Macmillan Publishing India Private Limited
707 Kailash Building,
26, K. G. Marg, New Delhi – 110 001
www.panmacmillan.co.in

Pan Macmillan, 6 Briset St, Farringdon, London EC1M 5NR
Associated companies throughout the world
www.panmacmillan.com

ISBN 978-93-89104-64-6



1 3 5 7 9 8 6 4 2



Typeset in Dante MT Std by R. Ajith Kumar, New Delhi
Printed in India by Gopsons Papers Pvt. Ltd., Noida.

*At the holy feet of*

*Ma*

*whose blessings made* Kratu *a reality*

# CONTENTS

# FOREWORD

Dear Samarpan,

This was a royal gift indeed, and like all priceless gifts, given to me freely, for which I thank you, my brother and friend in need.

I have been moved beyond words by the tale of Kratu: immense in scale, encompassing the *tri kaal* of past, present, and future. Your work of inspiration reminds me of the words of Rajaji who, in describing the Mahabharata, said (as I recall, without Kratu's gift/curse of perfect memory): 'Ordinary novels aim to thrill the senses, exciting the emotions of the reader, to reach "happily-ever-after" fairytale endings, or in terrible tragedy and destruction. The divine tales of Ramayana and Mahabharata, however, take us through the journey of human nature, and elevate us in the end to the consciousness of the Ultimate Divinity.'

Indeed Kratu had this effect on me. I thank you and, through you, your entire *Guru-Parampara* and Ma Durga Herself, for giving this unworthy human being such a marvellous experience.

The tale weaves its magical way across an immense timespan, threaded with masterly skill, truly like beads on a thread, as Kratu grows through his experiences to fulfil his sworn Karma. The tale is filled with pearls of eternal wisdom, scattered without a care across the pages, with the generosity of a Kubera of Knowledge. Aphorisms hang like ripe mangoes from the boughs of this tree of knowledge and deep learning. I marvel at the spontaneous inspiration of the author that the entire work was conceived and penned in a matter of 8 weeks. Only divine inspiration could have made this possible. The quick interludes with the Great Sages of our culture – Valmiki, Vyasa, Kapila, Shankara, Buddha and others – sparkle with spiritual light, leaving one in awe of the immensity of our civilization. I, for one, am indeed convinced that we are indeed at the start of the next Satya Yuga, and our land has the strength of culture, knowledge, and discipline to lead the way to the Indian Renaissance of the 21st century. This book is not only a reminder of our heritage, but also the harbinger of our destiny.

**K. Gopalakrishnan**
Eminent Scholar and Technocrat
Singapore

# PART ONE

# 1

# THE ROCK

The huge, insurmountable rock – standing majestic amidst the spread of smaller ones – was the meeting ground of the divine and the profane for the local people. The elderly talked about the legends centring around it, while the youngsters inscribed their names and the names of their failed loves on it.

Unconcerned with the meanderings of human nature, a yogi sat immobile on the rock by stopping his consciousness from becoming many. Living only on air for years on the height, he was now mere skin and bones; his clothes had tattered away long ago, and his matted hair was used as a nest by small birds. People of the area had not seen him come there and so they did not add him in the local legends.

The march of progress does not care for the secular or the sacred. It now demanded that the monolith be blasted away to make space for fresh dreams. The team assigned to do the job had drilled holes in that rock and had planted explosives to complete the inevitable.

'All ready, sir.' cried the foreman of the team, asking for the green signal for the blast.

The project manager thought of climbing up the rock to have one last view of the surroundings from its top before it was smothered into nothingness forever. However, its sheer steepness deterred him. He looked sadly at the majestic rock: 'Millions of years of being going away in a *twing*!'

Shaking his head vigorously, he drove the thought away. He was not paid to philosophize but to carry out orders.

Looking around to make sure that all was safe, he gave the thumbs up with '*Alfred Nobel ki Jai*', musing at the irony of Alfred Nobel being the creator of major destructive power and also the bestower of the Nobel Peace prize. 'Irony, thy name is power.'

'*B-O-O-M!*' was the response from the splintering rock.

One now became many; the individual degenerated into the collective; the inert became mobile and the mobile went dead. Birds fell to the ground, animals went flying through the air, heavier trees were uprooted, lighter ones swayed wildly, and rocks boomed all around. Energy, milked from the universe and preserved in the dynamite stick, *hoosh*-ed back to its freedom, flattening everything that separated it from being one with the universal.

The yogi on the rock was among those who faced the fury of the once-trapped. Unseen by anyone, he was thrown up into the sky on a parabolic path. His indifference towards the world had come back as its cruelty towards him.

The shock of the boom and the fall of the flight pulled the yogi's mind from the great to the small. By the time he hit the grassy surface, his mind had become one with his senses and his organs competed for attention. After that, it did not take long for him to be one with the multiplicity of Nature. The yogi, downed from the realm of consciousness, now belonged to the world of senses.

Dazed, he lay amidst tall grass, watching his consciousness spread over his body. When fully conscious, he felt weak and weary. Lying there for a while, he gained some strength and then he staggered to get some food, wondering if his body would tolerate the intrusion of food after such a long break from it. 'Long break! Yes. How long ago was it that I last felt the world?'

No one in the world had the answer.

Weak foundation makes a heap of a structure. The yogi got up, but his legs failed him. He collapsed like the fame of the respected whose hidden sins get exposed. He panted under the weight of his frailty.

Breathing slowly and consciously, he gained a little strength. With that, he encouraged his feeble limbs to drag him to a point from where he could get a sweeping view of what lay around.

His attention was caught by the asphalt road on which cars and buses were moving at a distance. He looked at them intently, wondering what those things were. Chariots? Carts? But where were the horses? Camels? Or bullocks? How could these be self-driven? Had he by some chance reached the heaven where the gods had self-driven vehicles? He could also see wires stretching out on huge structures to the infinite, as it were. What were these? He felt confused.

A big black ant crawled up his body harmlessly. The tickling caused by it told him that he was in no heaven, which was confirmed by the chiming of a bell in a nearby temple. He remembered something. Yes, there had been a Shiva temple near the rock where he had gone to sit for meditation long ago. He concluded that he was not in any heaven, rather he was in the same place where he had originally been.

Familiarity gives confidence. The yogi felt confident of getting some milk at the temple. After all, people did pour milk on *Shivalingam*, the symbol of Shiva. He hoped that the practice had not changed over the years, as is the wont of the world.

He had crawled barely some feet when he heard the conversation of a couple coming down the narrow path. The turn had hidden them from view, and now he was plumb in their path, barely a minute away.

The lady's voice made him conscious of his lack of clothes. 'What to do? What to do?' He panicked. There was no place where he could hide his nakedness.

The couple, returning from the temple, had been married for some years without having any child. Someone had advised them to walk miles and pray at that temple to have their wishes fulfilled. The boom of the dynamite just after their prayer was taken by the lady as a sign from God. 'Shiva has listened to us!' said she.

'Coincidences are not signs, dear,' said the husband.

'You are so negative! I wonder why I chose you for myself.'

'Ok, ok. It must be the sign if you say so.' The gentleman wanted to retain his poise after a deep religious moment.

On their way back from the temple, they talked about the choice of the baby, not knowing that a naked yogi lay in their path.

Stupidity, the Siamese twin of panic, took over the yogi's rational mind. 'Baby! Hmm, baby. If only I were a baby I would have been saved from this embarrassment of my nakedness.'

Before his thought could form fully, he felt waves of

unconsciousness taking over his limbs and mind, and his senses started withdrawing from their respective apertures.

The yogi went inert.

When his awareness returned, the yogi found himself as a baby in the arms of the lady who had been to the Shiva temple. The lady, surrounded by many others, was cooing over him, the baby, calling out adjectives like 'precious', 'prince', and 'gift from God'.

People laugh at the fallen, while fallen ones cry.

'Oh, no! Not again,' shrieked the yogi-baby in unfathomable agony, 'I am no one's prince or precious. Lord! Lord! Why this! Why this! How I wish I was saved from this ordeal of getting a new body. Now I will have to go once again through the trauma of growing up and the terror of learning; bondage packaged as love from parents, siblings, friends and frenemies; sacksful of tears wrapped in laughter; buckets of disease and baskets of decay. Oh Lord! How I wish you had saved me by letting me be where I was. But what do you care for others when you did not save yourself from being exiled and getting crucified? No wonder people refuse to accept you the way you are.'

Words are the privilege of the evolved. The lamentations of the baby did not come as words but as cries because of his underdeveloped vocal system.

'How cute he is,' said one. 'How cutely he cries,' said another.

Tears, the integral of pain, now accompanied the words of the yogi-baby. More than anguish, the words carried a soft complaint towards God.

Why thou push me once 'gain
In the band of broken tunes
Shrieking, yelling, noise loud
With soothing note of real me
Fizzing away in bitter, vain.

I was not with aught or naught
But as 'art and beat of all—
Beyon' little, half and part
Beyond count one or two
Free of body, senses, thought.

Why you wielded magic wand
To make me one with light seven
In the realm of rearing pain,
Smiles masking tears roaring
Birth n death's this murky land.

He cried his heart out till he was too exhausted to continue and feel asleep.

A smile is the product of certainty, good or bad. Once he was up from sleep, he was filled with, 'been there, seen that' feeling. The absurdity attached with his situation made him laugh at himself.

'How beautifully he smiles! A wonder kid he is.'

'Why not? Isn't he a blessing from Lord Shiva?'

His torment was multiplied when his nappy was changed and when he was breastfed. 'Yuck...,' he cringed and let out a long wail. He also closed his eyes, to hands touching his helpless body when he was bathed.

The naming ceremony for the baby was performed, which is one of the age-old customs, coming from the Vedic times. It is one of the sixteen *samskaras* – life rituals of a Hindu – through which a person evolves in social and spiritual existence.

There is a lot to names than one cares to understand. A name is the outrider of the form, representing the aspirations, hope, capabilities and essence of a person. In turn, the right name augments one's nature. So, Indians put a lot of stress on naming a baby and treat the ceremony as one of the major events of life.

After some deliberation, the baby was named Kratu. Kratu is one of the great sages of ancient India. The word also means 'sacred act'.

Everyone in the family loved the name. 'Hmm,' the yogi-baby reacted, 'New form. New name. New acts. The cycle goes on. What a pity! Worse, even if people knew this to be a fact, they would continue wishing for the same again and again, hoping to have better luck next time. Haven't I seen the same story repeated all through my existential memory?' He let out the yawn of the bored.

'What a cute yawn!' the guests clapped.

Kratu's grandmother had died some years before his birth. Remembering her, his grandfather smiled gently at the baby, 'Your grandma would have been so happy to take you in her arms.'

'Hmm,' he responded in boredom.

The obnoxious fawning of the family on Kratu ended when his sister, Anvi, was born. The new toy in the family meant fresh joy for the emotionally challenged. This gave Kratu space to explore life.

Exploration, knowledge, freedom. Life had revealed its secret to Kratu in simple steps. The absence of these three meant bondage.

Kratu started taking in the world of beings and happenings. His intellect, honed on the grinding stones of silence and purity, was now so fine that it could pick up the tiniest strand of knowledge from which he had been away during these years of absence. Electricity, mobility, connectivity – the three modern wonders – revealed their secrets to him in no time. The gadgets soon became slaves to him instead of being the masters.

Unlike gadgets, music fascinated him endlessly. His parents were surprised to see that instead of the fast beating of drums that kids usually like, Kratu remained transfixed while listening to classical music.

'Looks like Tansen is born in our family,' said Ma.

'Wait till he gets exposed to percussion and then starts breaking the household items,' said Pa.

'You are so negative,' retorted Ma.

Kratu paid no attention to these bickering; he was used to the behaviour of the doting.

His observation of the surroundings revealed that the world had undergone a qualitative change, unlike the linear change that it usually goes through. The Indian word '*samsara*' for world means 'that which keeps wandering', and so there was nothing unusual about the change. Even then, some changes were stark. People had moved away from the ideals of life to having life as the ideal. Packaging in life had taken over, replacing completeness. Even moms were now part time. Exclusiveness was no more a vice but way of life.

'Time, you spare no one. Even values get crushed under your juggernaut,' said he. 'How long can a society survive like this?'

Change or no change, he did not like strong emotions. One day he said, 'Ma, you were angry yesterday, so I got very scared.'

'It is ok, *beta*. Ma is not angry anymore. Can Ma be ever angry with her dear one?'

'It is not that, Ma. I got scared so I cleaned up your bathroom.'

'That is not needed, son,' she laughed, 'we in India do not like our kids to work. Once I am dead, you can work as much as you want. This is time for you to enjoy life.'

'I mean I cleaned the bathroom with your towel.'

'You did what?' laughed out Papa.

The sweet words of Ma fermented in a trice. She was furious. She remembered that the towel was wet when she was using it and she had wondered at the reason for that. Probably it had fallen down, she had thought.

Angry, she was about to scream when Kratu said, 'Please don't scream at me. I get scared and then do foolish things.'

The next time when Ma got angry, Kratu did not wipe his butt clean after going to the toilet and informed her about it the next day. He added, 'I cannot do the same thing every time I get scared. So I think I will have to hide in the drain or in the overhead water tank next time.'

That was the end of Ma's anger with Kratu.

'See how your son has taught you anger management and saved thousands from the counsellor, ' said Pa.

'Do you want to learn a few things in humour management?'

Kratu's grandpa had been a schoolteacher. In his time, schools were treated as temples, and education focussed more on man-making than money-making. This demanded sacrifice and discipline from the teachers, which they passed down to their students.

Grandpa's self-discipline and routine had earned him respect from his students and also from his family. After his retirement, he applied his lifelong discipline in improving his inner self through puja, *japam*, *dhyan* and reading of religious texts. He believed that after a certain age, one should pack up one's affairs and get ready for the onward journey. 'The world is the training ground to give up everything so that one can attain God. To remind us of this fact, death forces us to give up all that we have. However, foolish that we are, we refuse to learn and so suffer.'

Years of selfless service at the school and spiritual detachment in old age had given him deeper insights in human nature. One day he told Kratu in private, 'I am not a yogi to know who you are. However, my intuition says that you don't belong to us and that you will leave us one day.'

Kratu laughed, 'After your long stint in discipline, you seem to be taking a break from it, Baba. Your sense of humour is finally blooming in the desert of your sternness.'

*Baba* is the honorific address to grandpa.

'This is no humour, *babu*. My one request – mind it, it is only a request – is that you don't leave us till I am alive.'

Grandparents love grandchildren unselfishly and so their love is intense. There is no give and take in it, nor is there any fine print of future expectation attached to it, as parents generally have.

'*Baba*, you are so funny! Old age is bringing out the child in you.'

'Will you keep my request? Please.'

Kratu was in a dilemma. To cover his conflict, he laughed for a while, firmed himself up and then said softly, 'I will be near you at your deathbed, *Baba*.'

Grandpa felt happy and relieved. Death did not matter with him. However, the presence of loved ones while roaming here did matter. The small joys of life!

By the time Kratu was eight and Anvi five, they were studying in one of those schools that nurse the ego of the parents more than nurturing talent. The failed aspirations of parents make them have high expectations of their wards, for which they lovingly spend a fortune.

This was not to Kratu's liking, who often laughed at his school with, 'Ma, do you realize that our schools produce more salesmen than men? Once we get a degree, we get down to milking those in need, instead of serving them with our skill. Of course, we too get milked in turn when the time comes. Do you really want me to be a salesman?'

Ma wanted to make an angry reply but the fear of Kratu getting 'scared', restrained her.

Anvi loved her brother but she did not like to go to school, even though it was with him. It did not help much when Kratu often said things like, 'Anvi, we must go to school so that we can learn to swim in the ocean of words to reach the shores of degrees and then be successful salesmen. If you are lucky, you may also learn to shoot your mates dead, like students of distant lands whose clones we are.'

A frightened Anvi shed tears, Ma glared, while Papa laughed with, 'We have Socrates, the wise, in our family.'

Ma often wondered wherefrom Kratu picked up all those strange ideas. She had been tracking his internet search, without finding any clue.

The situation was not congenial at the school too. Complaints against him were more frequent than was advisable. He topped in every subject and was idolized by his friends whom he regaled with stories that seemed unbelievable. He could also answer questions easily from History and Geography, the two subjects that most students abhorred. However, his observations and comments drew frequent glares from the teachers.

One day, when the mathematics teacher was explaining the class about zero and its importance in computing, Kratu broke in, 'Do you know how zero came into existence, sir? Long ago, the sages had a disagreement about what would be the result if infinity was taken out of infinity. Those who thought the answer was infinity, came to be known as Vedantins, and those who thought that the result would be nothing, a mere nothing, although arising out of something, came to be known as Buddhists, the worshippers of *shunya*, the zero.'

'What is Vedanta, sir?' asked one student. Others laughed.

'Meet me after the class,' said the teacher.

'Why punish me for telling something very important, sir? I only wished to inform that while every number is the product of the human mind, 0 has a sacred origin, which makes it a quite interesting number, if you like to call it a number. It has no value of its own, and yet it increases the value of any number exponentially when placed in front, while it leaves the number unchanged if placed in the back. Added to any number, it creates no impact, and when multiplied... boom... the number vanishes into nothingness. Divide it with any number, and it retains its identity, and if you divide any number with 0, then consequences can be quite strange. Funnier is when you use 0 as power; it brings down every number to the socialistic equality of 1. One can build any social or economic theory based on this principle of 0, which has such similarity with life. Life is not 0, but zero is so much like life, isn't it, sir? Just like life, it can surprise anyone with its unusual behaviour. I hope I did not bore you all with these trivialities, sir?'

The class looked at him in shock and the teacher gave a bewilder look. 'Ok, ok. Sit down now and don't talk such gibberish.'

Finally, one day a teacher's patience imploded when Kratu wrote in his essay paper, 'Joy lies in being free of burden. We do not even realize that life is a burden; the body, mind, emotions and memories are a burden. The aim of life should be to get rid of these burdens to get the joy of the free. No wonder many prefer death over life.'

Kratu's parents were advised by the horrified class teacher to consult a psychiatrist right away, failing which Kratu was not to be allowed in the school. Ma cursed the teacher, hinting at his unstable behaviour because of his bachelor status, while father wondered if Kratu was one of the ghosts of Lord Shiva, sent to them to show that God too has a sense of humour.

'Lucky me! Some years ago I would have been taken to a *tantrik* to smell burning chillies or be beaten up by a broom for this. At least I will now have a couch to sit and relax and talk to these children of Freud for whom libido and mortido were the two forces making the world go round or whatever.'

'What is libido?' asked Anvi.

'See how your son talks.'

'Oh! Now he is my son? Why do people want to own only success?'

'See, see, now I am "people"! This is what happens when you allow too much space.'

'Look who is talking? You give space? You won't give an inch to a dying virus.'

Anvi intervened, 'Papa, do not fight with Ma. It is not good for the parents to quarrel. Let that remain for us.'

Embarrassment.

The doctor was a familiar name in the higher society. He was learned, wise and compassionate. His experience showed in his bald head and long beard. Rich people came to him to unburden their boredom and purse. The doctor obliged them with both.

The doctor examined Kratu well by asking serious and trivial questions. There was nothing wrong with him. He went deeper into examining him. The result was the same blank.

'Well, Kratu is certainly odd, although I am not sure what exactly it is. Probably an antithesis of Peter Pan,' said the doctor.

'Excuse me doctor sir, why do you have issues with the odd? Do you realize that life in reality is more odd than even, since oddness brings variety to life. Try whatsoever with even, it will remain always even; something predictable and flat like the Gangetic plain. Now look at odd. It is odd in the company of even, and even in the company of odd. The odd thing about odd is that it is odd only when it is in the company of even. Blame not the odd, sir, blame company. Get the right company, and you will be even, sir.'

Even long years of practice had not prepared the doctor

for this barrage. Smilingly, he offered not to charge for the consultation.

'This is how he talks, Doctor. I keep checking on his computer to find out where from he gets all this information. Unfortunately, I have never come across anything remotely connected with the things he talks.'

'Ma! You are keeping me under surveillance? Is our family a failed state that it would need to keep an eye on its members?'

Ma felt embarrassed. The slip was situational and not intentional. Even then the damage had been done.

Kratu continued, 'As for me being trapped in the wrong body, sir, you may see for yourself how everyone is trapped. Why else do people aspire for something? The very idea of aspiration and ambition implies the need for growth. And, why? Because one wants to outgrow the body and mind in which one is trapped to become what one thinks oneself truly to be. Look at yourself, sir,' Kratu pointed at the doctor's greying beard, 'you too aspire to be a philosopher or a sage by growing that beard.'

The doctor broke out in loud laughter. It was not often that a patient counselled him, 'I would love to meet you more often, young man.'

There was nothing more for the doctor to do than to wish the family luck.

There were tears during the return journey.

Anvi was frightened.

After dinner, when everyone went to bed, Anvi asked Kratu the meaning of odd.

'Odd? Odd is a fiction. There is nothing called odd.'

'That is no answer,' Anvi thought. So she asked him to tell her a story that would explain odd. The story had to be long. If possible, it had to be never-ending.

'Story, yes. We are all stories, sis. Each one of us.'

It was beyond Kratu to love anyone. The little semblance that he had of love, was for Anvi. Who knows? She might have been a companion in some previous life. He knew only his story and not of others, so he could not be sure.

From that night onwards, Kratu narrated stories from his life to Anvi without naming the source. Anvi wanted the hero of every story to be Kratu, her big brother, so things remained uncomplicated for him during narration.

The reality of Kratu was now a story for Anvi. Like a good narrator, he left out the philosophical detail and focussed only on the palatable parts.

He went back in time to when all this had begun.

# 2

# ANGI

'How long ago it was? May be eight or ten thousand years ago. Or more,' thought Kratu, when he started narrating stories to his sister. There must have been events prior to that but he neither remembered them, nor cared.

Following the practice of the land and age, Kratu was taken to an ashram by his father to learn the Vedas when he was around eight years old. The ashram belonged to Sage Angi, respected for his learning, simplicity and contemplative nature, the three essential qualities of a great teacher.

Kratu's father handed over his son to the sage with all humility, 'Acharya, please accept my son as your pupil. We have trained him in the basics of pious life. Now you please bless him so that he may attain his worth.' Kratu then offered *samidha,* the sacred wood used in *yajna,* to Sage Angi, as an indication of his willingness to be accepted by the teacher.

The sage accepted the gift happily, 'Kratu is now my responsibility.' He then called his wife, known as Guru Ma, to introduce Kratu to her. It was her responsibility to feed the students and take care of them, even though the family was a portrait of poverty.

With everything settled, Acharya patted the head of Kratu, 'Welcome to the life of learning and purity!'

Education in those days focussed on two kinds of knowledge: intuitive knowledge about God, and the practical knowledge about the world. Learned sages and brahmins were entrusted with the sacred duty of shaping children with twin ideals of their growth and service to the society.

Kratu's journey in learning began.

'When God created the worlds,' began Angi, 'He gave the responsibility of preserving the knowledge of the universe to the brahmins with the condition that they must never acquire fame and pelf, the twin poisons for the wise. This being the sacred promise made by your ancestors to God, you must stay away from these.'

The kids nodded their heads in agreement. For them Guru was God.

Angi had learnt the Vedas from his teacher in an unbroken tradition of *guru-shishya parampara,* at the end of which was God, the teacher of all. God had breathed knowledge in the form of the Vedas – which are the sum total of all knowledge, revealed and yet to be revealed – when the creation began. Memorized and maintained through oral tradition, the Vedic knowledge was preserved by the families of sages through the succession from father to son or from teacher to the disciple. No one ever questioned the sanctity of the sacred.

Kratu was now a link in that chain.

Angi spent his time in teaching the young learners and performing *yajna* by pouring oblations in the sacred fire with chants from the Vedas, known as mantras. These mantras were considered divine and hence were not written down. The students were marvellous at memorising them, although the knowledge encapsulated in those words seldom trickled from the heads of the learners to their hearts.

Innovations, experimentation, and questioning by students were considered impolite and unbecoming of a student. Anyone who violated the sacred traditions of Vedic learning was looked down upon. The learners knew all this from their family tradition too.

Everyone at the ashram had to do a lot of work, which included collecting alms from the village, looking after the cows, working in the fields, performing household chores and collecting material from the forest. The physical labour involved in these activities effectively cleansed the mind of the excess energy of the students, which otherwise would have resulted in restlessness and then sloth; the two great enemies of serenity, without which knowledge can neither be acquired nor retained.

Like any other obedient learner, Kratu studied and worked as expected of him. He was given the task of grazing the cows and collecting firewood from the forest that lay on the outskirts of the village. He had to get up before dawn, bathe, perform the morning rituals of pouring oblations in the fire, recite the Vedas and then take the cows to the forest. Once there, he often reclined against a mango tree and chanted aloud what he had learnt.

The mango tree against which Kratu reclined was the meeting ground of contradictions: it had given good produce in its time, and it had also stopped anything from growing under it; lonely travellers rested under its shadow to regain strength, and kids played under it to expend their excess energy; villagers came up to this point to bid farewell to those who were leaving them, and gathered there to welcome those who were returning after a long stay away from them.

The tree had stood its ground for centuries; a long time for a mango tree. Its long years had made it infertile. However, this gave it the scope of seeing its children and grandchildren spread far and wide, who sent the news of the happenings from their part of the world through the net of their roots and occasionally through the roots of the grass. Like any old man's love for gossip, this patriarch of a tree loved gathering and dispensing information unceasingly.

'Information, my kids, information; information is the key to power in the world. We have been left behind in the scheme of evolution only because we cannot store information. So, never let the networking peter out. Remember that we will be the ultimate winners in this race of evolution against the humans, provided we can manage our info system well.'

Unaware of the memories and hopes of the tree, Kratu sat under it every day. The cows grazed and accumulated what they would ruminate later, and Kratu ruminated on the learning that he had accumulated earlier.

The mango tree mused at the conversity.

Kratu was not alone in grazing the cows there.

Many poor lads from the village were employed by rich families to look after their livestock. Millennia later, Lord Krishna would glorify this profession, although at the time of the story, cowherds were on the lower rungs of economic hierarchy, although it did not attract the social frown that was plastered on it in later times. The caste system, which became cast in stone in later ages, was still plastic. Young ones could take up any profession of their choice, provided they could get a mentor.

Aswin was one of the cowherds from an economically challenged family. To carry the burden of his family, he had chosen to carry the workload of others. Nature, however, had not been unkind towards him. What he had lost in prosperity, he had gained in talent with mango seed flute. When the mango seeds fell to the ground and sprouted, he plucked them out, removed their outer shell, rubbed the core against a rough surface, and a flute of sorts was ready to produce music. At times, he punctured holes in it to play some form of crude tune to amuse himself.

Music was not yet fully born. People had a rough sense of notes which they used to set their songs, using three notes the way Vedic hymns were chanted. These chants were raised, lowered, and flat. When chanted alone or in company, the deep resonance of the sacred uplifted the minds of the listener.

Some sage had come up with the idea of five notes. This helped some hymns of the Vedas to be sung on a *veena* in five notes, which was not really adequate for a fully grown music composition. The village folks did not have any idea even about the five notes.

Kratu did not know much about these things. He lived his routine under the mango tree and often listened to the crude music played by Aswin. Soon they became friends and started exchanging stories from their life.

He explained to Aswin the basics of the Vedas which left the illiterate shepherd amazed. 'If the mantras be recited properly, one can get anything – child, wealth, empire, destruction of detractors, rains, sunshine – anything. Believe me,' said Kratu. Aswin's eyes grew big in wonder.

The charm of the Vedas was lost for Aswin whenever he thought of the strict discipline that Kratu had to follow at the ashram. He once commented, 'How can you live a regimented life? Look at us free birds; we are poor and illiterate but we are free.'

'Nothing grows without boundaries around it, brother,' Kratu explained.

'Tell me, why do we need to grow?'

'Growth is life, stagnation is death. Either you grow or you decay. This is the law of life, applicable to us, animals, objects and ideas. If you think that you are not growing, then know for sure that you are degenerating.'

Thus they talked day after day.

One day Aswin commented, 'How wonderful it would be if we all knew what you know.' The company of the learned has its own virtues.

'Luxury of freedom hates the discipline of knowledge. To acquire something, you have to give up a lot, which you are not ready to do. That is why knowledge can never be for the masses,' Kratu said.

'I know that you are learned, and you are great. Now tell me, whether you are compassionate too? Will you someday help me with your knowledge if I am in distress?'

Kratu laughed, 'One who has to demand has no friend, Aswin. A true friend will never give you the chance to ask for a favour; he will do for you whatever is required even without your asking for it. I am your true friend.'

Aswin's face lit up.

Kratu continued, 'A man can attain God through true friendship. Know for sure that I will be there for you in heaven and hell, and will use all my might to pull you out of any situation that you may not like to be in. For that I will face even the frown of God.'

Aswin bent his head under the weight of friendship.

One day Kratu was sitting under the tree, chanting the hymn, *"Aa no bhadrah kartavo yantu vishwatah"* (Let noble thoughts come to me from all sides) – now aloud, now silent, deep in the state of contemplative silence – the state in which the empire of words is left behind. He contemplated on the meaning of the words he had been reciting and waded in the deeper realms of silence. Things around him appeared far from him and yet more alive and vibrant. He was distantly conscious of all that was before him and was also oblivious of them.

In that state of lucidity, Kratu had a vision. Or, as he would later think, it was a dream. Two identically beautiful birds appeared before him.

'You invited us through your chants, so we are here. Now choose between us.'

'What do I have to choose from? And why?'

'We, the twins, are the two aspects of ideas. When God created the universe, He created us to guide the worlds. As ideas, I represent fame and my sister is anonymity. Every achiever has to choose between us. Now accept me and be famous.'

Kratu felt that there had to be a catch in it. Life can never be all blank; a loss had to be compensated by some gain. He said, 'If everyone accepts you then you must be quite common. I would then rather choose your sister.'

'Be not stupid in your youthful idealism. Invite not tears for eternity.'

The stubborn of the learned woke up in him. He said, 'I chose what I chose. Thank you for your offer.'

The fame-bird left in a huff.

The other one told Kratu, 'It is rare to come across one who chooses me over my sister. I bless you that you will serve in anonymity. Fame will elude you, but fulfilment you will have.'

Saying so, that bird too flew away.

Kratu woke up, as if from a trance. It took him time to come back to the plane of reality. Or was the vision real and this state of awareness make-believe? He was not so sure.

What worried him was if what he perceived in that altered state of awareness was correct, then he was heading for tears.

*Choices we make! Ah, choices we make.*
*Anonymity hither, craving for care*
*Silence of the loud, tear of the lost*
*Yonder be happiness, brimming with pride*
*Dream of the starving, mirage of the parched*
*What to pick and what to leave!*
*Choices we make! Ah, choices we make.*

The roots of the mango tree were going hysterical, passing on the breaking news to its kin. 'Kratu is the name, kids! Born to the anonymity of the great. Born to serve. Make sure that he is never deprived of shelter and fruits when he is near anyone of you.'

The change came over Kratu imperceptibly, like dew falling on a rose bud to make it bloom in the morning. It was marked by his growing contemplative nature.

One day he was sitting under the mango tree, sinking deeper into the realm of silence. In the distance, Aswin was trying to be melodious on his mango seed flute. Kratu's thoughts started synchronising the inputs from his surrounding with the inside of him.

Thoughts – music – notes – mango seed. Kratu was enjoying the deep dive in the ocean of thoughts when a new world lit up before him. He realized that music could be stretched to seven notes and that songs could be composed and played on seven notes instead of five or the limited three. Yes, it was easy. In fact, it was quite simple.

The joy of deep churning made him ecstatic and silent at the same time. He lost all awareness of time till he was woken up from the depths by the impatient mooing of the cows. It was time to take them to the ashram.

Kratu gathered his cows to return. For the first time, his face shone bright with the light of discovery.

Knowledge requires techniques to make it practical, the way it requires photosynthesis to convert sunlight into plant life. The technique for conversion of new knowledge into practical use may come in a short span or over generations. In case of music with seven notes, it took only a few days.

Like a baby growing inside a womb, the knowledge about the seven notes grew rapidly within the psyche of Kratu. Soon it was kicking to come out of its hold. His body-mind duo was unable to contain the gift of the gods, and one day it expelled itself, thus giving birth to the new format of music. And, like a fast-growing baby, it refused to stay within the confines of

Kratu; it demanded to be taken out. The baby now belonged to the world.

Kratu named the seven notes Sa-Re-Ga-Ma-Pa-Dha-Ni-Sa. Of these, Ga stood for his homeland, Gandhara. The later musicians refined these notes to come up with the enchanting Indian music.

Kratu first tried his discovery with the mantras that he knew. Yes, it could be done. He then tried one of the village songs. Yes, the rustic song sounded divine. 'Ah! Music, liberated here you are! I wonder what price I may have to pay.'

Angi had cautioned his students never to use the sacred for anything secular, so Kratu did not know what to do with the revelation that he had regarding music. Knowing the violent reaction that the inmates would have at his discovery, he kept quiet about it, working silently on ways to make it fit for the public, as and when possible.

He experimented with setting popular village songs to the new notes, which then appeared to have brilliance with no rival. Kratu then went a step further. Taking a cue from the mango seed of Aswin, he invented a flute with seven holes to play music. He felt as if music had been released from the captivity of the *gandharvas*, the custodians of music.

Aswin felt proud to watch the unfolding of Kratu's discovery and its application. He started learning the art of singing and music from Kratu. However, rapid developments sucked him into unfathomable darkness.

The summer harvest was beginning when Kratu had invented the wonder, music. The villagers celebrated the arrival of new grains by preparing delicacies with them and offering to Indra and Agni, the two chief gods of that period. The days were getting hotter, but the nights were still pleasant. Freedom born of opulence and leisure was used in organising night festivals soaked in singing and dancing. Most of the festivals were an offering to the gods, whose bountiful nature brought prosperity to the locality.

It was also the marriage season.

Society in those days favoured girls opting for her groom. A prized girl often opted for a *swayamvar* in which she chose her partner depending on the quality of the suitor.

Aswin wanted to marry Usha, who was a proud beauty, from a nearby village. She also liked Aswin. Unfortunately, she had already opted for *swayamvar* in which the condition was that the winner had to present something unique to the bride.

A tear-laden Aswin asked for help, 'Do something for your wretched friend, Kratu. I will die if I cannot get Usha.'

'I know. I am myself shaken. Now tell me what do we do?'

'Perform some *yajna* for me. Get something unique from heaven for me. I have been hearing so much from you about what the mantras can achieve and what *yajna* can get. Now is the time to use your knowledge to save your friend's life.'

'I am not a master of *yajna* and I am not sure if it can produce something suitable for you,' said a teary Kratu.

'In that case I pray that you never talk to me about the Vedas and its powers. What is the use of the exalted knowledge that cannot save even the life of an ordinary person like me? Friend, I refuse to believe in a wisdom that cannot save my life here but will give me heaven after death. You can carry on with your esoteric beliefs, friend, but allow me a break, which will not be for long. I will soon be dead without your intervention.'

Kratu was upset; very upset. He thought of burning down the village as a unique gift to the girl, but he gave up the idea as impractical.

A thought then approached him, probably from the goddess of anonymity, that he could sing a song set in the new melodies that no one had ever heard. 'I am sure that no one can bring the damsel a more unique gift than this.'

Before the thought could take over him, he vigorously shook it away. He could not do the unthinkable. But ideas are persistent.

'Life or way of life, Kratu?' said he to himself.

'Of course, I will choose the way of life. *Ashram* life is everything for us, the young brahmins.'

'Think again of the choice you make. If Aswin dies without your help, your conscience will never let you be at peace.'

'No I cannot commit the crime of presenting the sacred before the public.'

'You can perform penance for the mistake. But how will you atone for the death caused by you, mister?'

'Religion is everything; the Vedas are sacred. I cannot do that. No. A big no.'

'Life is above everything, Kratu. You can make compromise with anything to save a life. Think again.'

Kratu's conflict seared him through the middle.

*Bound to uphold the sacred*
*And to serve a friend in need*
*Twain tear me asunder*
*And heart they viciously knead*

The situation was such that he could not even consult anyone. Why consult when the answer is already known?

Kratu's head buzzed with thoughts that were at the throats of each other. Not very happily, he settled on singing during the *swayamvar*. If need be, he would perform penances for the transgression. If he was lucky, something else may crop up, thought he wistfully.

Usha means dawn. The Vedas had some beautiful hymns in praise of the goddess Usha, who heralded the day, which was then utilized in performing *yajna*. Coming to know of this, Aswin had composed some simple lines in praise of his Usha, which Kratu now converted into songs with seven notes. Aswin was not sure, but it was definitely better than a certain loss.

The night of the *swayamvar*.

There was a dust storm in the evening; a signal for Kratu to stop. The retracting force seemed to overcome the strength of his legs.

'Protect dharma and dharma will protect you.' This was a well-known saying among the brahmins. Dharma, the right conduct, is easy to define, and is learnt by every kid before he turns ten. That is how a simplistic religion or belief runs. Life, on the other hand, is too complicated to run on simple principles. Even to make the right decisions during conflict, one has to pass through the fire of conscience.

Taking a deep breath, he hardened himself and slipped out of the ashram in the storm. Fending off rain and falling branches, he reached the *swayamvar* site, all soaked and looking wild. There sat Aswin, with a ghostly face, at the thought of the imminent loss of his loved one, and then his own life.

Seeing Kratu, he jumped up like a fish at the full moon. He ran to embrace his friend, confident that he was there to save him.

Most suitors offered what they could, which was nothing much to boast about.

Kratu offered his music to the would-be bride as the 'never heard or seen before' gift from Aswin. There were murmurs of curiosity.

'Listen all, listen to the music that none of you has ever heard,' declared Kratu.

'We need to listen that.'

'Sure. It is for you.'

Taking the first step on a new path is difficult. The second step simply follows it obediently. When Kratu crossed the boundary of the ashram at night, the first step had been taken. It should not have been difficult for him to take the second step in transgressing the sanctity of the Vedas. He, however, wavered. He hoped for a miracle. Maybe the elders present there could be satisfied by his words, instead of a practical demonstration.

Nothing like that happened.

Steeling himself one last time, he made the plunge; a dive from which he would never again come out clean. The plunge was going to make him its slave forever. He began his soft singing of the song written by Aswin and set to music by himself.

Music, caged till then, was freed forever, for everyone. The music flowing from the lips of Kratu was like the sacred Ganga racing from Gangotri to Haridwar to expresses her freedom from the matted hairs of Lord Shiva: dancing, gyrating, gentle, wild, loud, whispering, curvy, straight. Like the mischievous adolescent Ganga in the Himalayas, the music now flowed, slowed, flew, alighted, hit, caressed, gave, tempted; above all, it drained and fulfilled.

The audience went numb.

The elegance of what was before them, had not been experienced even by their forefathers. Kratu's voice, mellowed by regular chanting of the Vedas, and made rhythmic by the new notes, took the villagers to the realms of delight that they had thought to be reserved for Indra, the king of the gods when he was entertained by *apsaras*.

No one could move. The wind, moving through the nostrils of the assembled, stopped moving. The leaves of the trees stopped to catch the strands of the music through their ill-formed senses. Crickets in the bushes went silent, ashamed of their cacophony.

People did not know how to react.

Usha got up in a daze with the garland and moved towards the suitors. She stopped before Kratu and felt confused. She raised the garland to put it round Kratu's neck, at which he screamed, 'What are you doing? Stop. Your garland is not for me but for Aswin.' Saying this, he ran – ran fast – to his ashram.

The village was back to its senses. Usha, now feeling normal, put the garland in Aswin's neck. The marriage was fixed for the next day.

The failed suitors were not going to let their bitterness fade into nothingness. It had to be taken out on someone, and Kratu was the right choice. Bound by the ties of the ashram code, Kratu was like a tree that could be mutilated by anyone, without letting out a murmur of protest.

'Sir, you are going to be famous,' said one of them to Angi.

It was beneath the dignity of Angi to talk to the spiritually challenged. The daring of these youngsters made Angi raise his eyebrows. He was then informed about the exploits of Kratu the previous night.

Disbelief – shock – fury.

The anger of the calm can burn the world. The anger of Angi was about to burn the spiritual world of Kratu. 'How could you put the divine on the stage of the commoners?' Angi quivered in anger.

Kratu stayed silent. What he had done was wrong. However, he had been left with no choice. The demons of dilemma had torn him apart before he had released the beauty hidden in his bosom.

'You know well that the Vedas and anything associated with them must not be paraded before the commoners. To add to that, you attended and sung at a *swayamvar*! Unpardonable.'

Kratu felt guilty but he held his head high. He felt that his convictions had made him do what he did. Moreover, he had not sung the hymns as a song and so he had not sinned. He remembered how past masters had talked about *apad dharma,* the acts that one can do during an emergency. What he had done was to save a life.

'Acharya, I did not use the hymns for the song.'

Angi's breathings were now well pronounced. 'You ignored my instructions and paraded the sacred before the rustics! Well, you deserve a special curse for this vicious sin.'

'What are you saying, Acharya? How can you even think of that?'

Angi thought for a moment and then pronounced, 'I curse that you may never again forget a thing. Stay cursed till eternity.'

'What!' screamed Kratu. The real impact of the curse was to unfold much later. However, he could understand even then what a disaster had fallen upon him.

It is an irony with the sages that, even though they have been the custodians of serenity, some of them are more famous for their anger. Sage Durvasa is known more for his anger than his wisdom, while Viswamitra and Vasistha are probably cursing each other even today.

'Acharya! Acharya!'

'And now leave this place.'

Dumbness.

Kratu bent down to touch the feet of his master, who withdrew. He then tried to look at the face of the master one last time, but the Sun's rays hit him square in the eyes. Numbed, Kratu got up, folded his hands in *pranam* to all that he had held dear for years, and then dragged his feet towards nowhere.

When Anvi and Kratu had grown up a little more, Kratu, curious about his past, wanted to know how his land of origin was faring these days. In the past, one had to travel to a place to know about it or had to depend on gossips of the traders. Now it was Google – the great info god – who informed him that the area where his story had begun was now no more an Aryan land. Gun-toting non-believers had overrun, and now ran the sacred land of Angi.

Kratu mused, 'Price of exclusiveness!'

'What happened to Kratu when he had to leave the *ashram*?' Anvi asked. She was fascinated by the story that seemed so near yet so far.

Kratu walked up the road of the story and led Anvi along.

Nowhere implies anywhere. Kratu's legs now carried the dead weight of his destroyed mind and dispirited body to nowhere in particular. He just walked away: from the ashram that had given him knowledge, and the village where he had translated his knowledge into music for the world. His feet trudged on the dusty road in the Indian summer. No goal, no purpose. Time stood before him as eternity.

Time.

Time is born in the mind, it stays in the mind and is one with the mind. When one remains conscious of the mind, he becomes conscious of time, and when one becomes too conscious of one's mind, then time appears as eternity to him. To let go of time, one has to go beyond one's mind.

Time lay as an ocean before Kratu. To save himself from drowning in that ocean, he walked in the summer heat to take his mind away from his mind.

Indian summer.

Everything was dying from outside and drying from the inside. The Earth, heated beyond its tolerance limit, was giving up her green garment. It seemed to pant for the rains from above, but the scorcher was cruel; it was not yielding. The dust kicked up by Kratu's dragging feet flew up to touch the sky for a lick of moisture, but returned disappointed from there to inform others of the futile effort. The wise particles, made heavy with experience, did not even bother to break their summer hibernation.

The Sindhu flowed at a distance from Kratu's ashram. The Vedas praised Sindhu as:

*Like floods of rain that fall in thunder from the cloud*
*So Sindhu rushes on bellowing like a bull.*

Sindhu, the cradle of Indian culture, rages like a bull in the monsoon but trudges like an ox in the summer.

Like any human being, India has three distinct bodies: physical, intellectual and spiritual. The spiritual body of the country got its core from the sages and saints; the intellectual body was shaped by the greats like Vyasa and Valmiki, and its physical body is tended by its rivers. There are lakes and wells to sate the thirsty, but the rivers of India are the sites of its history. Stories, legends, myths and history spring up in India not from the wells as in desert lands but frolic around the riverbanks.

Kratu walked by the lean river to reach an old *peepul* tree which was believed to be haunted by spirits. People avoided walking past it in the darkness of night and during the loneliness of noon. There Kratu sat, withdrawn from the external world and inner sanity. The cool of the shade above and the water before him calmed his mind to the point that he could order the events and watch the churnings inside him. His sadness cooled into tears that now flowed freely from the windows of his face.

It was customary for the students of the ashram to listen to stories from the religious traditions. These were known as *narashamsi*, which were later woven into the stories of the Puranas. One of the stories in it was about *samudra manthan*, the churning of the ocean by the gods and asuras. The asuras are the step-brothers of the gods but are always involved in a vicious power struggle. Once, they both decided to churn the ocean to get *amrita* out from it so that they could become immortal. When the great churning began, with Mandar Mountain as the churner, the first thing to come out of the ocean was deadly poison that threatened to burn down the creation. Lord Shiva then absorbed the poison so that greater things and beings could prevail. Finally, *amrita* appeared and made the gods powerful.

A *samudra manthan* of a different kind was going on in the mind of Kratu. The truth of life is that whenever there is a churning, first comes the froth of poison. Only if that poison can be absorbed, then one can expect to attain better things.

Sadness – disorientation – hopelessness.

'Of what use I am now to any? What will my parents say? Why live? Let me be of some service to the aquatic life at least.'

Determined, Kratu entered Sindhu.

Homo sapiens are children of light and hence they want light at the time of their death, while members of other species drag their bodies to darkness before they become history. Suicides are a different matter. Those who cannot bear the light of life, opt for death in darkness. That is what Kratu did while waiting under the *peepul* tree: he waited for darkness.

Unknown to him, a storm, far more intense than the one he had withstood last evening, was on its way.

Dark. Dangerous.

Time moved slowly.

Kratu watched and remembered the verse from *Nasadiya Suktam* that described creation: 'There was only darkness wrapped in darkness.' The approaching darkness seemed to match the Vedic description. However, it was not the seed for creation for him; rather it was the blow of annihilation. Soon the darkness inside Kratu matched the darkness outside.

He entered the river. Ankle, knee, thighs, waist, chest, chin, cheeks, lips and finally his nose was inside water, and he was gone.

His consciousness spirited away.

The news network in the villages has always been sturdy. It makes sure that no news is ever lamed or maimed, as is done by the present-day reporters. It was through this network that Aswin came to know of Kratu's expulsion. He came running to meet Angi and asked for forgiveness.

'Kratu will die outside the *ashram*. I know how much he adores you and the knowledge that you impart. Please forgive him and save him from imminent death,' wailed he.

Angi had calmed down by then. He was a master of *Jyotish Vidya* – astronomy – which was one of the six supportive subjects of the Vedas. It dealt mostly with astronomy to work out the correct timings for rituals and ceremonies. Some sages applied this knowledge to individual and cosmic events to come up with the art of astrology. With that, a new form of astrology, known as *Prashna Jyotish,* was coming up. A master of this art could answer any question put to them by calculating the planetary position at the time when the question was asked. Angi was a master of this art. He came up with the conclusion that Kratu still had a lot of life left in him. He said that much to Aswin.

Guided by some kids, Aswin ran up to the Sindhu to find his friend. To his horror, Kratu was struggling and drowning in the river. To save him, he jumped into the river, only to be swept away.

Usha had come running on hearing of the rapid developments. The scene before her was so pathetic that she too jumped into the river.

The storm gained momentum.

Kratu did not realize that he had been freed from his body. He could see and hear things around him just as before. Looking around, he was surprised to see people on the bank running and screaming, in spite of the approaching doom in the form of the storm. For them, the doom before their eyes was far worse.

Curious, and also to caution them, he ran towards them, oblivious that he had been running on the river without drowning. Midstream, he saw the body of Aswin floating lifeless. He tried to lift it up. His shock now knew no end when he saw that his body passed through the body of Aswin.

'Oh no! I don't have a body. I am dead,' screamed Kratu to no one in particular, which, of course, no one heard.

If not having a body was a big jolt, then realising that someone had given his life for him was devastating.

And then he saw the body of Usha floating in the river.

The crowd on the bank cowered in the storm.

The winds whistled, shrieked, shrilled and screamed. Wind, breath, vitality, energy; everything comes from Vayu. When he sustains creation, he blows rhythmically, and when he wants destruction, his flow becomes eccentric. Vayu was moving like a thousand inebriated frogs. It was as if *Vinash Yajna*, the sacrifice of destruction, was being performed by Vayu, in which he was the priest. The living and the inert was the offering, the churning winds was the sacrificial fire, the screaming winds carried the offering towards heavens, and the outcome of that *yajna* was destruction all around.

Spirits of all kinds – ghosts, goblins, banshees, *churails* – and of all forms and shapes were there: one eyed, multi eyed, one eared, multi eared, one legged, multi legged, one fingered, multi fingered, headless, multi headed, single bellied, multi bellied, hairless and thickly haired. They shrieked, croaked, whispered and bellowed.

Kratu was frightened to see and hear the forces surrounding him. He then remembered that he was one of them and so he was within the boundaries of safety. Fear of the known is mere pain. The real fear is of the unknown.

Most spirits were there for fun while others had malicious intents. They introduced themselves as products of accidental deaths, wars, suicides and murders. None had a natural death and they all longed for their lost bodies which by then had been burnt or destroyed.

Kratu moved with those spirits in the storm. In spite of the gloom that he had felt a moment ago, he felt happy in his newfound freedom. He was like a toddler who cries for his mom but finds momentary fun in a new toy. He went up, down, sideways and at an angle to verify his powers.

The storm reached the ashram. Angi and his disciples had hidden inside the cottages to save themselves from the falling debris. The sight of the ashram filled Kratu with a sudden rush of anger. Along with that came the memories of Aswin and Usha, floating dead in Sindhu.

Emotions are devoid of intelligence. Additionally, anger does not differentiate between high and low. An angry man, howsoever well-trained and cultured, can insult and harm even the respected ones. Kratu's anger, born of pain, loss and death, was ready to destroy.

He let go of the gratitude towards the place that had given him so much. His inner restlessness made him pounce on everything of the ashram. The spirits found it funny and so they joined him to give extra power to the storm.

The wind howled like a dangerous beast out to tear apart its prey. The thatched roofs of the cottages shook helplessly. Kratu and the spirits made another run on the ashram, 'This one for Aswin!' The spirits echoed the words, not knowing the why or what of it. A crowd, even if it be of the spirits, stays stupid.

'Something is not right,' felt Angi. 'The storm is not supposed to be so vicious.'

He contemplated for a moment. His mind, made pure by sacred practices, could see things that were not visible through eyes. What he saw then was painful and also shocking. Kratu was leading the hoodlum spirits.

'How can he be dead, when he has so much life left in him? And how can he be with the scum of the universe! Lord! Lord!' Angi felt sad for his disciple. He did not want to harm him, but he had to save those who were with him. He decided to use a mantra to scare away the dead.

*'Stambha!'* shouted Angi after he had recited the mantra. The storm stopped abruptly.

The spirits, caught unaware by the sudden stopping of physical movement, got thrown in all directions; some of them crash landed nearby, while some others were blown away far.

Kratu was quite light compared to other spirits because of his noble qualities. Inertia of motion blew him away far from the ashram and deposited him on the bank of river, where he lay inert, lamenting over the loss of his all.

The dead lay there dead. He had nothing to do even if he got up.

*There was a queen and there was a king*
*They both went dead, story went ping.*

'*Bhaiya*, your story was something like this. Where is the explanation of 'odd' that you promised to tell me through the story?' said Anvi.

'Patience, sister, patience. A delicacy takes time to cook.'

'And why do we have so many deaths in this story? There must not be any story that has death in it.'

'A story is no story if it ends with death. A real story runs stronger after death and rings in every home,' said Kratu smilingly.

'Now tell me, why so many people have to die in your story?'

'Why listen to a story if you have already decided what it should contain?'

'You always put me down.'

'I am not putting you down; I am only telling you what you should know.'

'I am not happy,' said Anvi and became quiet. She was still years away from teenage, when she would develop skills to win in every situation.

Kratu, the loving brother, consoled her, 'There is nothing called death, Anvi. You only go from one place to another as Kratu did. Of course, your memory is wiped clean at the time of death, so you cannot recognize your old ones and your old ones cannot recognize you because of your new body.'

Anvi could not understand that. She believed that death was the end of everything; a big finish. Now that her brother was telling otherwise, it must be correct.

Kratu, her brother, was her hero who could never be wrong.

# 3

# COSMIC CORRECTION CENTRE

Darkness of the spirit sucks. Even if that be of the dead. Kratu had lost everything connected with his body and now his newfound associates from the spirit world had been left behind. He lay where he was and thought over what had been and what could have been; what was right and what was more right; what he had lost and at what cost. He would have been saved from all those thoughts had he not been cursed by his teacher. Others in a similar situation would be luckier.

The thread of his thoughts, released unending from his mind, wound tight around his psyche, forcing him down for a long time till he was yanked up by two very angry looking spirit police.

The police of any land are scary for the noble. Law enforcers with batons in hands are a sign of unacceptable transgressions followed by the unpleasantness of 'why' and 'what next'. Noble persons cannot take such harshness. Kratu had been noble all his life. So, a direct approach by law enforcers took away the little strength that he had been left with.

The spiritland, as the ghosts preferred to call their land, had its own dynamics of existence. To keep the unruly spirits within the bounds of spirit laws, rowdy ghosts were given charge to keep them tamed. These spirit police, vicious as they were by virtue of their vices, presented their toughness through their rough speech.

'We have been looking for you everywhere, you dung eater. Instead of showing your shameful rotten pumpkin of a face to the President of spiritland, you have been warming this place with your back, as if you inherited it from your forefathers, you scum of a scoundrel,' said one of the men.

Kratu trembled at the language. Sanskrit, the language of the cultured, did not permit crude expressions, which made its speakers refined in their tastes.

'You bug of a cabbage, you did not even care to be where you were after arriving in the spiritland, blessed be the holy land,' said another one, and advanced towards Kratu with cruel intentions.

Kratu felt like a squeezed balloon.

'You also joined the spiritzens in an illegal manner to destroy an area that was not assigned you. You have thus violated the sacred spirit code.'

Kratu's boisterousness as a storm rider the previous day, or whatever day it had been, was now producing luscious fruits of pain.

'Follow us, or else...' The guards, unhindered by physical bodies, increased their size menacingly.

'I humbly present myself as a law-abiding spiritzen. Please do not scare me.'

'Law-abiding, you said? You, who have been breaking all the laws of our sacred land,' saying so, one guard gave him such a kick that he went flying through the space to land inside the gates of the spiritland.

The spiritland has ghosts, goblins and other spirits as its spiritzens, some of whom had been with Kratu during the storm. The USP of the place was dissatisfaction. Only those who were intensely dissatisfied with life ended up there. In turn, whenever these spiritzens made rounds of the lands within their empires, which included Earth, they pushed their pain into receptive minds so that they could get company.

Anvi interrupted the narration, 'Ghost stories are so exciting, *bhaiya*. But do they truly exist?'

'You are listening to a story so why should you worry about philosophy?'

'I am just curious.'

'The answer is both yes and no.'

'It is no answer.'

'Mind is composed of matter and it can know only that world which has the same composition as itself. When you know our world, you cannot know spirit world and when you know spirits, you cannot know our world because the compositions of the mind are different.'

'So?'

'Memory is associated with mind. So, even if, by chance, you reach the spirit world and learn all about it, you won't remember it here because your mind is fit only for that world which it knows. Your memory of that land will not work in this land because the composition of the mind has to be different to know different kinds of world. And what you don't remember, that does not exist for you. Your experiences are all in the mind, which get recalled as memory to refer to new kind of knowledge. Without a memory, your knowledge is a big fat zero. You are what your memory is. Kratu's memory, because of the curse, remained intact wherever he went.'

'My friends say that ghosts exist.' Anvi kept it simple.

'Most people who see ghosts need to consult a mental doctor.'

Once inside the gates, the guards escorted a terrified Kratu through the streets of the land of lost individuality where people with failed opportunity came to work out their karma.

'Hey, you rascal, you did not bow before me while crossing me!' shouted an angry spirit, 'Do you know who I am? I am the greatest that ever was. How dare you cross me like that? Bow before greatness to acquire some merit, you buffoon.' He then blocked the path like a hoodlum that one meets in a mean street.

One of the guards went up to him and gave him a big kick, making him clear the path. The spiritzen kept shouting, 'You do not know me! Just wait till I have you hanged by your ankles for eternity.'

Kratu trembled at the thought of being with such beings.

'O Sweetener of sweet, brightness of light, shine of the moon, please drop a drop of your kindness on this wretch and take me to my moonfaced, star-eyed, cloud-haired, air-light beloved of mine once, only once. Help this luckless whose hopes are lost in a black hole and whose memories are in the echoing well, and have my words that the mighty Lord will take you to great joy, o dear, spiritzen!' cried one with pathos dripping from his poetic words. Delicately, it came forward and held on to Kratu's legs like a python holding on to its prey.

This time, it was the turn of the other guard to give a kick to the demanding. The guards then hurried to reach the court of the spirit president.

Unknown land, unknown authority.

The rules in the spirit world were kept dynamic whenever it suited the rulers. At other times the rulers were unbending and were declared to have come from the divine. In the past, spirits believed in having a divinely ordained king but because ghosts do not breed children, there was the problem of successor. So, they changed the rule to accept democratically elected president. The dissent concerning violation of divine command was overruled by a voice vote.

When Kratu reached the spirit world, Pret Vardhan was the elected chief of the nefarious. The election was conducted every ten years of the ghost year, in which ghosts with unusual viciousness were considered for the post of the president and then election was conducted to put the stamp of approval by the stupid.

Viciousness demands sharpness of mind; crude minds can be violent but not vicious.

Pret Vardhan was as vicious as vicious could be. Once in power, he selected dolts as his consultants and appointed the violent ones as peacemakers. Within a year, he sat smug on power pyramid without any fear of change or coup. What this gang of the powerful lacked in moral authority, it made up through authority.

There were some noble spirits, serving lighter terms there. Their murmurs of protest were silenced through privileges or penitentiary. The tricks of democracy, coupled with Pret Vardhan's savvy personality, had successfully won him elections for many terms, often unopposed. He had been serving a long term in that spirit world, so he was in no hurry to give up power, nor was he going to be out of it.

Kratu now stood before the democratically elected dictator.

'What will happen? What to do?' thought a scared Kratu. His heart was pounding faster than the cyclonic storm that he had ridden.

One advantage of learning is that it sharpens the mind and thus helps it think even in dire circumstances. Thinking furiously, he worked out that only two types get into attacking mode: those who are cornered, and those who corner the victim. Hitting for pleasure is the privilege of the perverts. Kratu hoped that the president was not a pervert. As a spirit, he had broken some rules unknowingly, which did not qualify for cornering or getting cornered. He felt a little comforted.

'It is gross misconduct to move around freely without proper authorization,' said the law enforcing minister. He then rattled off the sections of the spirit penal code under which Kratu was guilty.

The stay there and flow of words around him, gave Kratu some confidence. Hearing the charges against him, he thought sarcastically, 'Criminals talking of protecting constitution!'

'You said something?' asked the minister.

'No sir.'

Kratu had indeed not said anything, but that place being the spirit world, mental waves could hit others.

'You said that our President is stupid.'

'I did not say anything like that, sir.' Kratu protested.

'Ha, ha! One always protests when caught. Do not try to act clever, spirit. You know that we know what you intended to say,' mocked the evil.

'Please do not put words in my mouth.'

'You are contradicting me! You know who I am? I am the minister of this spirit court. You are in revolt! You want to start a rebellion here.' Saying this, the minister turned towards the President and requested that the new entrant be put into hard labour for ten years for criminal conspiracy.

Pret Vardhan smiled satisfactorily. From the moment that Kratu had entered his presence, he was feeling uncomfortable. 'The fellow is either noble or learned. Why else I should be feeling uneasy? He has to be locked up to avoid any awakening.' The minister had made his job easy.

'Confinement!' ordered the President.

'I have done no wrong. How can you do this, sir?'

'Now you are challenging our sense of rightness? Another five years.'

'This is *atyachar* and *anachar*; absolutely bad form of governance. I strongly object to it, sir.'

'Anarchist! You are an anarchist. Guards! Get this anarchist to prison.'

Two bulky guards now approached Kratu to show his place.

Fear moves the universe. It makes one talkative, silent, amusing, vicious, frozen, jumpy; anything. It can make one sleep and also keep him awake, can make him shed tears and also make him laugh hysterically, can root one to a spot and also make one run, can make one sweat and also go dry. Kratu was afraid. He had never been so afraid in life. Even while returning at night from the forest to his ashram, he had never felt any fear. The idea of confinement and the associated feeling of being trapped made him sweat. He panted.

When crushed to the core, one's essence oozes out. That is how grape gives wine, mustard gives oil and stone gives dust. Anyone in that situation would have clung and cringed at the feet of Pret Vardhan. But Kratu's dignity, born of religious culture, made him stand tall amidst the debris of his security in front of the evil spirits. From his crushing, came out a prayer from the Vedas, '*abhayam mitrat abhyam amitrat, abhyayam jnatat abhayam puro yah*': Let there be no fear from friend, no fear from foe, no fear from the known, no fear from that which lies before us unknown.

Dignity! Ah dignity!

Kratu had been taught that Vedic prayers, if uttered correctly, had complete control over the world. These mantras could bring even the gods down from the heaven to the earth. He was now witness to the miraculous power of the mantras when chanted with a focussed mind, although the focus was born of fear. The two guards, approaching him fell down unconscious in the court. Even the ministers trembled in fear.

Pret Vardhan felt nauseous at the chants. In extreme agony and anger, he screamed, 'Who are you? Get out of here. You have surely brought something nasty and unspeakable from some other world. Get out before I kill you.'

The power of the mantras seemed to have awakened the strength in Kratu which showed in his humour, 'Can a ghost kill a ghost? I am just curious.'

Pret Vardhan blared like a broken foghorn. 'I get my power from Yama, the god of death. With the power bestowed unto me, I banish you from here.'

Before Kratu could understand what was happening, he was shooting through the void to land before Yamaraj, the god of death.

Yamaraj is the first one to have died. Since he had lived a righteous life, performed *yajna* and *tapasya*, Brahma, the Lord of creation, made him the lord of death. No created being can ever transgress his authority, which is not delegated but is born of virtuous conduct. When it comes to ruling over others, there is nothing like moral authority.

In the physical world, Yama rules through the laws of disintegration, and in the world of souls he rules by regulating their entry and exit. There have been cases when some powerful fool tried to overrun his jurisdiction. They were, however, all humbled before his virtuous power.

'Oh, is that you, Kratu? One who does not forget anything? Welcome!'

'You know me?'

'I know the past, present and future of everything. I am the lord of life and I lord over death.'

To stand before someone known in an alien land is the greatest confidence booster. Kratu felt good. Good was now good for him, without any riders. Much later he mused over this emotion. Does fear add weight to make one feel weak, or does it take away strength to make one collapse?

'What is my future, O Lord!' asked Kratu in true humility before the virtuous. Humility before the fake is mere fake.

'Let that remain the privilege of the astrologers. They too have to eke out a living.'

'You probably do not know the future.' Kratu felt that he had nothing to fear from Yama, the noble.

Yama laughed uproariously, 'Clever, eh!' He then said, 'Every life has a pattern amidst chaos. Why chaos? Because you don't see pattern in the existence of others. Again, your story has a pattern for you, but it is all chaos for others. To be free, you have to read your story fully and the pattern underlying it by experiencing it. Once you have read your story fully, you will be free. You will then know the story of others too.'

'Lord! Do you mean to say that freedom is the ultimate future of all, as disintegration is the future of all things on Earth?'

'These questions will be answered to Nachiketa when he comes here after some Earth-centuries. Till then you can have your conclusions.'

'My Lord! Will Nachiketa also be under some curse?'

'You will know about that in due course. Now, till your time to stay here is not over, you enjoy the place as you wish.'

'I suppose so. If I have to go back to Earth, I will at least have some nice description of all this.'

'Who will believe you? You may even get crucified for telling the truth.'

'Lord!'

'And make sure not to commit suicide in future. I do not want the balance of this place disturbed by you with the knowledge from Earth.'

Kratu's purity, born of austerities and learning allowed him freedom to move. However, the sin born of suicide forced him away from wherever he was. He was thus constantly on the move. Sometimes he moved very slowly and at other times he was dragged fast. He ate while on the move; slept, washed, conversed, and thought while on the move.

Anvi clapped. 'How wonderful!! I also do things while on the move. I am so like Kratu in heaven! In fact, we all behave that way all the time.'

'Yes, life is more or less uniform.'

Time went on like this for a while. Once, Kratu chanced to be in the august presence of Yamaraj again, who smilingly asked about his welfare. Kratu bowed in reverence and when asked for some wish, he requested to be shown Hell. He had seen a lot of Heaven.

'Hell? What is that?'

Kratu told the popular beliefs that he had about Hell.

'Oh! You earthlings can come up with any kind of a nomenclature and then follow it with your vivid imagination. There is nothing called Hell, there is only CCC, Cosmic Correction Centre. Yes, some folks are sent there to let out their spiritual pus.'

'Can I visit that?'

'Correction Centres are not a tourist place. You have to be its inmate to be there. So, I will do a favour and send you to see the Futuristic Correction Centre. Our architect, Viswakarma, is busy constructing the place for the spiritually sick of the future.'

Yamaraj then asked escorts to take Kratu to see the futuristic Hell.

The Board on the gate read, 'Futuristic Cosmic Correction Centre'.

Viswakarma was the divine technocrat. Of his many great acts, he had acquired fame by creating the invincible *Vajra,* the weapon for Indra. The special weapon required special material to build with, so Viswakarma suggested that it be created with the bones of the great sage Dadhichi, who was established in such purity that just his bones could destroy the vilest of impurity. The gods then approached the sage who gladly agreed to give up his body for the welfare of others.

Kratu knew the story and had been uncomfortable about the fact that the gods had chopped off the head of the sage for their personal gain. He asked that much to Viswakarma, who was the cause behind that bloody act.

'Why do you attach so much value to your body?' said Viswakarma with contempt. 'Dadhichi's sacrifice is the greatest that the world will ever see and will learn from. He gave up his body willingly for a cause that did not concern him or his people. People are so attached to being exclusive that they won't even piss if that benefits others. It is natural for such self-centred ones to expect sacrifice from others and yet condemn those who make it possible.' Viswakarma's beard quivered in agitation.

'I am sorry if I offended you in any way, sir.'

'The world runs on sacrifice. Light comes when oil burns and the light of life shines when people make sacrifices. If everyone thought like you, although that is not possible, then there would be no creation left and our Cosmic Correction Centres will remain ever full.

'May we have a look at the great creation that you are engaged in? Yamaraj was very appreciative of your foresight.'

Viswakarma calmed down on listening to the praise of his creation, as everyone else does. He rarely had the privilege of showing off his creation to any, so he went about it in great detail, 'What we are working at is futuristic,' said Viswakarma. 'God is all knowing, and so is Yamaraj. But I am just a god with some insight in the mind of my masters, who want this next-gen correction centre constructed. These humans are a mighty naughty lot. You cannot predict with them what they will do with their mind. So, let me give you a virtual tour of what I am going to work out.'

The sign on the door said, 'Garrulity Correction Centre'. Viswakarma opened the doors to take Kratu inside. 'Talk. Talk to me. And keep talking,' said he.

Kratu began, 'I am Kratu, cursed by my teacher. I have landed in this futuristic hell hole made by Viswakarma.' He suddenly stopped. He could not hear himself talk.

He repeated the sentences loudly. Still there was no audio feedback.

Viswakarma encouraged him, 'You can try a little harder.'

Kratu now shouted at the top of his voice, reaching the endurance limit of his vocal chords, but he could not hear anything, whereas even the whisper of Viswakarma was audible to him.

He turned vicious, 'IAMKRATU!'

His words were drowned in silence. His common-sense confirmed that he was neither insane nor gone dumb. The failure to make himself hear was making his blood, or whatever fluid was running inside him, boil. He felt that he would burst.

When he was about to get violent, Viswakarma took him out of the room, which made everything normal. 'So, as you saw, this is the correction centre for those who talk too much.

The screamers, screechers, shouters, protestors, sermonisers; they will all have to be in a place modelled as per this room. The inmates there will be able to hear others but will not be able to hear themselves. This will keep them crazy till the time they are here.

Kratu panted in disbelief, 'Believe me sir, you are a torture king.'

Viswakarma took offence, 'Why do you plaster me with abuses? You people commit mischief, God wants to clean you up so that you can be with him, Yamaraj orders the cleaning house to be prepared, and you blame me, the architect, for what you will have to undergo! What kind of sensibility is that?'

'Sorry, sir! May I see some more of your original ideas, please? I got carried away because of my pent-up words. Forgive me sir. Your work shines of brilliance.'

Remembering the command from Yama, Viswakarma continued the tour. The next door read 'I, Me, Mine Centre'. Entering, Kratu found himself with a sackful of coins. They appeared to be made of gold but the moment he touched one, it appeared to be fake. For no reason, Kratu started crying, 'My coin is a fake.'

In no time, Kratu forgot himself and became one with his streaming tears, crying, 'I have been cheated.' Viswakarma had difficulty pulling him out.

Once outside, Kratu felt pretty foolish. To hide his embarrassment, he maintained a straight face and entered the next room, 'Speed Correction Centre'.

Viswakarma waived his hand to bring into life hundreds of animated creatures, all busy doing and achieving, while Kratu was left motionless. 'I want to move; I need to run; I must run,' screamed Kratu. To his dismay, he stood fixed at the spot while everyone seemed to be in motion and enjoying. 'Release me. Now!' shouted Kratu. But there was no release, making him go pensive and then violent.

If Viswakarma had not taken him out, he would have gone insane, he felt.

'We will add some more features to it.'

The idea was frightening.

'However, I feel that it is all useless,' began Viswakarma. 'No one ever gets corrected in these places. Folks from all over the universe come to our centres, spend time and then go back to their respective places more or less as they were before.'

'Then why have all this?'

'I think, this place does leave some impressions in the mind, although not much. Creation goes on and so continues the mischief of people. On Earth, a thief stays ahead of the police. Here, we are many steps ahead of the mischievous, and thus successfully create futuristic centres. Even then the world continues to keep us busy.'

'What will you do if everyone becomes good? You will be left with no engagement.'

'Would you like to visit some more prototypes?'

Anvi loved this part of the story. '*Bhaiya*, can you tell me more of such stories?'

'I will, once Viswakarma gets down to creating more of his Correction Centres for the future public. For the present, I know only this much.'

'What do you mean? A story is a story. What has Viswakarma to do with that?'

'Leave that, Anvi. There is a far more interesting story waiting for you.'

While on the move, Kratu once saw his old friend Aswin going steadily in one direction. Aswin had drowned while saving his friend. His death being unnatural, he could not go to proper Heaven, nor did he have to go to the spiritland. Now he was going wherever he was, humming a tune that Kratu had composed. His memory of Earth had gone, but the impressions of what he had learnt had remained, as it was to remain forever.

Excited, Kratu ran after Aswin, calling out his name loudly. But Aswin did not seem to hear him, or may be he did not care.

Kratu sped up to reach him and said, 'Aswin, it is me; Kratu, your old friend. You are humming the tune I had composed for you.'

'Sorry, spiritzen, we do not seem to have been introduced. And I don't know what you mean by Aswin.'

'What do you mean by not getting introduced? We have been friends since our cow-grazing days.'

'You may be a good spiritzen but you are a bad storyteller. Every good storyteller sounds convincing. And, regarding the tune, let me tell you that folks like to take credit for anything that appeals to their tastes. You are no exception, spirit.'

Kratu felt upset at the words. How could his friend, for whom he had lost everything, behave that way? Undeterred by the rebuff, he followed his friend from the Earth, walking rapidly down. Kratu sped up to be with him without catching up. Aswin's time to be in the Heavens was over and so he was moving on. Kratu did not know that. From a distance, Aswin gave one last quizzical look at Kratu and was gone. Down somewhere.

Following his friend, Kratu too spiralled down uncontrolled, till he landed with a soft splash in a river full of strange creatures that could have been friendly or vicious. He struggled to get out of the river when he saw a mugger approach him. The normal crocodiles generally do not attack humans, but muggers are a different breed. They love human flesh. The mugger started closing in, swimming in ever decreasing circles.

'Help! Help!' cried out Kratu. The mugger closed in.

Kratu closed his eyes in fright when a saintly figure descended near him and lifted him out of the waters. He was Narada, a great sage born of the mind of Brahma, the God of creation. Narada did not want to marry so he was cursed by Brahma to be born in the *gandharva loka*, where the divine beings are expert in dancing and singing. Another curse from Daksha, a sage, made him homeless, and thus Narada was now a globetrotter, singing on his divine *veena* the devotional songs that he composed on the tunes learnt in the *gandharvaloka*. Although always on move, he helped the distraught and created troubles for the haughty.

Narada lifted an unconscious Kratu from the river before the mugger could catch him and placed him on the banks. He then went his way singing divine songs glorifying Lord Vishnu, without waiting for a 'thank you'.

Kratu lay on the bank of the river thinking of all the things that had happened in such a short while. Or, was it a long time? The scale of time being different in the spheres, one cannot be sure about these details.

When it was morning, Kratu realized that he was not on the bank of the same river where he had fallen last night. This disoriented him. The river had earlier appeared to be vicious, but now it was an image of calmness. He wondered if at night he had crossed *Vaitarani*, the river which every soul has to cross while moving from sphere to sphere. He was not sure. The wonders and mazes of life were slowly unfolding before him.

Anvi interrupted to ask Kratu if life after death was true.

'There is not much difference between sleep and death, Anvi. Life continues in both these states as a continuum, but it appears like a set of broken lines in case of rebirth. The change related to body, mind, memory and world is slow, and hence imperceptible, during the period that one sleeps. However, the change during death period is spectacular with these four, making it appear as if the new appearance is a new beginning: now visible, now gone. Imagine someone sleeping in his bed in Delhi and waking up in Kolkata in someone else's bed. It seems improbable and also frightening. Naturally, most people refuse to believe the idea of rebirth. For them, life is like the one-time appearance of a dot from nowhere which merges in nothingness after a time,' explained Kratu.

A lady was approaching the river with a pitcher to collect water. The Indian subcontinent is famed for deep wells, particularly if the land is near a river. In such areas, the river sucks the ground water away like the resourceful taking the wealth away from the poor. So, people had to collect water for daily use. This made riverbanks a hotbed for gossip and exchange of titbits.

To know his coordinates, Kratu got up to approach the lady,

but he felt waves of unconsciousness coming over him. He started losing track of all that he was aware of. The memory was fading temporarily.

After the gestation period, he was born to the lady with the pitcher.

Kratu shed a tear in memory of all that had happened so long ago. 'Master, Master,' he said softly in memory of his teacher.

Anvi had fallen asleep long ago.

A lot remained unchanged for Kratu since then. He remembered all that entered his mind through his five senses, thoughts, imaginations and dreams. His life kept etching marks on the space-time graph, without losing a shard of memory, excepting when he was in some womb waiting to develop some kind of receptor for memory.

Whenever he was born in a new body, he shed a tear or two.

In 326 BCE, Alexander reached the western borders of India. The valorous looter claimed himself to be the son of Zeus, the king of Greek gods. This impressed many, terrified others and made many people scoff at the idea. Galloping, pillaging and plundering, he reached Punjab and succeeded in crossing Jhelum, which the Greeks called Hydaspes; a crude name for a cute river. Things then stopped working in favour of this son of God, so he had to make an about turn; not an honourable thing for a divinely ordained world conqueror.

His teacher Aristotle had wanted to interact with some

fine oriental minds, so before going back, he wanted to take a brahmin with him. The king sent his men to get Dandi Swami, a famous sage in those parts. The sage laughed at the adjectives of Alexander and, without even raising his head from the bed of leaves, he commented, 'God is not a source of violence but provider of water, food, light and life. Your king cannot be the son of God, since he loves violence. He is a mere mortal.' Strong words for an unarmed man to say to the powerful.

When threatened, the sage said, 'Even if you take away my head, you cannot take away my soul, which will depart to my God and leave this body like we throw away old garment. We brahmins do not love gold nor fear death. So your king has nothing to offer, which I may need. Go and tell your king that I, Dandi Swami, will not come to you. If he needs me, he must come to me.'

Alexander came, saw and was impressed by the great sage. He also realized that neither sword nor gold could make the sage come with him. So, he persuaded Kalyan, another brahmin to come with him.

Kalyan was a physically weak person. To attend upon him, Kratu, who was young and belonged to a non-privileged class in that birth, was hired. Unfortunately, Kalyan died on the way, with the prophetic words to Alexander, 'We shall meet in Babylon.' To everyone's surprise, Alexander, who had no plans to go to Babylon, went there and died under mysterious conditions.

All this did not deter Kratu from his desire of seeing distant lands. He continued with the journey and reached Greece, the land of wisdom and western learning in those days. There he learnt how Socrates had been condemned to die by the elite, simply because the saint was showing the light of learning to the young of Athens. This stunned Kratu. 'Here too!' exclaimed he.

The one consolation for him was that Plato, the disciple of Socrates and Aristotle, the grand disciple of Socrates, had rocked the Western thought process. 'Progress, thy name is sacrifice. Human blood has to be sprinkled to sanctify the path before the convoy of progress passes,' thought Kratu pensively.

He was no more interested in the West. He travelled back to India. On the way back, he decided to forgive his teacher. 'If it is in our nature to stay calcified, why blame any one person?'

# 4

# THE POTTER'S WHEEL

The story of Kratu from the past was a living story for Anvi, without her ever realising that it was the story of someone so near to her. She loved the story and belched out its content whenever the situation appeared promising.

Devpuri, the city of Anvi and Kratu, had many clubs, forums and societies that invited speakers to teach people how to breathe, laugh, cry, sneeze, walk, talk and sit. Some of them had arrived in their art and some were pushed to their arrival by the media managers. Of course, their talks helped people unburden their time, emotions and purse, and hence word-makers were in great demand with the lazy and the crazy. They were also available on screen for the less lucky.

Anvi's parents attended many of these talks. The sense of belonging to the herd by joining the talks gave them confidence, and participation in discussion on the trivial gave them standing among the big.

The family once went to listen to a famed speaker from YOLO forum, who believed in the idea that you only live once. Rich in his expressions, the speaker could use words which were even beyond the ken of dictionaries. He used his magical qualities to dismiss ideas about God, religion, scriptures and afterlife as fertile products of idle minds.

Language, words, reasoning, quotes: what else remains to decimate a docile opposition? The crowd cheered in approval at the charisma of the famed. 'Lucky to be born in the age of enlightenment when we have such great minds,' was the silent refrain of the audience. He concluded with, 'Liberty is what makes us unique. So, take up the vow to liberate yourself from the weight of the age-old dead. Fossils are best left in the museums, and not as ideals for the living. Give up the lie and be free.'

Kratu clapped with enthusiasm. The speaker looked at him in admiration, 'A positive transformation, I suppose.'

The audience was still clapping when Anvi got up the stage with, 'I wish to tell you that what you have been talking is all wrong.'

'May I have the privilege of knowing the reason for the young lady's disagreement?'

'My brother Kratu is the best brother in the world. He knows everything. He has been narrating to me a story in which rebirth, afterlife, heaven, gods, everything is true. I can tell you, Mr Speaker, that my *bhaiya* is never wrong. This means that you are wrong.'

'My dear young lady, this is what I, a noble servant of truth, have been trying to convey. The concepts that do not meet the eyes are wild fantasies; a sack of stories. Why should we go believing that no one can show or prove?'

'My brother Kratu can prove you wrong. You do not know him. He is the best.'

Anvi's mother hid her face in shame and hissed at Anvi's papa, 'Why don't you do something?'

The speaker addressed the audience, 'Ladies and gentlemen, if I am ashamed of something in my life, it is the baggage of my link with the society that is mired in intellectual bad debt. I feel sorry for the parents who push minds of their children into the sty of nonsensical beliefs.'

Anvi's mom was in tears. The image that she had created of herself in the society was getting ripped apart in public.

Papa mustered his courage and went up to the dais and apologized profusely to the speaker, who nodded in a knowing way, 'This is what happens when you feed garbage to your kids,' he seemed to be saying under his breath.

'Why must we apologize when I am telling the truth?'

The usually dignified clapping of the audience had turned into a wild expression of interest. Kratu was on his feet and clapping vigorously. Ma glared at him into silence.

The meeting ended in chaos.

On the way back, Anvi was angry with her brother who did not come to her rescue when she needed her most.

Ma vented her fury by throwing a volley of uncharitable expressions at the traffic and the traffic light. With the angry energy spent on a neutral object, she screamed at Kratu, 'What stories and what rot have you been pushing into the mind of the innocent girl?'

Kratu let it go. When asked again, he said firmly, 'Anvi likes to hear stories and so I told her what I know.'

'You and your imagination! You two are not sleeping in one room from today.'

The unilateral decision by the seemingly powerful resulted in war. Anvi stomped her feet and refused to obey the instructions, 'You are my mom and I respect you for that. But your Hitlership cannot enter every area of my life.'

At night, Kratu consoled his sister, 'Wisdom and emotion are not for public display. Words of the wise are more precious than gold for a miser, and so they seldom speak in public or before the uncultivated. Waste not your words on insensitive or shed tears on the unworthy. That is the mantra for inner peace.'

Most of it was lost on Anvi. She demanded that Kratu continue with the story.

Kratu was born to the lady who had come to the river with her pitcher. She belonged to the caste of the potters, who took great pride in being what they were. Poverty and lack of respect stemming from caste connections had not yet taken roots in the society. One could be rich and gain respect by being true to one's profession, the choice of which was partly hereditary since it gave advantage of developing life skills since childhood.

As Kratu grew up, he was pushed into the finer points of the family traditions. 'Look son,' said his father, 'look at this big wheel that we spin to give shape to soft clay to produce anything that fancies us. Brahma makes the wheel of the universe spin to create beings, and we spin the wheel to create things. Do not think that I am being proud. Just look at the whole thing impartially and you will realize the fact for yourself.'

Kratu was not sure if he was impressed but he looked at art of pot making with appreciation. Clods were beaten into fine dust, mixed with water, kneaded thoroughly, made to spin on the wheel, given shape and then put to dry. If there was even a little imperfection in the product, it was not passed off as style, but was put back in the wet clay to make it go through the process again. Once the perfection was achieved, it was put in fire to be given permanence. Never again was it to go through the cycle of kneading-wheeling. 'It appears so similar to the life process,' thought he.

However, he was not at all happy with his situation. He had tried telling the family that he was actually a brahmin boy under curse. His father always replied, 'Yes, yes. I know. I was a king in my previous birth,' implying that Kratu's words were a ploy by the lazy to avoid work.

The Vedas prescribe four kinds of worship that may be performed by all: daily worship, special worship, motivated worship and purificatory worship. Following the tradition, Kratu's family once wanted to perform a special puja on the occasion of *griha pravesh,* entering their newly built house.

In those days, puja was performed as a *yajna*. The *yajnas*, performed by noble brahmins, were believed to bring favourable results and even gods were believed to come down from the heavens to accept their share of offering made by the sages, although they were visible only to the eyes of the spiritually evolved. A successful puja required right material, a good brahmin and proper performance of the rituals.

Priests, particularly village priests, are not sages. They somehow maintain the tradition, with an aim to earning a livelihood by imitating the sages, although they have neither the capability nor the renunciation of the great. However, that is how life runs; one has to take the ordinary with the great. If one wants to have only Einsteins and Darwins in universities then a lot of government expense on education will be saved.

When the puja was being performed, the priest kept uttering

the mantras improperly. His wordings were poor and the intonations were all wrong. Kratu was watching respectfully the rituals and rigmarole of Vedic worship, with which he had been so familiar, but when he found the mantras so pathetically presented, he objected vehemently and uttered aloud with perfect intonation, the first mantra of the *Rig Veda: Agnimede Purohitam Yajnyasya Devam-Rtvijam, Hotaaram Ratna-Dhaatamam*. The mantra is in praise of Agni, the fire God.

'How dare a potter's son find fault with my divine knowledge? You are not trained in the finer arts of the Vedas. You are good at turning the potter's wheel and you better stay confined to that,' screamed the priest.

'There is nothing divine about what you are doing. You are cheating the gullible, and if things continue like this, I am sure it will be the second nature of the brahmins to cheat the innocent. As for me, I know more of the Vedas than all of the brahmins of the village put together,' retorted Kratu.

'I tell you,' said the priest to the family, 'this boy is possessed by the ghosts. For his and your safety I advise you to take him to an *ojha*, an exorcist, right away.'

There were worried looks and tears all around. The whispers making round seemed to confirm what the priest was telling.

The silence all around encouraged the priest. 'Actually, I too know how to exorcize ghosts, but after this insult I refuse to have anything to do with you people. So, you better go to the village *ojha* before it is too late for you.'

Kratu refused to go. Instead, he started chanting more mantras from the Vedas to prove what he had been telling. The family was now convinced that some powerful ghost, possibly a *brahmadaitya*, the ghost of a brahmin, had possessed their child. His mom cried for her son.

Unable to control an agitated Kratu, the villagers tied him with a rope and dragged him to the *ojha*, who lived on the outskirts of the village. The privacy gave him the advantage of secrecy in which he could hide his ignorance.

The *ojha* performed elaborate rituals to exorcize Kratu. He first protected himself with mantras that no one could understand. He then drew a circle within which Kratu was kept confined, burnt a large quantity of red chilli and looked at the contorted face of Kratu, who could hardly breathe. His eyes, nose and face were burning. In a grave tone, the *ojha* confirmed that Kratu was possessed by a deadly *brahmadaitya*, who could be thrown out of the boy's body by giving him a sound beating.

The onlookers were amazed at the great powers of the ojha. They tried remembering all the brahmins who had an untimely death. Was it so and so or someone else?

Kratu screamed to be released. But who listens to the wise when the world runs on ignorance? Watching keenly the screams, the *ojha* confirmed that the demon was getting restless and hence dangerous. To put the ghost in great trouble, he put more chilli in the fire and signalled the drums to be beaten with force. He then started dancing in frenzy, making Kratu wonder if that fellow himself was possessed.

Kratu was now worried about his safety, 'Why did I have to tell these dolts who I really am?'

The last part of the ritual began. The *ojha* picked up a stout stick, making everyone shriek in anticipation. If there was any doubt in the mind of Kratu, it bid a final farewell, and Kratu blurted out, 'Yes, I am a ghost. Do not beat me. I will leave this body.'

There were gasps of admiration.

'Tell me, who you really are?'

Kratu could not think of any name, so he said, 'I am Angi. Angi's ghost.'

The *ojha* put more chilli in the fire which made Kratu confess more of his crimes as a *brahmadaitya*. Angi, the great sage of some other time and place was now proved to be a vicious ghost who was out to commit the most heinous crimes on the innocent. The irony was not lost on Kratu. The sage, whose words had rolled Kratu in this plight, had now acquired the infamy of being a deadly ghost. Poor Angi! He might have been enjoying the fruits of his nobility in some heaven, without realising that his disciple had made a ghost of him.

Not satisfied fully, the *ojha* gave a few juicy ones to Kratu, who now admitted to every possible past and future crime.

When released, Kratu lay on the ground panting for some time. With the *tamasha* over, the crowd dispersed. Kratu's father tenderly put his arms on his shoulder and guided him to home. Kratu stayed silent throughout.

When it was dark, Kratu slipped out of his house and went straight to the *ojha*'s place to set his hut on fire. From there, he entered the village and did the same to the priest's house and then left the village forever. Next day, the villagers blamed the untamed ghost for the mishap and blamed it for the disappearance of Kratu. There was only sympathy for the priest and the *ojha*.

When the *ojha*'s hut was burning, the flames caught a few leaves of a nearby mango tree. In pain, it passed on the information on the root-net to all with some cuss words against Kratu. It also had some rough words for the patriarch who had asked them to remember and respect Kratu. Being of a different species, they never had difficulty recognising a person even in a different body.

The old mango tree had been dead for many years now. Its place was now taken by another old tree, who knew well that if criticism of the past elders was allowed, then the fire of revolt could catch the existing too. So he managed the youngster with, 'Calm down, kids. The road to greatness is paved with raw pebbles. There will be wounds and blood for a traveller of this path. Learn to respect the traveller without looking at his wounds.'

The junior mango trees obeyed.

Kratu's mom shed tears all her life for her lost son.

Anvi was upset that the hero of her story had burnt down something. She expressed her feelings to Kratu, who laughed at her with, 'Life is a package deal, sis.'

'What is a package deal?'

Kratu ignored the question and continued with his narration.

Thousands of years later, Kratu came to know about three magi who had been to Bethlehem to offer their salutations to the Lord who was born in the desert lands. The story was floating around as gossip. Finding out as much detail about it as he could, Kratu realized its significance and set for the second time to the West. The journey this time was mainly over land, so he had a far better time than what he had with Alexander.

By the time he reached Jerusalem, the story of Jesus was on its last page. He had been judged as guilty and was to be crucified. The word passed in the crowd that before his crucifixion, Jesus had said, 'Father, forgive them, for they do not know what they are doing.'

Kratu reached the site where the Lord stood crucified to the cross. There he waited till evening to offer his *namaskar* before the great went back to greatness. When alone, Kratu offered his prayers to the Lord on the crucifix and said, 'Lord, I know who you are. Accept the *pranams* of an oriental. But why did you have to tell the ignorant who you are!'

Jesus smiled, 'A time comes when one has to tell who he is.'

'My one prayer is that in future you please make your advent only in the holy land of India. There people will not wait for your death to adore you, instead once they recognize your divine nature, which India does instinctively, you will be worshipped even when alive.'

Jesus gave his beatific smile.

Kratu then saw the mother and sister of the saviour from this physical world approach the site. Knowing well how family emotions run, he took leave of the master. He visited the Lord everyday till he was gone from the world of good and bad forever. He would now be visible only to the pure in His subtle form.

After setting the two houses on fire, Kratu left the village forever. He could not stay in a place where hurts and pain would be the new normal. He also had to find Aswin whom he had seen falling from Heaven. The consolation was that probably he did not remember his past and so he was not suffering as much as Kratu was. Nevertheless, he had to be found out, thanked for his commitment and saved from any ordeal that he might be undergoing.

While on the run, Kratu vowed never again to talk about his past. The chilli in the fire and the stick on the back were great incentives for his self-promise.

He crossed the river and climbed the clay clumps of the slippery steep bank. Once on the top of the bank, he saw a huge meadow dotted with cows. Someone at a distance was playing on a flute.

Hungry and exhausted, he walked towards the source of the sound. There, he was, the flute player, under a mango tree, eyes closed, and his senses lost in the oneness of sound coming out of the wind instrument. The notes from the flute moved smoothly up and down, while the sound produced by this movement remained undulated. Music, musician and music instrument had merged to become one; only oneness, or maybe even the loss of that, alone remained.

The cows, alarmed by an unknown smell, acknowledged the presence with loud mooing, passed from cluster to cluster till it hit the ears of the young flute player. The flow of notes, dancing on a single tune, ended. The rhythm of creation snapped.

There was no need for a *deja vu*. Kratu remembered everything so he did not have to get a feeling of some remote past. 'Same set up, same story,' thought he. Only there was no way to know how many years had passed. The idea of a universal calendar to keep the count of years was still thousands of years away.

The young boy, tending the cows for his guru, was Ritam. He was young when his father died. His mother had sent him to the ashram where his teacher gave him some basic spiritual instructions and then sent him to the forest with some cows, asking him to return after some years.

Following the instruction of the great, Ritam had come to

the forest with the cows and had lived the life as Kratu had done years ago. Of course, Ritam knew nothing about Kratu or his great discovery.

Music, released from its captivity by Kratu, had spread like sweet fragrance, silent but effective. Skilled singers and musicians had taken to the idea of seven notes and many now preferred to play their music accordingly. Ritam had picked up the flute and its notes well before he had joined the ashram of his guru. He played on his flute, watched after the cows, and contemplated. The morning and evening were dedicated to worship based on the Vedas. He spent the remaining part of the day diving deep in the inner world which helped him fathom the limitless.

'What is a word if not a mere symbol of an idea or a concept?' Ritam thought. 'And, what is this world as perceived by me? Isn't it a bunch of ideas coming to me through my senses? So, aren't word and world same? Isn't then idea, object and word essentially same; only perceived through the triad of the sense and understood differently?'

He was going deeper. 'What might happen when there is no idea to convey, not even that of nothingness? Will that be the death of word and hence the death of the mind itself? Of course, yes. What will remain then: Void or fullness? It has to be fullness, since I am aware of it. Yes. Fullness alone exists. Fullness is joy. Fullness is strength. Fullness alone exists. Variety is the play of the full on the full.'

The infinite is infinite. It is neither something physical nor abstract that can be described, deduced, inferred or imagined. Diving deep in the stillness of mind one can feel the essence of infinity by becoming one with it. A pot of water is different from it only till it is not poured back into the ocean. Once poured, the question of oneness or difference does not arise.

In that state of oneness, time, space and mind: everything lose their identity. What remains, remains. It can neither be called one, nor zero, for there remains no existence to create the idea of distinction.

It was time for Ritam to go back to his teacher with the cows. He had been playing on the flute for the last time in the forest, full of joy of his spiritual wisdom, when Kratu arrived.

'Who might you be?' asked a surprised Ritam.

'I am Angi's ghost,' said an agitated Kratu. His hurt at happenings around him was refusing to leave him.

Ritam let out the laughter of the free. 'Indeed you look like a ghost with mud and grass sticking all over your body.' He then added, 'Going by your tone, you must be an angry person.'

'Sorry.'

'Looks like you took the world too seriously. How else can it give you such deep hurt? An arrow shot from a distance cannot pierce deep.'

The softness of sympathy melted Kratu's stubbornness. Tears trickled. Only a while ago he had vowed not to tell his story to anyone, but the poise of the young sage made him open up. He narrated his story.

Ritam's face shone with the joy of the happy. He embraced Kratu and said, 'How wonderful to meet the conduit through whom music flowed down from the *gandharvaloka* to this Earth. Blessed are you friend. No suffering can ever be too high a price to produce what you have. I feel privileged to meet you. The wheels of the world are greased by the likes of you. Blessed you are.'

Kratu stayed silent.

'I will be returning to the ashram with the cows. Will you care to join me?'

Yes.

Driving hundreds of cows is not easy even for an expert cowherd, what to say then of Ritam who was a mere brahmin boy! He somehow managed to keep the herd together with the help of Kratu and moved slowly towards the ashram.

On way, Ritam narrated his story in brief to Kratu and then said, 'Friend, I have realized that all this is one, and I am that one.'

*The universe rises in me and sets thither*
*Alone do I exist, none else is there*
*I am intelligence pure and one*
*Not body, senses, nor mind ever*

Kratu found it difficult to believe. He hazarded, 'Isn't it difficult to believe that the bull in this herd and you are one?'

'Indeed what you say is correct when seen through the prism of the mind. But when you realize that fullness alone exists, how can one distinguish an object from another? There is the essential oneness behind everything. Between the river that you crossed and the waves that you saw, the river alone is true. Its waves are born of the river, exist in it and merge in it. There is no independent existence of wave away from the river. When you see the wave, you don't see the river, and when you see the river you don't see the wave. Blessed is the person who sees oneness behind everything.'

'What you are saying is so counterintuitive!'

'Information always appears logical, for it is processed by

the mind, whereas knowledge seems counterintuitive, for it is actually intuitive.'

'If I am to believe you, then time too will lose its meaning. There will be no present, past or future.

'How correct you are! Indeed time is a manufacture of the mind. Once the mind is stilled, time too stops. Past, present and future have no meaning in the absolute.'

Kratu looked blank.

Ritam explained, 'Look at the sight before you. You can see the whole of it. Now imagine a situation in which a blinder is put on your eyes, with a pin hole in it, and you are allowed to move your head only in one direction. What will be your perception then? You will have past, present and future. Everyone in this world is moving around with a blinder with a pin hole: the mind.'

'I appreciate your arguments, but I am sorry to say that I do not find it reasonable.'

'It should take struggle of many births to realize this truth, sir. However, it is not as complicated as you might think. Let me explain. Tell me, how much is two and two, and how you get the answer?'

'It is simple. We learnt it in our early days to get the answer as four.'

'So, why do people often make mistakes while answering a question, whatever the subject that might be?'

Kratu kept silent.

'It is because you reach the right answer by giving up every wrong answer, although you do not realize it.'

Ritam then pointed at nearby tree, its branch and then a particular leaf on it, 'What do you see?'

'The leaf.'

'Where are the tree, branch and the surrounding gone?'

Ritam then explained further that when one focuses on the right thing, then every other possible existence vanishes, even though they might exist for others. 'To get the right one, you have to first give up all the wrong ones. This is true of the supreme reality too. To know it, you have to first give up all that surrounds it, which are like the possible, but wrong answer. You think that you are true, the world is true, the Vedas are true and the universe is true, because you are surrounded by all these wrong answers. Give them up, and then the right answer will become self-evident to you. You will then know what I have been telling.'

Kratu persisted, '*Yajnas* can produce anything, sir. Even the gods are bound by the power of mantras recited during *yajna*. Of what use is this oneness, or whatever you say, is?'

Ritam smiled. The smile carried the power of inner silence and conviction of truth. 'It is difficult to be great, but it is more difficult to see greatness in others. It takes ages of patient learning to appreciate others.'

Kratu felt hurt. He felt that he had greatness by his side. Wasn't he who had given birth to seven notes of music? However, there was something in Ritam that made Kratu silent.

'Fullness is knowledge, fragmentation is ignorance. Knowledge is joy, ignorance is death. People do not die of starvation; they die of ignorance. Ignorance makes people die again and again through their many births.'

Kratu remained silent.

Ritam continued, 'Have you seen a river when it is full? Even if you be frightened of its breaching the banks, you can never miss the majesty that such a river carries with it. Anything that is full – the full moon, a full river, a full ocean – are all images of fullness, which verily is the outreach of God. Joy lies in fullness.'

'I mean, why would anyone try what you have achieved? It has no practical value.'

'Why do we need to judge everything by market value? You are so gross.'

'Not even a fool engages in an activity without a purpose. Your knowledge, even if that be great, does not have any purpose.'

'Knowledge is an end in itself. *Vidya* is the ultimate result of pursuing it all one's life. However, *vidya* can produce any result that one may want. I know nothing about your *yajnas* but I can produce anything that you or your teacher can produce.'

'Joking, you must be.'

'Just look around and say which one is the real you.'

Kratu looked around to see nine facsimiles of him surrounding Ritam. There was no way, simply no way, to tell one from the other.

'Who is the real Kratu?' asked Ritam,

They all vied for the honour. Each one of the ten Kratu knew everything about the erstwhile Kratu.

'Stop! Stop!' cried one of them.

Ritam smiled, and there was now only one. It was difficult to say which Kratu remained, the original or his copy.

'By giving full, one becomes full. Learn to give whole of you and you will become one with the whole. Multiplicity is *maya*, seeing the part is *maya*. Get out of *maya* and you will be one with the whole.'

'Must be,' said Kratu politely.

'Look brother, my *ashram* is approaching, and we will not be together for long. There is a saying that if two persons walk seven steps together, they are then bonded for life. We walked together for so long, so I owe you a favour. If you want, I can take away the curse from your teacher. The burden of memory is heavy to bear.'

Kratu thought for a moment and then said, 'No, noble sir, let the curse remain. I need to find out my friend Aswin who gave up his life for me. I won't be able to find him if my memory is gone. I will rather live with pain than be damned in my own eyes as being selfish.'

'That is fine. Just remember that fullness is joy.' Saying so, Ritam entered the ashram, and Kratu walked towards nowhere once again.

# 5

# HOMA

Higher reaches are achieved by giving up one's attachment for the lower. Yet, even at those higher planes, one has to carry the baggage of one's body, which demands food at regular intervals. Unlike the machines that humans have made, the body needs nearly the same amount of food when passive as when active. A lot of crime, passion, wars, development and goodness percolate the society because of the demands of the belly.

Kratu had left his connections with the potter family but he had to pay the belly tax by finding a way for livelihood. Moving all over the land, doing odd jobs, begging his way around, he once met Isan, the woodcutter.

Like the potter family, Isan took pride in what he did. Illiterate but wise, he had given himself to doing what came his way with all sincerity, leaving the outcome to fate. Restraining thus the emotions born of success and failure, he had gained complete control over his mind, which he valued most in his life. No one had ever seen him lust after anything, nor was he ever seen angry.

When Kratu approached him to be taken as an apprentice,

Isan happily agreed, believing that anyone who came on one's own was a gift from God. Such a gift should neither be rejected nor should one try to hold on to that when it wanted to move away. He often sang:

*Wind blows and light shines*
*Never being they of mine*
*Why hold then me on to what*
*Comes in life ever unasked*

Soon Kratu learnt to trudge the routine of Isan. They both left for the forest with their axes in the early hours of the day. The shapely trunks felled by them were used by the rich to quench their vanity and the chopped branches were used by the poor as firewood for their survival.

The duo took their lunch break when the sun started its downward journey, blowing off powerful blasts of unpatterned energy which causes only ruin and burns. Isan had been long enough in his body to know that one can face the brutality of the powerful, but it is impossible to parry the assault of the marauder whose hold on power is nose-diving south.

During the break, Isan took rest while Kratu sharpened his axe on a stone. They also exchanged titbits of their life then.

One day Kratu realized that Isan never sharpened his axe, while he had to do that daily. He asked as much.

'Son, any work of yours that does not enrich you, is a sheer waste. The goal is to make your inner self rich and not merely to complete a task.'

'Oh!'

'People and objects, whose help you take in accomplishing your work, should also benefit through you. When you use the axe, its edge should get sharpened, instead of it getting blunted, as happens with it all the time. Only the selfish use persons and objects without caring for them.'

Kratu's embarrassment ran wild.

To hide his discomfiture, Kratu changed the topic by pointing at the nearby oak tree, 'How about getting that big, fat tree down, master?'

Isan went silent for a while and then said gravely, 'No one can cut down that tree, son. Not you. Not me. Not anyone.'

'What do you mean by that sir? I don't know about your strength, but I do know that my muscles are powerful, and my axe is fresh. Give me any tree and it will be lying head down in the lap of Mother Earth in minutes.' Saying so, he steamed up with an inner fire that only the young are privileged to have; his muscles twitched, lips quivered, eyes blazed, hairs bristled, and his breath became heavy. Unable to control his feelings, he twirled his axe. The reflection of the bright sun from its sharp edge caught the eye of the master, who blinked.

'That is how I too felt at your age when my father told me what I told you. However, one has to taste humiliations to learn humility.'

'What has humility to do with cutting down a tree, sir? My axe, when wielded by my powerful arms, can take care of any cutting other than chopping off the head of God, if he has one. Allow me to proceed. Please.'

'Go ahead,' said the calm master.

Kratu reached the oak tree in one bound and struck ferociously at one of its lower branches with his weapon.

It is said in the Puranas that the legendry Parasuram had wielded his axe against the warrior class to get rid of them twenty-one times. What ferocity! Kratu might have known the story and was probably emulating him. Unlike Parasuram, however, Kratu's axe drew a blank. Instead of the sound of the falling branch, there was a big 'BOOM' like a mighty hammer striking an unmovable block of steel. Kratu's axe went flying through the air and he himself was thrown on the ground by the force of the recoil.

Anger, the inseparable friend of failure, made Kratu jump up from the ground, pick up the axe, and hit the tree hard – all in one single motion. The boom this time was louder. However, the axe did not go flying; Kratu had held it firmly and had planted his legs carefully.

The mocking boom from the strike angered Kratu further. His emotions were now a jumble of frustration, anger, humiliation and pain. But the tree was unrelenting. The rapid strikes only made the forest sound like a foundry in frenzy.

'Enough!' said the master softly, who had arrived silently near Kratu. 'Stop wasting your vitality on the immortal, son.'

Kratu stopped. In frustration, he kicked at the tree viciously.

'Let me tell you the story centring around this tree. We all know this story and anyone who wants to have a career in wood, has to know it. It is a long story so we will have to stop work for today.'

Kratu grunted.

The master began the story, looking at the legendary tree.

'Our forest shelters everyone the way a grandma pampers the young,' said Isan. 'Sages scorched by the world, bandits with blood on their hands, outlaws seeking safe havens, the rich looking for a break, and the poor struggling for bread – all get refuge here. The forest rejects none and demands nothing in return despite its body getting dismembered everyday by the greedy and the needy. It is thus that generations of villagers have lived around it, maintaining their lives and building up legends.

There are, however, occasions when the net of safety of the forest gets blown away by the higher forces of nature, of which storms are the worst. Many years ago, a storm of unusual brutality struck this area. Inhabitants of the forest trembled with fear. The unlucky ones were sucked up and thrown far away from their marked area, with their limbs telescoped. They could not even get burial in the land of their birth. The unluckier ones panted under the dead weight of the fallen wood, praying to be relieved of the misery of their existence. The less unlucky ones ran from one shelter to another, only to lose a limb or two to the savagery of the cruel and got pain and tears in return.

For the forest, it was the night of terror, loss, and destruction.

When the morning sun came out sheepishly, its heat was toned down hugely. It probably knew that it had been at the root of all the destruction previous night, so it was being gentle to its children.

The Sun was a welcome relief for the dazed denizens. The living slowly limped towards life after the sun had taken a few paces towards the west. Birds, reeling under the shock of unprecedented loss last evening, dragged the dead weight of the personal losses they had just suffered. It is the great irony of nature that when one loses the external weight of relationships, he starts staggering under the increased emotional weight. Those are the moments when one wonders whether relationships are extra luggage, or are the contraptions to lighten one's emotional load!

The junglefolk looked around warily at the surroundings which now looked so unfamiliar. The landscape itself had changed for most of them and many others had lost their known landmarks along with their dear ones. The blooming forest a day earlier was a mass of debris, of which a lot had been brought from outside. There were roofs from distant villages, big and small objects from all over and dead ones from other parts of the forest. The weak cried, the strong went mute and the kids tried to suppress their glee at the newness of events.

Every dance of destruction results in a rhythm of creation. Nature, like a miserly house maker, never allows wastage of its resources and so finds ways to optimize its loss. A small bird, not belonging to that forest, lay panting on the top of one of the heaps of debris.

Overcome with compassion, one bird asked it, 'What is your name?'

'Mom,' replied the shaken bird.

Some young ones arrived to watch the new one. Like any other young, they were indifferent towards the miseries of others. They giggled at the answer of the birdling with the whispers of 'a foolish one!'

'Where are you from?'

'Mom.'

'Where is your mom?'

'Mom,' said the teary eyed baby.

The tears of the birdling set the young ones tittering. 'Silly, isn't he?' whispered a young one. 'Who allowed this mama's baby to fly?... I would have died of shame before crying in public.'

A sparrow couple who had lost its brood in the storm, offered to adopt the baby. No one objected. A little gain or loss during such a calamity carried no importance.'

'Hierarchy, the spine of any society, is well pronounced in the avian world, as in our world,' said Isan. Eagles, famed for their sharpness of eyes, swiftness of limbs, and stinging intellect, were the clear toppers for the post. There were vultures, of course, but being carrion eaters, they were never considered in the hierarchy. The sparrows were more or less perpetually on the bottom of the ladder.

Whatever the social status, everyone wanted a good name for their nextgen. For the purpose, the sparrow couple took the baby to Mister Flamingo, who was surprised to see the baby bird. It had thin, shapely legs and longish wings. Despite his anguish, he looked straight in the eyes of the wise, something that not even the eagle did out of respect. The kid definitely had an inner fire – Homa. Yes, that had to be his name.

Without looking directly at the sparrows, Mr Flamingo suggested the name. 'Homa signifies strength and power. The baby was born out of the power of storm, so this is a befitting name for him.'

That is how Homa, the unknown bird, got his name, identity, and address.

'Do you know how creation takes place?' asked Isan.

Kratu knew all that the Vedas had to say about creation,

he, however, chose to stay silent to hear what this illiterate woodcutter had to say.

Enthused by Kratu's silence, Isan began.

Brahma, the lord of creation, creates the universe through meditation and his mental power, from which sages and noble personalities come into existence. In turn, they too populate the world through pairing up. Sage Kashyap was one of those greats, who with the help of his many wives helped the creation grow. The sage was also the father of the divine bird, Garuda, whose mother was Vineeta.

The family of Garuda birds evolved as the powerful of the avian world. Of these birds, Garuda stayed in Heaven, the Homa family chose the heavenly space as their home and Argenta came down to live on the Earth. Because of gravity, Argenta became the smallest of these mighty, with a wingspan of less than twenty metres, while the other two had larger wings.

By virtue of its choice of abode, Homa enjoys its freedom in the space, but it also has the problem of instability. Whenever a mom is heavy with egg, it has to come down towards a planet due to its increased heaviness. When the egg separates from the womb, it keeps falling towards the nearest planet or star, during which the egg hatches. When the newly born chick comes quite near the surface, it realizes the impending danger and then takes the upward route to the safety of its mom.

This chick had been falling through space for days when the fierce storm started raging.

'See mama, no wings!' The birdling exhilarated.

'Careful baby, these are dangerous airs. Come up right away.'

Before the baby could understand what was happening and why, he had been sucked into the vortex and pulled down towards the Earth.

'Mom!' shrieked the baby in terror.

The lack of training and its tender baby wings made it plunge a lot lower than the safety limit permitted.

The mom-Homa was horrified at the turn of events. She screamed and dived but it was too late for her to save her baby.

The baby went into a free fall and finally crash landed in the forest in its new avatar as an earthling. And like any other earthling, it was now subject to the vagaries of internal and external nature. Worse, its body was now far heavier than that of a fully grown Homa bird. It meant that it could not fly out of Earth's gravity to space.

Flying helplessly, high above the clouds, Mom shed tears for her baby who was now trapped in gravity with a body. Caring mom she was, but she was helpless.

In exasperation, she approached Indra, the king of gods, and pleaded against the injustice meted out to her baby by Vayu, the god of winds.

'Neither I nor my baby has done any karma to deserve this fate. Nor have I offended Vayu in any way. O Lord! I want my baby back. Please,' cried she piteously.

Indra was unmoved, 'I can understand your pain. However, neither I nor our creator God Brahma can do anything about it. Even Lord Vishnu, who is the lord and master of all, can do nothing about it, for there is no magic in our existence. We can only wait till your baby makes effort to get out of the mess he is in. We can try to hasten the process but there is no abrupt way to end this. When God incarnates, even He cannot end His stay on the Earth or any other sphere magically. He too has to go through the phases and emotions of the sphere, although He is not affected by the karma of all that. Now, we are not Lord Vishnu. We have to face our karma here and also in any other sphere.'

There were more pleadings and more tears. When nothing came of all that, she cursed Vayu, 'Let the curse of a crying mom be on you: you sucked my innocent baby to Earth, so you too will be harnessed by the Earthfolk. Your flow that had been unhindered till date will be one day channelled and regulated as per the wish of human beings whenever they want.'

'How do you know all this in such detail, master? You sound as if you were present all along at the site of the events. Are you making it up,' asked an incredulous Kratu.

'There are truths, lies, stories, legends, history and many other forms of words. You cannot say that a story is true or false, since every narration is an extension of the narrator. Take up any story, or even history – these are all reflections of the narrator in words. The same story told by two persons will be different for obvious reasons. So, whatever the facts surrounding Homa, the story is what I am. I am true, so this story is also true.'

'Do you mean to say that all the stories in the Vedas are like that?'

'How do you know what the Vedas contain?'

'I just heard it here and there.'

'Well, you are correct. The stories of the divine are in fact the personalities of the sages as presented in words. They are neither true nor false.'

Kratu thought.

Isan continued.

Ma sparrow made extra rounds of the forest to feed Homa, whose hunger never seemed to sate.

Pa sparrow made fun, 'Good investment, I am sure.'

'Why you male folks always have to calculate in terms of good and bad investment? For me, the smile of the satisfied baby itself is the best return of my labour.'

So, when Homa could fly out of the nest, there was a big relief for Pa. Ma, on the other hand, felt pangs of loss at the joy of feeding the baby. Caring that she was, she always kept an eye on where Homa went and what he did.

She made sure that Homa grew up as a good sparrow.

Homa was growing up and so were growing his data inputs, which were organized in the growing pattern of knowledge, but his dreams refused to fit in with what he saw, heard, smelt, felt and tasted. He often dreamt that he had become an unbound flier in the open space where stars and planets lived.

Learning is the process in which one learns to fill the incoming data in the existing frames, existing in one's mind. If one has a large number of frames, gained through exposure, he is then known as learned. The new data entering such a person's mind has a better chance of becoming a 'proper noun' instead of being a 'common noun'. A cowherd knows every cow individually, while an onlooker sees all cows in a herd as merely 'cows'.

As one grows up, one gets plenty of exposure and thus succeeds in creating many more frames in which he can fill new data and make sense of memory, dreams and imaginations that keep invading his space.

Unable to cope with the dream data, Homa told his parents about his predicament.

'I often saw myself as the king of birds in my dreams till I got married to your mom. The reality has never been displaced since then,' said Pa sparrow.

Ma wondered aloud if it was time to get a bride for Homa. Scared, Homa kicked away the ephemeral unreal for the tangible real. Soon he became an ideal sparrow, fearing all and depending on leftovers of the powerful.

Dreams are not real, yet at times these can be pointers to the real.

In spite of Homa's commitment towards becoming a good sparrow, his inner urges pushed him beyond the permissible limits of a sparrow. Without letting his mom know about his exploits, he started exploring the forest. That is how he met Sukarna, the vulture who mostly stayed in a state of rest in deeper recess of the forest.

Sukarna welcomed, 'Oh, is that you Homa, the sparrow who is not a sparrow? I have heard about you.'

'I also know about you, sir. You sit the whole day and eat the dead. If it be true that one becomes what one eats, then you must be a dead bird by now. So, am I talking to the dead?' laughed Homa. In spite of the huge power within the wings and beak of Sukarna, Homa felt safe with him.

'Witty, aren't you? Wit is a gift of God to the special ones. What are you doing by wasting your precious life behaving like a sparrow?'

'Come, let us have a fight. That will be a good engagement

as per your suggestion. But promise that you won't tell about the fight to my mom. She gets very angry whenever I have a fight with any.'

Sukarna laughed uproariously and said, 'Mama's baby! I can't fight with you, Homa. Accept my defeat.'

Homa was too young to recognize humility born of strength. When asked to explain, the vulture narrated his story.

In the beginning of this cycle of creation, every species fought for supremacy in the world. However, ultimately the two races of gods and asuras became true contenders. You should know that despite their eternal enmity, they are step-brothers whose mothers were sisters.

Our ancestors were great fighters and had softness for the godly forces, so they joined Indra, the king of the gods in his fight against the asuras, and helped him win many wars.

Indra was pleased but was also worried about the appetite of our ancestors. Left to ourselves, we could have wiped off the creation in no time. Aware of this, Indra devised a plan. You know, in spite of being godly, he is quite scheming. Believe me Homa, many devils hide behind godliness and unspeakable cruelty lies beneath beauty.

Indra said, 'O king among birds! We grant you the privilege of being the divine mount of Lord Vishnu. We also bless you that whenever Lord Vishnu is in any crisis in any of his avatar, your descendants will have the privilege of serving him.'

After the blessings, Indra laid the bait, 'In the mortal world, when someone dies, his soul leaves for different spheres of existence depending on the kind of action it has performed. For this, a soul must not be allowed to linger long near the cast-off bodies, for which they have weakness. Human beings dispose off their dead by burning, so their soul transmigrates easily, but the birds and beasts tend to hide in darkness at the time of their death, so their soul keeps hovering there. It would be great if you kindly agree to finish off the dead bodies of whatever species, quickly. That will help their souls wend their way to other spheres. We, the gods, request you not to refuse this service to all.'

In return, Indra gave my ancestors additional boon to see far and to stay invincible against enemy.

The truly strong are innocent at heart. They neither scheme, nor can they understand that others can be scheming. My ancestors were strong, so they fell in the trap led by the godly. Since then we have stayed true to our words, although we would prefer even to turn vegans than to be cadaverous eaters. But even the vegetables are living beings and hence we cannot eat them.

'So, my dear Homa, I hope you can understand how I cannot abuse the privileges accorded to us, and nor can I outstep the bounds of vows.'

'Fascinating story. So, do you accept that I am the winner?' said Homa.

The king of birds smiled at the naiveté, 'Not many come to visit me. As a reward to your kind gesture, I promise that I won't eat your dead body. You can consider yourself the winner that way. If you want, I can admit that much before your mom.'

A frightened Homa flew to safety.

An unknown bond between Homa and Sukarna developed. Whenever free of foraging food, Homa landed up to meet the big bird, making sure that his family knew nothing about it. Sukarna, old and wise that he was, told the baby many stories about the forest and realities of life, the underlying message being, 'Be strong, be free'.

'You need to be strong, Homa, strong to the point that your acts will be effortless and spontaneous. For that, you have to give the whole of you. Once you are established in strength, you will be able to give whole of it to anyone. The miserly always keep something back for them, but the strong do not hesitate to give all.'

Another time he said, 'Passion, young one, passion. Where is your passion? Where are you consistent? You take up one thing and then another thing the next day. It shows lack of passion, which is a pointer to your lack of strength.'

'Are you strong, sir?' asked Homa.

'I know it, the world knows it and you know it. I don't have to blabber about it in the world. My humility about it shows that I am strong. You show off only what you have in limited supply.'

Homa loved listening to Sukarna, without understanding much and rarely putting them into practise. Sukarna once told him, 'You may not be able to practise all that I say, but it is always good to know truth. Knowledge creates aspiration which turns into achievement. Never stop learning.'

Sukarna loved Homa more dearly than he had loved his own birdling. What the sparrow family had done in matters of shelter to Homa, Sukarna was doing the same in matters of training him up. 'Be free. Strength liberates you; fear binds you down.'

Unknown to Sukarna, the winds of change had started

blowing softly in the personality of his pupil. It was soon to become a whirlwind and shake the forest.

The crows were the second-tier scavengers after the vulture family. They found it offensive that Homa was hobnobbing with Sukarna but not with them. To straighten things up, Budhiraj, the leader of the crow community, one day addressed Homa as 'orphan'.

One takes offence at lies and also at truth if it demeans them. To demean someone is to squeeze him in a smaller space, the consequence of which is invariably brutal.

Homa objected to the adjective used by the crow, who in return taunted with a 'truth hurts' jibe. From there it was an easy go for the verbal to become physical.

'You orphan, what are you? A coward, hiding in a sparrow family. Look at me. My sharp beaks can tear through the hardest hide and my wings know a hundred types of flights, something that you may not even have heard of. My flights include: rising up, swooping down, whirling around, coursing straight, proceeding gently, advancing speedily, moving forward, going sideways, flap and glide, hawking, hovering, zigzag and myriads of their combinations. You may not be an achiever but at least learn to be humble before an achiever,' said the crow.

'Like any worthless, you are a braggart. The greats know one; the ordinary know many. I know only one kind of flight and I can beat you with that in both height and distance.' Homa's squeezed space was oozing out anger in torrents. Onlookers gathered to see the conclusion of the conflict.

Angered, the crow attacked him laterally, to which Homa gave him such a powerful kick that the crow went into a tailspin to the ground, injuring himself massively.

On getting the news of the hurt, the crow community gathered, cawed and then went in a body to attack the unprotected sparrow couple, and threw them down in blood. Not knowing of the developments, Homa sat near the crow, full of sympathy for the fallen till some birds came hurriedly to inform him of the death of his parents.

Homa rushed home and was shocked at the sight. Furious, he went and attacked the crows, who counter-attacked him collectively.

The challenges before him and the fury at the loss of his parents awoke Homa's strength and speed. After that, countering a bunch of the cawing was an easy deal for him. He went high up like an arrow shot from a powerful bow and from there he dived on the crows, taking with him quite a few of them at the same time. The onlookers were surprised to see the height to which Homa could reach, and the speed at which he ascended or descended to annihilate the fighting power of the crows.

Sukarna, with his long eyesight, watched the unfolding of strength.

Cowards that the crows are, they dispersed in fright, cawing loudly.

When Sukarna and Homa met next time, Sukarna said, 'I am glad that you fought and won easily. In future, learn to hold back your strength. The truly strong also have the strength to hold their strength in check.'

'Sure, my master.'

With parents lost, and his own strength on public display,

Homa was now welcome on any tree, including the oak tree around which the story centres, said Isan.

Homa's divine mom in the heaven was not sparing Indra, who could do nothing to take Homa out, although he was in the know of his affairs. When Homa's fight with the crows was over, Indra said, 'Now he will soon be trapped and be out of the place.'

'How, my Lord?'

'Strength is weakness and weakness is strength; these are one and the same. Push one's strength beyond a point, and it will become the cause of his destruction. Similarly, the strength of a person lies in his weakness. Push weakness beyond a point, and it becomes his strength. Timid folks are weak, but that is what makes them survive more than the aggressive.'

'So?'

'Your baby, Homa, is gloating over his newfound strength. This strength will become his weakness soon and he will meet his fall. Let us watch how things unfold.'

'My Lord! You are only trying to put me away as any secure person does. If you were as insecure as I am, you would not have delayed my petition.'

'It is not that, divine-bird-lady. I told you before how we cannot interfere in these affairs. However, I assure you that Homa will soon meet his physical destruction. No one with this kind of power can survive on Earth.'

A new arrival in the form of a never-before-seen beauty in the forest awakened interest and also fear. Homa made friends with her who introduced herself as Mrini, someone from a distant land.

Homa's friends cautioned him with, 'Never trust the unknown.'

'Forget not that I too came as an unknown.'

'Yes, but that was during a calamity. The norms for peacetime and troubled times are different. You sure know that.

Sukarna, the wise, told him, 'We make ourselves susceptible to weakness and then bring misery upon ourselves. Why invite trouble of the unknown?'

Homa maintained the silence of the determined.

Sukarna felt the reticence and so continued, 'There is a story that when God was contemplating on beauty, He gave it to the male members of every species. This created a lot of resentment among females. God then gave beauty to the females of human beings, who are the only female to have beauty, as you can see all around. Later, God created another species with beauty, and to stay away from controversy, He did not create any male member of them. This species can stay in any form as they wish at daytime but become poisonous at nights. I am not sure if this new arrival is from that species. I have seen the world and never seen anything like this, so I am apprehensive. My fears are not the fears of the immature, but are the caution of the experienced.'

Homa was now more determined in his resolve. 'Yes sir. I will surely obey you.'

'These creatures procreate through viciousness, which fertilises them. So they use people, and abuse relationships. Do listen to me as you have always listened, Homa.'

'What makes you think, sir, that I will not listen to you? Life is too short to lose a teacher like you.'

Loss of a teacher or not, Homa would not let Mrini go.

Sukarna let Homa slip to fate, 'If my hunch is correct then even the gods cannot save him from this.'

He then thought of driving Mrini away from the forest. For that, he had to talk to her alone, which was nearly impossible. So he had a fight staged between the eagle and an ordinary bird who happened to be a friend of Homa. When Homa dashed to save his friend, Sukarna cornered Mrini.

'Look, I know who you are and what you are capable of. I do have a mind to give one peck at your slender body to make the end of this drama. But should I break our divine vow on a lowly creature like you? No, I should not. So, I request you to leave us and Homa alone and find someone more suitable for you.'

'I will find my way, master,' cried Mrini. Her tears told Sukarna that she was not going to leave.

'I am not scared of you nor am I attached to you. So if I hit you, the sin of hitting you will not touch me. I request you again to leave us.'

'Give me the deadly peck, my master, if you feel so. I feel sad to cause anger in a noble one like you. Anger is the ornament of the weak. How I wish that I take away your anger on me. Unfortunately, I do not have the power to make you do that.'

'Stop this *nautanki*. And not a word of this to Homa.'

'Yes, noble one.' Mrini quaked before the righteous. Mentally she was firm on not leaving Homa. When she was back, she told him all about the conversation. Homa vowed never to go near Sukarna again.

The forest was asleep, except for the prowling owls. One of them suddenly started to hoot in extreme agitation, which was more unusual than rising of the sun at night. Many woke up frightened and started shouting in their respective voices.

The tree on which Homa lived was on fire.

There was no storm or lightening to which the cause of fire could be attributed. Scared birds screeched and flew to safety. So did Homa and Mrini.

Sukarna sighed.

In the morning, Mrini told Homa, 'I am not suggesting anything. But is there a possibility that the crows, your old enemy, might have started all this?'

The strong are never shrewd. Homa believed Mrini and in great agitation he informed his friends, 'Believe me, these lowly creatures must have got the fire from the villages to burn me alive.' He then went to challenge Budhiraj for this dastardly act.

Budhiraj protested, 'Your lies are so unspiced that even a sage will have difficulty gulping it. You have power that does not mean that you will blacken us to suit your convenience. Go look in your own nest; the viper is there.'

Homa was furious at the hint. He pounced on Budhiraj to take out all his unspent emotions trickling in his heart since the first day that Mrini had arrived. However, other birds intervened, and the non-contest was averted.

Another tree caught fire after some nights. There were whispers and even the close friends of Homa gave him side glances. Some good-natured birds volunteered to keep a watch on the crows.

And more fires. The strange thing was that only those trees caught fire on which Homa was sleeping on that particular night. The conclusion was foregone.

Mrini was in tears, 'You know, dear, you are getting a bad name because of me. You are losing your friends. Allow me to go away. I will find a way for myself in this wide world. I don't want you to suffer because of me.'

'The weak love to be loved, but the strong love to love. I am not weak and my care for you is not because of any motive. So worry not.'

Mrini shed more tears.

'Tell me, how you are responsible for the fire? Or, how we, as a duo, are responsible? When two objects combine, sometimes they give birth to a new something that is opposite to both of them. But is that possible with us? Never mind what others think or say. You are under my care and you will remain ever so.'

Sukarna made one last unsuccessful attempt to save his *chela*, to which Homa offered stoic silence.

With all of his shelter and possible shelters gone, Homa now lived on the oak tree with Mrini. Afraid, all other birds left the tree.

Mrini's tears were not stopping. She blamed herself, beating her wings against her chest and wailing. Homa consoled her.

One night, Homa was having a nightmare that his nest with the sparrow family was on fire and that he had to save himself. He got up with a jerk to see that Mrini was not there. Looking around, he saw that she was down below, with her face resembling a snake and biting at the tree viciously. The tree caught fire.

Homa screamed, 'What are you doing! O Merciful Lord of all, what is happening here! Mrini, Mrini, so everyone was right about you all the time. Blinded by my ego, only I was not able to see the truth!'

Mrini advanced towards Homa menacingly and hissed, 'Now that you know my identity, you must die. God has ordained that we stay timid only to those who have not seen our face. Trees had to die for the same reason. Now it is your turn.'

'Haven't you ruined me completely? My friends, my shelter – everything is gone. Now what more do you want?'

'Now this,' saying so, Mrini advanced towards Homa and bit him furiously. Once, twice, thrice.

Homa's feathers and wings went up in flames.

Listening to the story of Homa, Kratu's mind wandered to feel how life was more or less uniform everywhere and at all times: what happened yesterday, is happening today and will take place tomorrow. No story was unique or exceptional. His own world had been burnt many times by noble looking personalities.

Isan had stopped for a while, noticing the distant look on Kratu's face. 'Are you bored?' asked he.

'No, no, master. Your story is so charming. Pray, continue.'

Homa screamed in fright and pain, 'What are you doing? Stop. Stop.'

'Don't you dare cross my path again,' hissed Mrini, 'I wonder how you are still alive.' Saying so, she gave another poisonous bite.

Feathers burning, Homa fell down. He did not hear the hisses or the last fanged attack by Mrini. He breathed very slowly for a while and then went dead to the world.

Mrini's viciousness had peaked when she attacked Homa the last time. This would now allow her to give birth to more like her and thus make it possible for creation in her species to continue.

The other birds were too scared to approach the burning tree at night. In the morning, they came near the tree cautiously to see the dead Homa.

Mrini was gone. To produce the likes of her.

The disposer of dead, Sukarna, arrived under the oak tree where Homa lay to say him the bye. True to his promise, he was not going to eat his dead body. He went near and took in the smell of Homa deeply. Surprised, he said to the assembled, 'He is alive. Wait for a while. He will gain consciousness.'

Someone brought water, some fanned him. An unrecognisable Homa, with burnt feather and crippled wings, opened his eyes, cried 'Mrini!' and collapsed again.

Loving care brought Homa's life back. He could now drag himself somehow, but he wished that he was dead, 'Death is better than pain.'

Sukarna knew the mind of his charge. 'Let us see what juice you have within you. If you die now, it would mean that death is your only reality. Like corn, you were born only to die. So, get up, kid and show your mettle to all. Show to the world and your detractors what you are capable of. You have a debt towards your friends and well-wishers. Repay that by showing what you can do. Get up. Up!'

'I am finished, master. I am finished. Break your promise once and hit me to end my story. Please. Break your bond once, only once.'

'You sound as melodramatic as the *koel* who is the star performer of the forest. She does not take care of her own brood but entertains all with her tales of sorrow.'

'Mercy, master.'

'Crisis is the portal to new opportunity. Now pull yourself up and work on the new opportunity that stands open before you. What stands tall amidst ruins, is the true you. Show us your true you.'

Ignoring the words, Homa lay there panting, and wishing for death, which did not come.

Lying under the burnt oak tree, Homa looked back at his life. 'What did I ever do with the precious life that I got?' He mused further, 'Life is such a beautiful chance to achieve and to give. I did achieve a few things in life, but what did I give in return? Trees burnt down, which used to be the shelter for many!'

When the inner pain overtook the external pain, he decided to do something unique for the forest. 'I will recreate the oak tree,' he said aloud. 'There is nothing that a true service cannot achieve.'

Determined, he dragged himself to the water pond that lay not far from the tree. He filled water in his beak, walked back and poured it at the root of the tree, with the prayer, 'May my life force be transmitted to this tree.'

Like a mom caring for her tender baby, there he was, caring for the oak tree that was as dead as Homa himself. No food, no rest; only the oak – pond – oak.

One day a crow came cawing to Homa, 'So, how do you feel big mouth? Like to teach us flying?' The noise attracted more crows. Each one of them had a suggestion or a threat for the brave who had been laid low.

Hearing of the incident, Sukarna left his shelter to stay near the oak tree. His silence was a great encouragement for the dying.

To everyone's surprise, one day a shoot appeared on the tree.

The life force slowly ebbed away from Homa, while the oak tree started getting new life. Birds watched the deed in unspeakable surprise.

Every step of Homa was now laboured. He panted, breathed hard, sweated, but he persisted.

And then one day Homa fell dead at the root of the tree. The oak had bloomed.

'That is not the end of the story,' said Isan.

The birds of the forest gathered near the dead. The crows were impatient to get their beak in the burnt, when to everyone's surprise, there came a huge bird out of the dead Homa. It was huge. Simply huge.

This new bird flew up in the sky with unmatched speed, and

from there it dived down to the oak tree with perfect, absolute perfect control, and sat on a leaf. Not a twig or a leaf moved. He seemed to have the body of lightning and as light as air. Or, should that be sunlight?

'Allow me to proceed on my journey of life, my friends,' smiled Homa. He then raised his one wing and bent his head in salutation to Sukarna, 'Thank you, master.'

The birds watched in awe. Unseen to them, Homa's mom had come in the sky to receive her long-lost baby.

Sukarna was in tears.

Homa started his flight up very slowly. He wanted the folks of the forest to have a look at him for as long as possible.

Finally he was gone. To his abode of mid-space. Forever.

'Thus', said Isan, 'was created the oak tree, from the blood and toil of the divine, making it imperishable. No one can break even a leaf of the great which was created by the sacrifice of the great.'

Kratu was lost in the story. He slowly woke up from the trance.

'There is, however, a way to get what one wants from the tree. Come, I will show you.'

Isan got up with Kratu and took him to the oak tree. There he made *pranams* to the tree, took his axe, made a cut in his finger, and put the blood round a twig, and then plucked it. The twig came off easily.

'That is how it can be done, son. That which is created by sacrifice, can be destroyed only by sacrifice.'

A sad Kratu commented, 'Why would someone give up his life to destroy this majesty? It is great the way it is.'

It was evening when Isan and Kratu left for their home without getting any wood.

The silence of night in Isan's village was countered by Kratu's riotous thoughts. He had to pay his debt to all those who had loved him. More than anyone else, he had to pay his debt to Aswin who had given his life for him.

'Repay the debts!' said Kratu to himself with conviction.

He left the wise woodcutter in the dead of the night in search of his destination but with no known path to reach that.

# 6

# PARAS, THE FISHERMAN

Memory or no memory, life is in motion, ever, everywhere. Birth – presence – growth – transformation – decay – death: the cycle continues unhindered. In this cycle of coming and going was trapped Kratu, who felt that he had many debts to repay but did not know how to do that. He often broke into song:

*The wheel of crusher, yoked to the moon*
*And to the glowing, travelling sun*
*Juices out tears and smiles of me*
*To offer to world for free and fun*

Unlike others, Kratu's trouble was his memory that made life an unpleasant joke. He lived waiting for death, and then waited for a new life in the world of the departed. 'Memory! What a curse you are!' He often mused. 'Blessed are the ignorant in the world, for they can enjoy life,' he would say in disgust.

Life was boring for Kratu; the king of spirit worlds where one went after committing suicide was fearsome to face; and

Yamaraj, the king of death laughed at him every time he reported to him. He once noted Chitragupta, the ever-serious secretary of Yama, raise his eyebrow at him. Since then he started feeling like a serial offender who gives joy to the jail warden whenever he returned to jail.

He remembered how the sage boy, Ritam, had offered to take away his curse and how he had refused to accept the favour in honour of his teacher. Or was it at that time his secret pride in his unusual power? He now regretted not accepting Ritam's magnanimity.

As the cycle continued, he became desperate till he heard of a fisherman named Paras.

The gossips said that he sat all day on the banks of a river with a fishing rod, but no one had ever seen him catch, sell or eat fish. He had no shelter, no family; he was believed to eat once a fortnight by collecting grains that fell in the marketplace. An unverified story making rounds was that if any beggar approached him on the day of his meal, he gladly shared his bread with him.

He was also a great story-teller which made him popular with children. The tales he told had never been heard before, and seemed to carry a message which no one cared to understand. When in the marketplace or the village, he gladly shared his laughter and stories, although he never imposed those on anyone.

Curious, Kratu reached the riverbank where Paras sat all alone with his fishing rod. Fishermen loved him, but no one ever sat near him with his fishing rod for fear of acquiring bad luck. Poor people have a lot of taboos to fear.

Kratu sat down at a visible distance from Paras. The river water was crystal clear like a mountain spring. One could see the bed of the river, which seemed to be nearer than it actually was due to refraction. One could also see every creature of the river, of which fish were the most numerous; floating, frolicking and foraging. They too appeared nearer than they actually were.

The angling hook of Paras, the fisherman, carried substantial bait.

The aquatic world and the training techniques for its members are quite different than that seen on land or that can one think of.

In the river on the banks of which Paras sat, there lived a large family of fish, in which Papa fish regularly instructed the young ones in the art and science of life, 'We are the greatest in the world,' said Papa fish and waited to see the impact on the newgen.

'When God created the world, He created everyone like us. We were all without necks, as we are. Then there were some naughty ones among us. God pulled them out of water and threw them where there was no water. In the process of pulling them out, their necks got elongated.'

The little fish looked at each other to see if anyone had a neck.

'Shameless that the landfoks are, they keep visiting their old world. Shameless! But how can we take back those who were thrown out by God, the Lord Himself? No, we cannot. May they suffer the aridity of land and air, while we enjoy the freedom and cool of water.'

The small ones made happy noises.

'God is a big fish, who once saved the world from the

great flood. Without our Lord, the two-legged would not have survived. And look at those demeaned ones! They are always out to catch us, the chosen children of God! They don't realize the sin they are committing. If someone asks you what God is doing, you can safely say that God is busy preparing stinking hell for humans where the smell of all our dead family members, bless them, will torment them till eternity.'

The baby fish gave a satisfied look.

Another time he said, 'Life and livelihood are intertwined but one must not give up one for the other. Life demands food and food may cost life. So, kids, you need to be careful while foraging for food. Do not risk your life in your struggle to get food.'

The small ones smelt fear.

Papa fish had to scout for safe food for himself and also for the shoal. After a lot of checks and experiments, he one day said, 'Thanks to our Lord! He has listened to our prayers and sent someone who is ideal for our purpose. Come. I will show you. With a little practice, you can easily trick him and get the bait without the hook.'

'That would be wonderful, Papa!'

Papa fish came with his brood where Paras sat with his bait with the twin aim of getting food and training the young.

'Now watch,' said Pa fish. He slowly moved forward, circled the bait, nibbled at it, moved forward and backward, and then rushed to safety just before the line was yanked out with a big 'Whooa! Got you, stupid fool!' By then the fish had swum to safety.

'Clever one! Survived!' said Paras with glee. He then took out the line, put fresh bait on it and threw the line in the river.

'This is the secret, children. Run for safety just when the line is withdrawn.'

'Yes, papa!'

They now took turn at the bait, now eating, now watching, now terrified, now swimming away.

Kratu watched the fishing for a long time. He had not seen such an entertaining sight for a long time, and he could not stop his laughter at the meaninglessness of the game by Paras. Only a real pro could jerk out the rod so clean, with the bait and fish both gone. Paras was definitely no amateur. Nor was he an ordinary person. Given the food habit and daily routine, Paras had to be a sage.

He approached the fisherman who welcomed him with, 'Hello Kratu! Nice day it is for fishing.'

Kratu had seen so much of the world that he thought himself immune to surprises. But there is no end to learning and surprises in the world. 'How do you know my name?' asked he in surprise.

'Isn't that quite simple?'

'It is not simple, and definitely not quite simple, sir.'

'What brings you to me?'

'If you know my name, then you also know why I am here.'

'Clever! Clever! Just like that fish,' saying so, he pulled the fishing rod out of water with another 'Whooa! Looks like you are an apprentice,' said Paras to the fish, which had escaped to the safety of his father's presence.

Papa fish told him, 'I told you not to be afraid. Just see how simple it was! Do not be scared of this foolish biped. He is God's great gift to us.'

Kratu glued himself to Paras. Except for sleeping, Kratu was always near him, pestering him to teach how to get out of the ordeal in which he was.

One day Paras said, 'Tell me what you know about creation.'

Kratu knew how the Vedas described creation. He had also learnt from Isan the Puranic ideas about creation. Now here was this sagely fisherman who was surely going to describe a new process of creation. 'Who knows? Probably there is no theory of creation at all, which would mean that a time may come when there will be as many theories and models of creation as there are heads. Too many theories mean no theory.' He smiled and then went silent, hinting that the sage may continue.

Paras let loose the thread of the fishing rod and took up the thread of conversation, 'God alone exists. There is no two in Him, which means that God is pure love. Oneness signifies love, while two or more signifies varied emotions.'

'So true.'

'Have you ever loved anyone?'

'No, sir. Not in the sense of being one as you are suggesting.'

'You will have to love someone someday to know what it means to be God. God is love and he can be reached only through love. The Vedic prayers, yajna, devotion – everything is a way to love Him only.'

Kratu stayed silent.

'If you think over the love that you might have ever had – maybe for your friend, say – you will realize that you can love only what you know. How can you love something that you do not know? Yes, Kratu, to know is to love, and to love is to know.'

'Oh,' said Kratu in surprise.

'And what can you know? Only that which exists. Even if you love something imaginary, that thing has to exist in your imagination, and the mind does not care whether the impulse that it gets is from real or imaginary. What does that leave us with? You can know only what exists! Whooaa!' Paras shouted at some of the young fish who had their share of bait by then.

'Since God alone exists when there is no creation, He is knowledge, He is Love. The three are one and the same as I explained to you.'

'Yes, I suppose so.'

'When God desired to create, He, the absolute existence, appeared as three – Strength, wisdom and love. Why these three? Because existence is strength. Strength allows you to be what you are even when everything around you crumbles.'

Kratu thought if he ever had strength when things were falling down around him. 'Probably I had strength. How else would have I survived?'

Paras continued with his monologue, 'Wisdom means to know that you exist, and you will continue to exist. That which will not exist, that which you are afraid to lose, is not true you and hence you should not even think about it, what to say then of brooding over it! Pain in life comes only because we want to hold tightly what we are not. That is the seed and tree of all suffering for everyone. No exception.'

'Whooa!!' shouted the angler, startling Kratu violently. A fish had nibbled deep, and Paras, as was his wont, had yanked the rod out in time to save it.

'Missed it again,' smiled the sage. He then put some more food on the hook, placed the rod in the river and continued with his narration.

'Didn't I hear something similar in the story of Homa?' thought Kratu. 'The philosophy of life seems to have a similar run at deeper levels.'

'And love?' asked Kratu instinctively.

'Come you big, fat one. Today you will not escape my hands! Whooaaeee!' shouted Paras. It was Papa fish who had mastered the art of flight before fright set in. It swam away majestically, demonstrating skills that needed emulating.

'Excuse me sir, you seem to be such a poor angler,' joked Kratu. He knew the truth very well.

'I caught you. How can I then be a poor fisherman?'

Kratu smiled.

Paras continued, 'Love means to be wise about your existence. You love your existence, and all that you consider to be the extension of your existence. No one can love what he does not consider to be himself. One loves wife, husband, children, gold and house – everything – only because he considers those to be himself.'

'How true!'

'Why then attach yourself to what you are not? Because love gives strength. When your love extends to the whole universe, you become truly wise and consequently you get established in strength. Love makes you free, so does wisdom and strength.'

The ideas were difficult even for Kratu.

'When God created, he appeared as three – Why these three? Because one can create only what he is. A horse cannot give birth to an elephant. God is wisdom; wisdom is love; and love is strength. These three are one and the same. Creation thus stretched on the warp of these three. Wherever the Lord was not, there was weakness, ignorance and hatred. All pain and suffering come only because one lacks strength, wisdom and love.'

Kratu looked at Paras in wonder. 'India! India! The land where knowledge walks on two legs! Who or what can harm such a land!'

'Coming back to creation, when the process began, the infinite states of the spectrum – strength-weakness, wisdom-ignorance, love-hatred, permeated the universe. The permutations of the shades of the trio came to be known as ideas.'

Paras was talking to Kratu but his attention was fully on the fish nibbling at his bait.

'The ideas,' said Paras, 'were actually a combination of aspects of existence, as I explained earlier. Each of these ideas, which would be as infinite as the number series, had a name for it but they did not have bodies. It was a funny situation: name and existence without a body! There was no fun in it for anyone. Fun comes from action and action requires body, which the ideas lacked. So, they went to God in a body, asking for a body.'

'Nice pun!'

Some village children had come to the fisherman to see his catch for the day. If he had not caught anything that day, then he had to tell a story to them, that was the permanent treaty between them.

'Baba! How we wish that you miss the fish so that we can fish a story out of you.'

'Welcome kids! Here I am telling a story to this gentleman. You can listen to that.'

'That will be boring, we know. We want stories of wars, fights and the good bashing the bad.'

'What I am narrating is far more interesting.'

The kids sat in a semicircle.

'God smiled at the request of the ideas who wanted body for themselves. He then willed that each idea has a body. The universe of the bodies, visible and invisible, was now created. There were the gods, sages, *gandharva*, *apsara*, *vidyadhar* and other divine beings – each one being the embodiment of an idea.

Then there were the *asuras*, demons and others. On our Earth, bodies of worms, snakes, birds, animals, fish and others came up. Thus frogs and fish, turtles and tortoise, snakes and snail were all an idea each, binding the species within its limitations of strength-wisdom-love, or lack of it.'

Kratu had been to some of these planes of existence so he did not have any doubts about the words of the great angler. Sitting on the banks of the ever-flowing river of life, Paras, the sage, had been angling for ideas and serving it fresh to anyone who was willing to take them, although there were not many takers.

A kid asked, 'What about us, the humans? Are we also ideas?'

'For that you first need to understand individuality and universality. One moves from the collective to universality through individuality. A piece of wood is as good as another piece of wood. This is the state of collectivity. When it is shaped into a chair, it gets individuality and also universality over wood, since it is a chair and also wood. This chair now has a collective existence with any other chair, but if it is turned into an ornamented chair, it now has added individuality, and consequently more universality, since it is also a chair, as well as a piece of wood. The series continues till it become absolutely unique and thus more universal. This is true of ideas too. There are ideas that are barely separable from each other, while there are ideas which are more universal, since these cover a lot of ordinary ideas.'

'Boring! Boring!' shouted the kids.

'Wait, wait. Patience my young friends.'

'Boring! Boring!'

'The prince of ideas was the ultimate universal idea. He was a prince and also a sum total of all other ideas. The prince approached God to be given a body like anyone else. God smiled and gave him the human body. Human beings thus have the strength to become everything that is there in the universe – he can become a god, demon, lion, snake – anything. He can also become the king of ideas – one with God.'

'Boring! Boring!'

'You are scaring my fish away, you naughty!'

'They escape even otherwise, baba.' Saying so, they threw some pebbles in the river to scare the fish away. They did not want their afternoon to be a complete waste.

Kratu knew the Vedas by heart. He had also contributed to the creation of music. In spite of all that, what he was hearing was fresh.

Paras continued, 'So, if you want to be free, Kratu – and I am sure that you want to be – then you will have to first master the world of ideas by becoming one with the prince of the idea world. Only then you can achieve whatever you want to.'

Here was the solution, but it appeared equivalent to climbing the Mount Everest.

'Master, existence continues in one form or the other even after death. In your words, we get a body to express an idea, in whatever world that might be. So how to be one with the prince of the idea world?'

'You have been a heaven trotter, but do you know what these truly are?'

'So, he knows about my stay in the heaven too! God!' thought Kratu.

'There are different kinds of matter and energy all over the universe. Broadly these can be classified as: physical energy that makes our Earth run, psychic energy that runs the world of ghosts and gods, mind energy that permeates the universe, and the mother of all energy – the will of God. These are the four forces that make each existence possible.'

Paras waited for Kratu to absorb this and then continued, 'Each of the worlds has its own dynamics and powers associated with it. A body in a sphere is made from the matter and energy available there, and hence, a body belonging to a particular sphere can interact only with the corresponding world, and that body will have only the powers associated with that sphere.'

He continued, 'The concentration of a particular kind of souls makes one world appear as different from another. Different souls reach different levels of elevation in each of these worlds. On this Earth too, there are people with power, wealth, status etc. in varying degrees, sticking together. One may grow in a particular sphere, but all will never be equal.'

'True.' That was what Kratu could mutter.

'People go to various spheres by the power of their good karma and thoughts. Interestingly, one can also do that by focussing one's mind. You do not have to die to reach this or that heaven, as many mistakenly believe.'

It was all absolutely new for Kratu.

'You can get the power associated with any of these spheres here and now. In fact, it will be quite easy for you since you have already been to some of those places.'

'Thank you. Now tell me what exactly to do.'

'Awareness increases eminence. The more aware you are of something, the more prominent it will become for you. Learn to be aware. Awareness – Eminence – Existence. That is the mantra. Understand this, practise this, realize its universality, and you will be free.'

Kratu needed to reach higher in the empire of mind and then go beyond it. This required a light mind; a very fine and subtle mind.

Paras explained, 'There are two types of gains: master the world through speed and strength, or master them through spirituality. Whatever the way adopted, one first needs to master his mind, which can be done through any number of ways. I will teach you the way through fishing.'

Kratu did not have anything to say. He had to learn anything that the great master could teach him to get out of the mess of life-death cycle.

'Choose any fish from the shoal that is moving in the transparent water. Then focus on it and think only of that fish, till you become one with it. Let nothing come between you two.'

Kratu did that.

The fish are a vibrant species, particularly the smaller ones, who are always on move out of fright or for fun. Watching them for the whole day was a good way to silence his mind. He watched and watched.

At nights, Kratu was to sit tight and contemplate only on the meaning of the *Gayatri mantra*. 'Your sit must be firm. You remember the story of *samudra manthan*? In that story God had taken the form of a tortoise on which the mountain was kept for churning the ocean. The tortoise was so firm in its seat that neither it moved itself, nor did it feel the huge churning going around him. Sit firmly like *Kurma*, the divine tortoise.'

'Sure, master.'

Days changed into months and then into years. Kratu's days were spent in focussing on a particular fish frolicking in the water till it went away from sight, and the nights were spent in prayer to the higher powers to enlighten his mind so that he could be a fit recipient of wisdom.

One day Paras said, 'I feel that my stay here on this Earth is coming to an end. So, let me teach you the essence of whatever I have to. Keep focussing on the fish till you master its mind, and know in advance what it is going to do next. Then you reach the level where you can dictate to it, through your mind, what it must do next. The rest of knowledge will come to you on its own.'

'Do not talk like this. Given the powers that you have, you can easily delay your departure.'

'My job is done for this life. Do me a favour once I am gone. The fish in the river gave me great company. So, give me *salil samadhi*. I will be able to give the fish one last meal, as I fed them when I was alive.' *Salil Samadhi* is when a sage is put in a water body, instead of giving him a burial or a burning.

'Where from will I learn master and who will guide me once you are gone?' sobbed Kratu.

'The controlled mind is your true friend, the uncontrolled mind is your great enemy, and a pure mind is your real teacher. There is no other truth to be learnt in this world, Kratu,' saying this, Paras exhaled for the last time.

Kratu had never cried so much as he cried at the passing away of Paras, the fisherman.

He gathered the villagers, tied the body of Paras to a stone and put it in the river.

The fish family could feel the going away of someone dear. They circled his body without nibbling at it. The natural forces of the river slowly disintegrated the body.

Awareness – Eminence – Existence. That was now the mantra for Kratu, which he had to practise to master the empire of mind.

At daytime, he sat alone on the bank, trying to phase his mind with the movement of the fish. At nights he focussed on the awareness-eminence duo. What he was aware of? Nothing but the external world, his thoughts, dreams and memories.

What if he focussed on something to make it eminent and then cast that aside? That is what he did. He focussed on the fish, made it eminent, and then let it go away from his awareness. This left him only with the awareness of movement, pure movement, sans the fish. He could now predict the movement of a fish.

When one does something, good or bad, it becomes easy to do that a second time. If continued, an act becomes easier to perform till it becomes one's nature. That is how a noble person or an evil person graduates. The evil ones make a mistake: when they do a wrong act a second time, they don't realize that it won't take long for that unpardonable act to become their nature.

Kratu's regularity in practise made him adept in meditation. He felt uncomfortable if he could not sit for long hours in meditation for whatever reason.

He then focussed on movement, made it eminent and then cast it aside, leaving only time in his awareness.

Time. It seemed to stretch.

When two events get enacted under same parameters, they are said to have taken same time. The sun, moon, stars, and everything else with a periodic motion maintain uniform rhythm that can be used variously to compare events of this world. Time, as perceived by the mind, is a measure of internal events. With no events taking place, other than watching time, the mind perceives time as being real big, eminent, and can see it stretch.

He then focussed on the fish again. What is a fish? An idea running through every fish. The so-called individuality of a fish is an aberration and not universality.

The veils that covered an idea were now dropping away. Getting out of his body was now a simple task for him; he had mastered the secret of human body as an idea.

New worlds now beckoned to him.

He could now make a fish move the way he wanted.

People are so attached to their body that they hardly realize what a burden they carry all the time. Freed from the baggage of body, Kratu sped away from photosphere, the world of physical lights and shot through a porous wall. The pores were just right to let him pass.

The sphere where he reached was full of beings with every shade of colour, ranging from dark to pale. No one seemed to pay attention to him till one being with a deep dark red complexion darted at him with, 'Is that you, Kratu? MY, MY! So nice to see you here. Remember me? You used me when you set out to destroy poor Angi's ashram?'

Partner in crime.

Reminding him of past sins.

Embarrassing. Kratu felt stripped naked.

'He, he! And then I came back to you with the rebound energy to land you in the land of ghosts. How was it? Enjoyed the stay? Sorry that you did not command me to be there. I could have been of some use to you there too. Of course the rebound then would have taken you to the real hell.'

So, these were emotions. He was in the emotosphere, the sphere from where emotions shoot out to take possession of beings, and then rebound at them.

People keep complaining why bad things happen to them, without ever realizing that their own thoughts, reflected from the great walls of the cosmic mind, hit them with redoubled force. That is how an angry man meets with violence.

'Your demand for service as the potter was also well served. He, he! You had to run a lot after burning the houses, wasn't it?'

Kratu felt guilty.

'If you earthlings with physical bodies, do not get angry, how will we stay engaged? We drive our power and sustenance from likes of you. Do give me a chance to serve you again.'

'Not in my life, sir,' muttered Kratu.

The exchange brought many more beings of various shades. They all vied for Kratu's attention, reminding him of how each one of them had served Kratu when he was in any of the related moods. The price in each case had been a rebound back at him.

There was a soft hiss. A beautiful serpentine-looking face came forward. 'Remember me from the story of Homa? I am Homa's lust. Remember what happened to him?'

Homa had flown back to his mother in the heavens, but his journey in the middle had been terrifying.

For a moment, Kratu felt rooted to the spot out of fear. After a while, he mustered up his courage to say, 'Lawful or unlawful, rest assured that I will never require your services.'

Mrini, or the emotion that represented her, spat and left. The place where her poison fell flared up.

From that time on, Kratu never let his mind dwell on lust ever again. If ever a floating thought came, he punished his body severely so as not to allow entry to the unwanted.

The other beings present there said, 'Do not take notice of her. Indeed she is not fit for you. But do allow us to serve you again, sir. *Seva ka ek mauka dein*. It was pleasure getting our vigour and strength because you allowed us to serve you.'

'I swear that whatever I may do, I will never demand your services ever again.'

'Ha, ha! That is what you all say when caught. Once you are free of pain, you indulge in same mischief.'

'That may be true of all. Who knows? I may be quite different.'

'Everyone claims to be different, but there never is a unique person. You all are made from the same template.'

Kratu stayed calm at the demeaning words. He had to proceed on a greater mission, so it was meaningless engaging with the base.

Freed of emotions, Kratu felt lighter, and shot through another porous wall to reach the logosphere, the world of words.

Ideas – words – forms. These are one, but they also have their exclusive existence. In the world of forms, physical matter gives birth to forms, while in the logosphere one can create anything by just uttering it.

The place was serene, full, and spaced out, unlike the previous worlds of Yama, gods or even emotions.

'Welcome friend, welcome!' The voice was soft and melodious. A sage appeared from nowhere, who informed him about the place and its speciality. Kratu had known from his Vedic days how mantras, if pronounced properly, could produce material objects. He was now actually in the land where it was the norm.

'Water', 'mango', 'bread', demanded Kratu. There these were.

'You are so crude, Kratu. Asking for the ordinary in the land of specials.'

Kratu wondered what would happen if a tiger appeared through his utterance. He checked his thoughts. Remembering Aswin and his own duty towards him, he asked if he could find his friend from where he was.

'Not really. But you can create a copy of him by just uttering his name.'

'I want to get the original. A copy is for consolation.'

'True.'

'Is there a way that I can have more powers?'

'Yes. If you free your mind of thoughts, you can then reach the higher sphere that permeates this one the way water permeates ice.'

'Sorry to be curious, but could you please tell me why you are stuck up here when you can go higher?'

'It is because of Trouble 69. To go higher I need to free my mind further. This requires *tapasya,* for which I need to get a physical body, which I do not want. Trouble 69, we call it. If you do it, you are in trouble; if you do not do it, then also you are in trouble. I am stuck up in trouble 69.'

That was the end of it. Kratu had to go back to Earth – the sphere that allowed freedom to do good and bad. Logosphere was locked in its goodness, without allowing one to grow, as the heavens were.

When he reached his old place where he had lived with Paras, he could not find his body. Some villagers had found his lifeless body and thinking that he was dead, they had burnt it.

'No problem. I will get a new body by the powers that I have acquired.' And there was a fresh Kratu, with the old mind in a new body.

He then walked to the marketplace to get some food. Seeing him, people ran in fear, thinking that he was the ghost of the dead Kratu.

'What a nuisance! I will have to be born again to lead a normal life. Absolute nuisance. Trouble 69.'

This created a serious problem for Kratu. If he wanted, he could have created a body for himself, but that would balloon into complications. He decided not to use this power of his ever. So, whenever he had a need, he had to be born. One consolation was that even God has to be born from a womb when He incarnates to do good to the world. His appearance is never magical.

Kratu decided not to waste time on rebirth. Instead, he went to a distant place down the river to engage in meditation. India being India, no one cared to verify the credentials of a wandering monk or yogi.

Kratu started his practices where he had left it. The good thing about meditation and its practices is that its effects never wither away. One can pick it up from where one had left it, like reading a book from the page where one had stopped.

He could now control the fish completely now and could create them by just uttering the word. But he needed to grow further, He focussed more. With time gone from his awareness, and ideas becoming pure ideas, without even his sense of awareness of them, he was ready to move on.

By his will, he could now reach the ideosphere, where he could create things by mere wish, instead of uttering the word. Eternal freedom, infinite wisdom, joy and strength lay just beyond the wall which he had to cross. He tried to cross over but hit against the invisible wall. The pores here were finer than he was.

'You can't proceed further,' said an unseen voice.

'And why so?'

'You have one desire left. Your mind is still weighty.'

'What is that, noble sir?'

'You have your love for your friend.'

Kratu was startled, 'How can the desire to help someone be cause for bondage?'

'Good and bad are all same here: these are thoughts. As gold and iron make no difference to a weighing scale, good and bad make no difference here. Till you have a thought, you cannot proceed further.'

'Whoever has heard of such reasoning!

'You need to know that space, mind and time are inseparably mixed, and so to go beyond one is to go beyond the other two. To be one with the infinite means to go beyond space and time. This requires that you go beyond mind. Till you have a thought, you have mind and you are trapped in mind.'

'Allow me to proceed, sir. I will make it. Believe me.'

'Who am I to stop you? You are stopping yourself. The net here is too fine for you to make the crossover.'

Kratu tried to force his way but he only hit against the crystal wall; he could see and feel the presence beyond, without being able to cross it. He tried this and that: he became big and then small, he thought noble and then evil, he smiled and screamed, he threatened and then pleaded. Nothing worked.

A sage appeared before him. Kratu felt that it was Paras, the fisherman sage. But the sheer dignity of the sage stopped him from asking any personal question.

'You cannot cross over till you have the thought of helping your friend. However, since you have been here, you now have the power to know any mind on Earth by touching him/her. But use it with caution; do not waste this power ordinarily or else it will leave you. With this power you can find your friend. You now decide what you want.'

Kratu's dilemma.

To serve or to be free.

Aswin had to be somewhere on Earth or in one of the lower spheres. To locate him, he had to go down, guess him out and then verify the fact with his power.

A long silence ensued and then Kratu decided to repay the debts of his friend even if that came for a price.

Birth – death – memories.

Fine. Be that so.

He did not have to tell as much to the sage. Everyone knew everyone's mind. The sage melted into hugeness.

Thus began a fresh cycle of birth and death for Kratu.

To get rest from the tiring cycle of birth-death, he sat in inaccessible places and meditated on the highest sphere. That way he could avoid being born.

A person, howsoever powerful, belongs to the relative world of thoughts, while the absolute power is beyond good or bad. This power broke Kratu's contemplative state every now and then. Coincidences, inexplicable events, accidents and other such cause forced Kratu to be born again and again. He could not locate Aswin in any of the past births; instead it seemed as if God sent him down to help others.

Kratu's story thus continued and now he was brother of Anvi, after he was blown up in the air from the rock where he was meditating. While narrating the story, Kratu did not tell this to Anvi. She was too young to understand the mysteries of existence.

# 7

# BHU BABA

Anvi's parents were committed devotees of Bhu Baba, a self-proclaimed godman.

Jesus Christ was crucified for saying that he was the son of God and Mansoor was hanged for uttering 'Ana al Haqq – I am Truth'. But India is different. Here, in this land of God, anyone can claim to be God. Instead of hanging or beheading such a proclaimer, some are sure to become his followers. Their argument usually ends with: if God can come in any form at any point of time, then why it can't be this or that *baba*. Good circulation of the real gives rise to the counterfeit, and so India has allowed fake ones to survive since ancient times. Even Ravan had taken up the garb of a *sadhu* to kidnap Sita.

An exponential growth of information and proportional loss of wisdom helps bloom the bluffers. It is true of godmen too. They had such a roaring practise in the info-age that the pseudos of the past were probably tearing out their beards in various Cosmic Correction Centres over their lost opportunity in the golden age of stupidity.

Bhu Baba belonged to the long line of the insincere.

During his early days of spiritual life, he had studied some popular religious texts and had done some *sadhana*. This had given him some powers with which he could control the fools more than he could control himself. Investing in trivialities, he made sure that his fame and following grew in proportion to his pretensions, which he covered with tempting tricks. To add dazzle to his aura, he changed his name or added adjectives to it every few years. He was now one of the top performers of spiritual *tamasha* in the country.

Unfortunately for him, his layers of lies were explosion ready. It now waited, patiently, for a simple trigger to go 'boom' and take his hypocritic world down. Disaster loves to build over time to create a lasting effect.

Entertaining the assembled with his wisecracks, incomprehensible Sanskrit *shlokas*, and showering the much-wanted blessings, Baba took turns visiting cities where he milked money in multiplied proportion to the talks he gave. He did not mind ending his talks abruptly if he was not paid as much as promised by the religious mafia who helped organize his talks, meetings and popularity.

He was coming to Devpuri after many years.

Kratu's mom was very excited, who believed that whatever she had, was due to Baba's blessings. She had hung his pictures at prominent places around her and never forgot to add 'Baba's blessings' and 'Baba's wish' while talking about the good in her life. The bad in her life was blamed on her bad karma which even Baba could not mitigate.

On way to meet the bearded baba, Ma cautioned, 'We will appreciate if you do not make an ass of us in presence of the Baba.'

'Are you telling me, Ma? Whoever has heard of such preposterous allegation?'

'Don't you act innocent.'

'I will stay silent as I am always.'

'You, and silence! Please son, please do not embarrass us.'

'Should I go back?

'Then I am also going back,' said Anvi.

'Now, please!'

Bhu Baba welcomed the family privately in his meeting room.

After paying the customary *pranams*, the family sat on the floor. Baba then pulled out a piece of paper from his table which had '3' written on it. He then addressed Ma, 'He, he! See, I had written this down even before I was informed about your coming. My heart was telling that someone with three will come. The paper says how you are coming with three others.'

'Baba, you are great,' said Ma with sincere devotion. Tears brimmed her eyes. 'We are blessed to take shelter in you.'

Baba gave a knowing smile.

Kratu wondered at the clever trick. Undoubtedly, the number was written beforehand, but there was the sleight of hand in presenting the interpretation. A trick, like scientific probabilities, requires clever interpretation to attract admiration. If he were the only child, then Baba would have claimed '3' to be the number of people coming. If Ma were childless, then he would have added something else to come up with number three!

'Wah! Such a simple sleight of hand to impress the gullible. He does not even labour to acquire better tricks. The privilege of the popular!' thought Kratu.

People love to mix magic and religion at a grand scale. Every juggler in India is thought to have magical stones and herbs, while publicity seeking *baba*s use tricks to pose as being spiritual. *Indrajaal,* the term for magic in India, is itself a mix of religion and magic. Indra is the most famous god of the Vedas who represents the mask of the Infinite, while *jaal,* the net indicates magic. The Vedas describe how Indra takes up many forms by the power of his *maya*. One appears to be many by the power of *maya* and non-existence appears to be existence by the same power. The jugglers in the streets are at least honest about the tricks they demonstrate, but these money makers are another thing!

Kratu looked around at the affluence that was sucked out of the unsuspecting. And to think that the *baba* represented the tradition of the greats who gave up all that they had to be one with the divine. There were Kabir and Surdas who lived in perpetual poverty, Mirabai who lived in a palace like she was in a forest, Buddha who gave up his kingdom. When tricked by his father through his son, Rahul, asking for inheritance, the great Lord had handed the five-year-old a begging bowl!

Kratu lost interest in the winded talker who was into self-praise, 'You won't believe the austerities that I performed at Gangotri. For years, I bathed twice daily in the ice-cold water to soothe the heat coming out of my body due to spiritual practices.'

Kratu wondered if the *baba* had even been to Gangotri. Instead of soaking in the dung of *baba*, Kratu revelled in the fragrance of his meeting with Buddha.

Kratu was living in Vaishali, a short distance from the present-day Patna, when Buddha was about to burst onto the world stage.

Freedom from fear and greed makes life enjoyable. Kratu was free of these two shackles; he had nothing to gain or to lose in the godown of nonsense. Instead, he observed people and indulged in gossip, without any attachment, to add spice to his existence. Kratu was never in the committee of the critics, but he loved listening to those who shredded the reputation of respected persons with the passion of an achiever.

It was through this gossip that Kratu came to know of one Prince Siddhartha of Kapilavastu who had given up his kingdom, wife, and son to seek the truth.

'Just see how people can run away from responsibility,' said one.

'What is the world coming to? Why must one sacrifice one's own to be with the One?' said another wise critic.

'*Haan*, but great achievement requires great sacrifice, *bhai*.'

'Believe me, all this religion and spirituality is a big *tamasha*. Can there be a greater service and achievement than serving one's parents and family?'

Kratu laughed uproariously by thinking of Paras, the sage, changing the nappy of his kids instead of meditating on higher things. He had not yet met Jesus, or else he would have liked to add in his thoughts, 'And Jesus shaping wood planks to earn a dime to feed his mom!'

'You liked my words, *hai na?*' asked the one who had made the comment.

Kratu was no more listening to the froth. 'This is big,' thought he, 'I must meet this seeker who had the strength to give up the known for the sake of the unknown. His love for Truth has overshadowed attraction for the physical. He has to be great.'

Truth, in the Indian context, means to find a way out from the cycle of birth and death.

There were sages before Buddha who had given up everything, including the sacred Vedic rituals, to know the truth. Kratu had known from Ritam and other sages that to know truth meant to be one with it. It was the state where the duality of subject and object vanished forever. However, most people practised religion as rituals, recitals and righteousness and then outgrew their way of life to be one with realization. For an onlooker, it was a natural growth, although uncommon.

And here was the prince, who was opening up a new path to spirituality in which a person could get into the spiritual life directly from where he was.

'This is going to be revolutionary,' thought Kratu.

Gossip is like a chain. By holding one link and then proceeding on, one can reach the truth. Applying the process, Kratu reached Magadha, one of the major states since the Vedic times. He had heard about it many times, particularly when Jarasandh, its great king was killed by a trick suggested by Krishna.

The capital of Magadh was Rajgriha, a pilgrim town. There the gossip told how a different looking yogi had moved to a place near Gaya to meditate in silence. Kratu walked towards Gaya.

Gaya had been famous as the place where every practitioner of Vedic culture came to offer the ultimate rite of one's forefathers, known as *pindadan* on the banks of the river Phalgu, which like some other rivers of plateau region, flows wide during monsoon and lean during other months. However, unlike other rivers, one can find water flowing under the sand bed in Phalgu even in lean seasons.

Kratu found the flow of the river metaphoric; life flowed unseen through the universe, manifesting only where beings were present.

Aryans, the culturally evolved people of India, practised five daily rituals every day to repay one's debts to God, the presiding deities of nature, ancestors, humanity, and lower life forms. They believed that a person's existence is directly dependent on these five, and hence one must have a cosmic connect by praying and making offerings to them. 'A man may be breathing air, a sign of life on Earth, but he is like the dead weight of a corpse on Earth if he does not repay his creditors.' A sage had once told Kratu this. Since then he had followed these rituals religiously whenever on Earth.

Now that he was at Gaya, he was overcome with filial emotion. He went to the local priest and offered *pinda to* his ancestors, from this life and also from all previous lives, on the banks of the Phalgu. This ritual belonged to *Pitri rin*: repaying of debt to manes.

After the ceremony was over, he was filled with a sense of closure. He had repaid the ever-hanging debt on him towards all those who had given birth and nurtured him in his different life cycles. 'How many births, how many lives! Theoretically, I am beyond them, but when viewed in a practical way, I owe them this much. Dear bearers of my weight! Thank you for what you have gone through on account of me.'

Full of good cheer, he asked the priest about Prince Siddhartha.

'*Arre bhai,* this is the land where everyone aspires to become a monk in his old age. How do you expect us to keep news of all of them? And all these yogis and mahatmas are our enemies. They never come to perform their duty towards their ancestors. Disgusting. Just imagine what we will be left for us to eat if people start following them?'

The priest was so right. Buddha's sweep over the land was soon going to take away the bread of many priests. The eternal war between the prophets and priests is the story of religion all over the world. The prophets throw away the yoke of the priests for the time, although priests belonging to the new prophet soon come up with rituals to worship their prophet.

'Noble deeds have their own shortcoming,' though Kratu and moved on after haggling over *dakshina,* the priestly fees. The priest wanted to charge him for the time spent on conversation in addition to the charges for the ritual. Kratu talked him out of that.

Failing to get anything from the priest, Kratu walked down to the marketplace, which is always a good place to get news. The waiting rooms of barber shops are presently a good platform for that, but in those days, barber mostly used bricks instead of chairs, so Kratu had to find some suitable meeting places.

'Yes, there is an unusual yogi *baba* near a village not far from here.'

'Why unusual? We are the land of yogis, *bhai?*' asked Kratu.

'We cannot answer that for sure. However, those who have seen him feel that there is something unique about him, something that cannot be explained but can only be felt, which is not seen with other yogis and *sadhu babas*.'

Kratu reached the outskirts of the village where the great yogi sat under the Bo tree lost in meditation.

Yogi.

Paras, the fisherman.

Ritam, the cowherd.

Kratu mused. He wondered. He saw. He could recognize a yogi when he came across one.

Unknown to any, the yogi-prince, or the prince among the yogis, was on way to reaching the state of mind when it stops taking inputs from the world and then stops its modifications caused by its storehouse of memory, dreams and imaginations. Anyone can do that although very few do. Consequently, a non-yogi has to suffer the miseries of the world: its tears, burns, fire and flames. Even then, he never wants to control his mind. The setbacks and scratches in life make one want to leave the palace of pain, but Mother Nature comes with a new trick of hers to engage the disillusioned.

Kratu thought all this and waited near the tree to have a few words with the yogi, who was all out to stop his mind from rushing out to become many by identifying itself to thoughts and objects. If he succeeded in that then the future multiplicity coming to his mind would stop affecting him.

The yogi had gone skinny; all bones and a thin layer of skin. 'Ahh, prince! Great you are,' admired Kratu. Yogi Siddhartha was too absorbed to take a note of Kratu.

Waiting without success for some days there, Kratu took up

the job of a cow herdsman with the village head. That was a job he was good at from his days with the sage Angi. It took care of his basic needs and helped him in the vicinity of the yogi, with the hope that he would have a word or two when he opened his eyes for the world.

Kratu waited and waited.

One day finally the yogi opened his eyes. The mortification of the flesh was of no use in stopping the mind from becoming many, he had realized. It was not enough to break the never ending cycle of birth and death. He needed to find a different way.

The practices that Buddha gave up came to be known as *Hath Yoga,* which is still practised by sincere and also the showmen of yoga. What Buddha took up from that point, came to be known as Yoga, the real one. There is no glamour in this path; it is all about inner struggles and growth.

Kratu approached the yogi. 'Master is a great yogi,' said he with humility.

Yogi Siddhartha smiled calmly. His mind was beyond the relative of praise and abuse, good and bad.

'What might the great yogi achieve by this never before performed austerity?'

Siddhartha, the yogi, was surprised to see a shepherd asking this.

'Austerity is not my aim. Breaking the chain of birth and death is what I aspire for. That is the only way to get out of sorrow and pain.'

'Allow me the liberty of asking, O master! How his becoming free will help those left behind? There must be many who helped the great one in reaching where he is. Yoga is about inclusiveness. It is about compassion. How will the master shower his compassion to those who carried him on his shoulders?'

The yogi looked inward. What was he thinking? Or about whom? His father? Wife? Son? Who?

Sujata, a village girl was around. The yogi asked for some food. She ran home, prepared some *payasam* and offered to the great yogi, who took it haltingly and then sat under the Bo tree with the firm resolve of not getting up till he became one with the truth. His eyes looked one last time at the world. They would next see the world only when the master's mind had become one with the absolute.

How must have been that last look? A final bye? A relief? There is no way to know all that. Kratu himself had not reached that state.

When Mara, the great tempter, born out of the inner workings of a powerful mind, appeared before the yogi with his last temptation, requesting him not to spread his message, the yogi refused. The wisdom that he had acquired was for the welfare of many, for the good of many.

He was now Buddha.

The morning sun came out with pride to be the first to see Buddha, the enlightened.

When Kratu reached there with the cows, he saw the illumined face of Buddha that glowed the way Ritam's had glowed. He fell prostrate at the feet of the blessed, who looked at him intently and then said only one word, 'Serve'.

They then walked their way; both serving the humanity in their own ways. Kratu walked east and Buddha walked towards west. Soon the Master was to deliver his first sermon near Varanasi.

Bhu Baba had been talking about the meaninglessness of the world by explaining how it was all *maya*. Advaita is the truth. The suffering, miseries, pain; these are all *maya*. Forget all this and say '*Aham Brahma Asmi*'.

While expounding the hollowness of the world through his pompous words, Baba was keeping an alert eye on the distracted Kratu. 'What are you thinking, *beta*?' asked he.

'About the greatness of your tradition, Baba.'

Kratu's parents breathed free. 'My son is a little naughty, Baba. Please bless him. We are so dependent on you for your grace. We have reached so far in life only because of you,' said Ma.

'I know, I know. Kids will be kids. I was also like this when young. *Bolo beta,* what do you want?'

'Nothing, Baba.'

'He, he! You are so good. So I will give you this coin that will help you pass your exams and stay focussed. I wish I had something like this when I was a student,' laughed the Baba uproariously. He did not know that Kratu got best grades in all papers.

'You too, Baba!' said Ma laughingly. It is a big relief to know that the great ones too had their chinks.

'I need a coin more than *bhaiya*,' cried Anvi.

'Yes, mother. Here is a coin for you.' India addresses its daughters as mother. Young girls are also worshipped as Mother Durga, representing Shakti, all over the country by the devoted.

'The coin is definitely powerful Baba. It shows its power here too,' commented Kratu. He was hinting at the affluence of the room.

'Wonderful! Wonderful! You are so humorous. Humour is a sign of intelligence.'

'Thank you, Baba.'

The family left the august presence after offering a hefty *pranami*. Ma was satisfied beyond words, which showed in her tears.

Once out, Kratu begged to go back and meet the Baba alone.

'Yes, son. We are happy that you are impressed.'

'Sure, Ma.'

Baba welcomed him, 'Wonderful! Wonderful! Tell me what more you want. All your wishes will be fulfilled.'

Kratu asked for privacy. When alone, he said, 'Don't you feel ashamed cheating the gullible with your tricks? Do you realize that you have put on the ochre that was once put on by Buddha and Shankaracharya? Do you never feel like a worm wriggling on the canvass of the pure and sacred?'

'Are you mad? Do you want a slap?' Baba raised his voice.

'I am not mad. You are a charlatan. Do you realize that you represent the great line of the sage who gave a begging bowl even to his own son? Do you ever feel the weight of knowledge passed on you as spiritual heritage by the sages on your head, which seems to be filled with crow poop?'

'*Koi hai?*' shouted Bhu Baba.

'Here, take your coin back and give me the silly powers, if any, that you possess. This may push you back to the path of the ochre.' Saying so, Kratu touched the knee of the Baba and threw the coin in his lap. Baba could not understand what was happening to him. He choked and felt drained.

The coin, dropped in his lap, instantly changed into a hissing snake swaying its hood.

'Help! Help! Get him out! Get him out!' shrieked the Baba, with all his smugness gone. The volunteers rushed in, and seeing the snake, they concluded that to be cause of hullabaloo.

Kratu slipped out in the ensuing pandemonium.

'What happened, Kratu?'

'There was a snake in the room. So I ran away.'

'Oh, you lost such a great chance. People seldom get a chance to talk to Baba in private.'

'I am sure.'

'Have you kept the coin safely? It will surely help you move ahead in life.'

'Yes, Ma. It is as safe as it could be with the Baba.'

'Good.'

Within a few days, the news anchors were shrieking how *baba* had been arrested on multiple charges of fraud.

Ma was furious at nobody in particular, 'Jealousy! Jealousy! We, the people of India, have resolved to be jealous of everyone who rises higher than us. Jealousy has been the bane of every slave nation, and we continue to have this slave mentality.'

'So true, Ma. You are so perceptive.'

'Take my word, Kratu, India is never going to be great till the wretched ones do not learn to come out of their narrowness.'

'I fully agree with you, Ma. How I wish more people were like you.'

Ma was not confident if Kratu was truly complimenting her.

Bhu Baba was in a spiritual mess.

Physical bonds and calcified beliefs can be smashed down with effort, but spiritual imprisonment requires the greatest of spiritual powers to make one free.

Kratu was capable of pulling out the heavy from the sty. He decided to lend his hand to Baba, for which he had to wait for some years till he grew up to be independent of his family and emotional package that came with it. Till then Bhu Baba had to wait and suffer ignominy.

# PART TWO

# 8

# VIHAN

Anvi had graduated from listening stories to reading them, so Kratu did not have to narrate to her the stories from past. Nevertheless, a story is a story; it rolls on irrespective of a listener. Kratu thus glided in the present, wafted by the past.

She, however, often had discussions with him on issues that teenagers usually have. These stemmed from her curiosity as also from conversations in her peer group.

'Do you think that time travel is a fact?' asked she.

'It is happening all the time. How do you know that I am not someone from the past visiting you?'

'You always put me down. Why don't you answer directly, in scientific language?'

'Wait. What exactly you mean by being scientific?'

'The same that you mean and everyone else means. It means to be rational and to be consistent.'

'If a person is not rational then he needs to go to an asylum. However, even an insane person has his logic straight, as a child has reasons behind her imaginations. It is a different matter that their reasoning is valid only for them. If universal acceptance be the yardstick for calling something scientific, then most scientists will cease to be scientists. Do you know that Theory of Relativity by Einstein was not accepted as being scientific for a long time? And that Nobel prizes have been given for contradictory theories? Sister, truism is the great enemy of rationality. And, scientists are great at parroting truisms.'

'I mean, there is difference between faith and rationality.'

'No faith runs on irrationality. Only your faith is not my faith, and your cause-effect relation is not my cause-effect relation.'

'Where do you get all these ideas from, *bhaiya*? Anyways, do please say if time travel is possible.'

'No, it is not possible. By its very nature, mind can know something only in real time, and can never distinguish between past, present and future. For it, the present is the only reality and eternity.'

'Wow!'

'Living in the present, one thinks that he will never die; an unhappy person thinks that his misery will never get over; a change in plans disturbs one violently; achievement not meeting up with expectation makes one sad. To flavour things up, the mind adds adjectives to the past while feeling memories and dreams.'

'Wonderful!'

'The future too, like the past, has to appear before mind as the present only. Poor fellow! Pushed by the past and fathered by the present, the future has to remain an orphan. Worse, a mind does not have adjectives to add to spice it up. So, even if the so-called "time traveller" appeared before you, you will know her only as present. In turn, the visitor too will see everything only as present. Her mind can add adjectives of past or future, but her mind, if she has one, will see everything as present and only as present.'

'Gosh!'

'Yes, sis. The present knows no future, nor does the present know the past.'

Unknown to them, someone from future had landed in Devpuri just then. Of course, he was to appear only as someone from the present.

Devpuri, the city of Anvi and Kratu, was India in microcosm. Affluence, culture, religion, aspiration as also their opposites flourished side by side. So did politics, the national pastime of India.

Mr Jeshi was the leading politician of the city whose influence ran up to Delhi. The three trinkets of the rich – power, politics, and press – were at his feet, and in turn slaved to bring more gold to his coffers. He was a bit low in culture, which, of course, was a non-issue for him. With the power that he wielded, he had all the bearers of culture running after him for his kind attention. He had only two weaknesses – power, and his young daughter, Sibi. His wife had died during childbirth.

When Kratu was moving from sphere to sphere, he had come across many ideas in the idea-world who were sad that they were not getting proper bodies anywhere in the universe. They hoped that God won't let them down, and that their time will come some day when they too will have their fun.

The idea of power-pelf symbiosis had been one of those ideas. It had floated through different spheres in search of a body for a long time, but there was no luck for him. Finally when it came across Jeshi, it let out a smile of achievement, 'Here is the body for me.'

Jeshi had made his power-wealth duo grow hand in hand. He often told his coterie, 'Gold, my man, gold is the answer to all problems. Gold may not be god, but nor is it less than god. Look at America, the global leader of pragmatism. What do they have other than cowboy culture? But see how it has purchased learning by the power of its purse.'

His political dependents never contradicted him. Why stop the flow of gold by the folly of one's wisdom? 'Amazing sir! You are so clear!'

'Power comes from the clink of coins. Make sure to have enough of those and your ears will never have to bear your cries of agony.'

'Sure sir. Enlightening!'

Jeshi had been a lawmaker for many years now and he wished to die as one. 'It feels good to be wanted. When you get up in the morning and see people waiting to meet you in anticipation of getting favours, you then feel blessed. What better way to start the day and what better intoxicant one can think of?'

In democracy, votes count, which Jeshi got in plenty through his overt and covert ways of persuasion which were not always worth emulating. Through all this, he had kept his ladder connected with the law makers' body for years. His opposition was permitted to let out the steam of their frustration, in measured amount, during the election campaign only. The only ones who did not tow this line were the members of Peace Party.

The party was a pan-Indian phenomenon which wanted to spread its tentacles all over the world. Its followers were ready to kill and get killed in the name of peace. When scared, which they were often, they behaved like creeping worms, and at other times they struck like cobras.

The party had a dream origin. Some time ago, the founder of the party had a dream in which he heard a voice telling him that peace must be achieved in the world to make it a heaven. As if, people did not know that already!

The inspired dreamer got up hurriedly from the bed to write down what he felt to be divine words. When he could not find any paper on the table, he rushed to the toilet and wrote down the words on the toilet paper. On an afterthought, he added, 'I am the Truth. He, who does not agree, will perish.' He then came back to his bed and slept, dreaming of the happy hunting grounds that awaited him.

In the morning, he had a foggy remembrance of what had happened at night. When he saw the toilet paper, he remembered the great blessing that had dawned upon him. He was now ready to lead Devpuri, India and the world in that order. India, the storehouse of all that has been discovered and practised in the world ever, howsoever inane, does not discard anything. Thus the party thrived.

An intelligent member had come up with the slogan, 'Sense barrels from guns'. Since then bullets were used more freely than words to convince non-believers. The corollary was that anyone who followed the cult was to be blessed eternally, and those who objected to their ways were to perish sooner or later, preferably sooner.

Because of the origin of the cult, the critics called it 'Toilet paper gang'. The Peace Party members made a list of all such 'jokers' and if someone from the list went missing, the city knew who was behind it.

Jeshi, the living glory of power in Devpuri, was one of the opponents of the party. He had created many roadblocks for them, personally as well as professionally. The members had vowed to drive sense in Jeshi's head through bullets of various calibres. If all that failed, then he was sure to walk unhindered through the gates of hell.

Regarding the existence of hell, the cult was divided. Some believed in its existence well below the Earth, while others said that it was within oneself. Whatever the opinion, they were unanimous about Jeshi cruising to hell after death. Given the option, they would have loved to make his life a living hell.

Making a master plan, three members of the Peace Party one day succeeded in cornering Jeshi and his little daughter, Sibi. The innocent girl had planned a visit to the city mall with her father without much of security. Unknown to them, the killers were waiting for them with the intent to kidnap Sibi so that they could make various demands, like release of the members from the jail.

Jeshi was entering the mall when the random firing begun.

Without realising what he was doing, Jeshi ran inside the mall while Sibi was still a few steps behind. That was of course a chance slip. Jeshi was shrewd but not crude.

Once inside the safety of the mall, he looked for his daughter. She was nowhere to be seen. He looked outside and was terrified to see his daughter facing the men with guns. He let out a shriek and ran for her, but the guards prevented him from a certain death.

The sudden firing in the market took everyone by surprise. People looked helplessly at the terrified girl, with foregone conclusions.

A gentleman was standing quite close to Sibi. He calmly

took a few steps towards Sibi and stood in front of her, facing the guns.

He was Vihan.

A learner from future.

A visitor from tomorrow is an oxymoron, as Kratu had explained to his sister. So, no one would know who Vihan was – the man from tomorrow where the present of today is the past of yesterday.

Much had changed where Vihan lived. Also not much had changed. Civilization had moved ahead, people had evolved, psychosomatics had metamorphosed, and kids learned all that was to be learnt before becoming teens. Schools were needed mostly for social interaction.

Kids learnt fast, used their learning to advance the knowledge bank of their society and then waited for death, sometime patiently, sometimes aggressively, as people do at present. Society had not changed much in that.

Words were used mostly as time pass. 'So kids,' would say the teacher, 'We have mastered the art of acquiring knowledge and being happy. We have all that we need. The venomous vipers of the universe do pose threats at times in different forms, but we also have the technology to tame the untamed. We have learnt the art of mastering mind, materials and machines, and have thus evolved from the savage state of our ancestors some thousand years ago.'

'So boring you are, sir! We know all that.'

The elders in the society felt that too much was being focussed on the future, neglecting the past. Not everyone agreed with that. 'These oldies want themselves remembered so that they can burden our present with the dead past.'

In spite of objections, the education council had made it compulsory for the students to learn the history of humankind from the time they could be called humans. The history lessons made the young ones laugh at the practices and beliefs of their forerunners. The kids were too far in future to value the sacrifices of the past to make the present liveable.

'Isn't it shameful for us to call these savages our ancestors? How if we change our past?' asked a kid.

'There have been cases when some bright ones like you tried to do that through the machine, the consequences of which were quite unfortunate. They seemed to have got lost somewhere in the past, about which we have no information. In spite of all the advancement in our technology, we cannot look for an individual in the hugeness of time-space spread. So, the government has banned any such misadventure.'

The teacher was referring to the Past-Present machine or PPM in short, which was used for travels of long distances. The machine shortened the time required to cover long distances through techniques that they had perfected. Using that, one could travel into the past too.

Once in a while, scholars with connections in high places travelled into the past for research purpose, with the undertaking that they would not try to change the past. Requests from lesser scholars were rejected sternly.

The intricacies of permission created the safety net for the travellers. Precautions and preventions were then taken up by the engineers to make the journey safe.

The future had maintained its past well. The details of history were preserved variously in museums and record rooms. Interested ones could have a look at the past freely.

Vihan was a bright kid with unusual interest in the living story of his ancestors who appeared to him like clothed savages. Whenever he had free time, he studied the details of human character and knew well the dress and food habits of people who belonged to earlier era. He had also picked up the language and could lisp it comfortably.

When he grew up, he was bored with the present, so he decided to explore the past. The real explorers are the bored people in the world. Curiosity leads to far fewer discoveries than boredom. A curious person stretches the reach of his mind while staying safe in the cosiness of his world, but a bored person rows out of his comfort zone to chart the ocean of the unknown.

Vihan approached the office that granted permission for the PPM. His application said that he wanted to study the living present of the past.

The officer in charge of the PPM called him for an interview and commanded sternly, 'You have been taught since your childhood not to think of any such thing. But it seems your learning has remained immature. We let you go with a warning. A repeat offence will invite punishment.'

'Yes, sir.'

'But the aura on your head disagrees with what you are saying.'

The aura referred to the particular kind of light that comes out of one's head all the time. The colour, texture, build and intensity of the aura are indicative of the state of the mind which can be seen by a powerful mid. People of Vihan's time-space were advanced enough to see aura of a person all the time and thus could know the inner working of that mind. This could be embarrassing in moments of passion. Kids, on the other hand, created fake auras out of fun to annoy the elders.

'Sir, it was the momentum of previous thoughts.'

'I caution you again. It is for your own good.'

Vihan stayed silent. He calmed his mind so as not to throw any defining aura.

The authorities put a special watch on him to make sure that he did not indulge in any misadventure. But the young will be young, whatever the land or time. In spite of outward humility and obedience, they will do what they set their mind upon.

The cost and speed of communication is the measure of progress of a society. Economists have come up with many theories to measure the wellness of a society. However, a definite way to find if a society is affluent and happy one has to see how fast its modes of communication are, as also the cost involved in that.

Vihan's society had made communication fast and cheap.

The scientists had come up with mind-machine twin, which was the manufactured twin of a person. The machine lived and grew with the original, knowing all thoughts and aping all actions of the person. It could move in air, on water and land at any speed when with its master. One could consult with it, talk with it, and live happily with it forever, if need be. These machines thus acted as a carrier, counsellor and consoler of a person. The only limitation of these machines was that they could not travel through time-space. For those travels one had to depend on PPM.

Everyone in Vihan's land had such a twin. The government

was prohibited from probing any mind-machine even after the death of a person. To distinguish a man from the machine, MM was added to the name. Vihan's twin was thus known as Vihan MM.

Vihan placed his dilemma to his twin, concluding with, 'So, do what?'

'You are the master. My purpose of existence is to be with you in whatever you do or think. I cannot judge your action.'

Discipline withholds freedom but gives security. Every inch of freedom lost due to discipline is compensated by equal measures of security for the community. When someone got proper permission to make use of the PPM, he also got the security cover related to it so that one could return from wherever he had been to. The mavericks, however, did not have that privilege. They lived with their sharp intelligence and died due to its brutality, stuck in some remote land in the forgotten past. Vihan was not to get the support to bring him back to his land if he landed in a mess.

'I may get stuck in the past. Being unauthorized, my superiors will not try to locate me.'

'I will surely reach you wherever you are and bring you back. You only need to send thought waves powerfully. I am not sure how long it will take those thoughts to reach me, even though these travel faster than light.'

'You think my thoughts will reach you?'

'We, I mean you and me, are more powerful than anyone in this land. I am sure that you will be able to reach me if you can send powerful bursts. I cannot accompany you there in the journey, but I am sure that I can reach you wherever you are, at least for a moment like a fleeting shadow, and take you out.'

'I know I can depend on you.'

'You make me laugh. You have to depend only on yourself. I am only your image.'

The past creates and the present breaks.

Vihan overpowered the fear of law and broke into the PPM, which was in a highly secure area. But can there be anything unbreakable for the Genext which has been created by the previous generation?

Vihan skirted through security protocols, entered the machine and pressed the go-green button. The machine let out a long wail. The designers had put that as the last security measure to alert the authorities of its use.

The wails brought the security folks running to check the intrusion. The higher-ups realized that Vihan had broken through the system.

'Get him!' shouted the authority, implying a complete shutdown of the system.

Excited to be out, Vihan ignored the 'get him' and instead waved at the angry engineers at the centre, 'So, long guys! See you soon.' With that, he sped through the space-time spread. Riding on the vanity of youth, he now had to rely on the buffeting waves of time-space. He hoped that his twin would help him get back if the need arose.

In seconds, Vihan landed near Devpuri, the city of Kratu's present.

The machine was indeed fast.

To know the particular, one requires special acumen even if he knows the general. It is one thing to predict the flow of the river, but it is impossible to predict the movement of one particular water particle at a fixed instant.

Seeing the city at a distance, Vihan walked the few miles and reached the city. His dress looked odd, but people took that to be the future fashion from some distant land, which in a way was correct.

Vihan knew the history of the human race but he did not know the details of the human character of all places and all time periods. His learning proved inadequate to face the unexpected in Devpuri. His five senses got stretched to their capacity due to their intakes from the surroundings, and his mind seemed to crash down in its struggle to process the strange and voluminous data that flowed through his five senses.

The worst of all was the stench. 'Do they carry dead animals in their pockets?'

Then there was sound.

Everything in Devpuri made noise: young and old, seller and buyer, idler and active, horns and bells. 'I wonder if they make noise in their sleep too!' Unknown to him, his guess was correct. Snoring was a major problem that only stopped short of starting wars. Bright minds even made money by offering a cure to sound coming out at night from the two horns that God has fixed on human face. In some places, it was a major cause for divorce.

'Where have I landed? How can these people live like this? No wonder they are savages. Maybe I should not have allowed my curiosity to take better of me.'

More dangerously, he was not able to see the aura of people around him due to his overburdened mind.

Vihan's people had mastered the art of controlling their mind by switching off the senses, imagination and memory, whenever they wanted so. Using his natural powers, Vihan switched off his olfactory glands, which did not help his mind much, so he switched off his taste and touch organs. That being not enough, he thought of switching off his ears too but then decided to wait for a while.

His mind was now able to process data a little more smoothly, and he could see the aura surrounding a person hazily.

He was not impressed by what he saw. 'How confused these people are! What to say about working out, they do not even know what they want. They are all running around and making noise. How can someone achieve anything with so much of buzzing in their heads? Even while sitting, their minds are like electrons inside an atom.'

He was looking around with disgust when he saw three persons with deep crimson aura pulsating over their entire body. The aura surrounding their heads was spinning, as if in a tizzy. If such a thing happened in his own land, then someone would send blue aura to neutralize and thus take away the inner violence of the person.

He was thinking of neutralizing their aura when he saw one of them whipping out a gun and firing to scare the crowd. People ran for their lives. However, like a predator focussing on an individual in the wildly running herd, these messiahs of death had a clear target in their minds: Sibi, the young girl who had been left behind by her father in the hurry for the need of security.

The buzz of fear and violence confused Vihan. He had never seen or heard anything like that. 'Looks like these people want to harm someone. But why? Why would someone want to harm one's own? The history books are so correct in assessing these people as violent.'

His mind went back to all that he had read about weaponry. When the apes first picked up a stone to fling at a victim, predator or prey, they made a stride both in aggression and defence. Then came the arrows, swords and gunpowder. These too had the dual purpose of protecting oneself and attacking others. When the atomic bomb was added in the arsenal, weaponry moved to killing only. If exploded, it killed both the predator and the prey. Vihan's society had moved away from such senseless violence, although they knew how to create shields to defend oneself. Violence was a strict taboo with them.

Vihan looked at the killers. With his tactile-sense switched off, it took him some seconds to realize that a kid was holding on to him and pleading for protection.

The murderous came near him with, 'Be not an obstacle in the path of peace, young man. Move or you die.'

'Excuse me, sir. I am new here. Could you please explain what this peace is for which you are ready to kill the little one?'

Vihan came to know about the founding and spread of the gang later. If anyone used such logic in his land, he was sure to get free bread for a long time in some asylum.

One member of the gang shouted at Vihan, 'No time to explain. If you want, you can join us later. Right now, move. Move, move.'

Vihan remembered how the folks of this period came up with brainwaves that they declared to be either of divine origin or as revolutionary. Precedence was given to persons more than principles. 'Stupid,' he used to smile.

He decided to shoot in the dark, 'Sorry sir, but how do you know that your founder alone knows the way to peace? Whosoever can have come up with such a silly idea?' He was confident that the idea must have come from a brain suffering from thought dysentery.

'You rascal! Son of a black hole! Worm of a lost missile! How dare you address our leader like that? He is to be addressed as Noble; the great. And you dare question his wisdom, you rotten fruit of hell! Since you are from outside, we will let you go by chopping off your hand after we are done with this girl. Now hand her over.'

'But, why all this, sir?'

'For a better tomorrow. For a glorious future. If a little blood is spilled for that, it is a small price to pay.'

'I am the future, sir.'

Sibi trembled behind Vihan, oozing fear through her breathing, the sound of which was painful to bear for the sensitive.

The gunman said, 'We knew from the start that sooner or later you will claim to be our competitor. This always happens. So, be ready to taste hell, you stinking product of sewage. All your dung talks about being new were a ploy to distract us.'

'You stink, sir!' said Vihan. He was confident that everyone in this place stank, so he was sure to be correct even with his olfactory sense shut. He also felt ashamed to use such words towards those whom he did not even know, howsoever uncouth they might be. His culture did not allow abuse or abusive words.

'Look, we are here to take this wretch, the viper in making.

That will bring some sense in the head of that snake of a man, Jeshi. We hope he learns to respect us after this. Now, move.'

The girl clutched at Vihan's legs fearfully. She did not want to die.

Silence.

'We gave you enough chance in the hope that you will join us. Now, here you go. Henceforth you will be visible only in pics,' said another one.

'I am one and you are three. Isn't it an unfair fight?'

'You brought it upon yourself, mate. We will forgive your misdeeds if you promise to join our fold.'

'I mean, aren't you people too inadequate for me?' Vihan said in a super chill tone.

People watched helplessly from a distance. Jeshi croaked with fear for his daughter. All his pomposity about gold being supreme was of no use here. He also wondered who the young man was, standing boldly in front of gunmen.

'*Bang! Bang! Bang!*' The gunmen fired coordinated shots at Vihan.

By then, Vihan had focussed on his body, making it rock solid. This was another development of yogic powers that everyone in the future had. The bullets clanged against his body, without harming him a bit. More shots were fired. Vihan stood still. The bullets got deflected.

In the next micro-second, Vihan hit the trio with such force that the glass panes in the nearby shops rattled, even though he barely seemed to have moved. Or, was he too fast? There was no way of knowing that. The threesome lay unconscious on the ground.

People were dumbstruck, Jeshi blinked in disbelief, Sibi cried in fear, and the approaching sirens of the police sounded ferocious.

Vihan felt terrible that he had hit someone, even though they were about to kill an innocent girl. 'Who knows? These fallen ones may be my direct ancestors.' He promised to himself to remain gentle and polite even if someone hit him in future.

When the police had bundled the attackers in their van, Vihan went up to them and apologized profusely for the hit. Seeing him close, one of the gang spat at him and shouted, 'Wait till we are out, which we will be soon. This time our bullets won't miss you, you filth of the leftover of a dog.' Vihan did not know how to react to this unprovoked barrage.

Jeshi was too shaken to stay in the market but he decided to offer his thanks to Vihan over a cup of tea.

'So, what did you say about where you are from?' asked Jeshi. Politics flowed in his nature, and so he never asked direct questions.

'I have not said anything about my place, sir.' Vihan was too straight to understand the nuance of the clever. He then added, 'From a little far. You won't be knowing about my place.'

Mr Jeshi concluded that Vihan was probably from a village somewhere in the Himalayas. People did come for work from such places to Devpuri.

'You said something about your education.'

'I am a student of history.' He ignored the indirectness this time.

'Wonderful! Not many read history here these days. You are such a wonderful person! Very nice, very nice. He, he!' Jeshi concluded that Vihan must be a complete idiot to read history in this age of studying science.

'Yes sir.'

'But you must be knowing about computers, the modern wonder? He, he!' Jeshi was being polite.

'What is that?' asked Vihan. His books on history did not mention this curio. His folks had long ago outgrown the need for such machines, the way people of present have forgotten the use of abacus.

'He, he! I forgot that you study history.' Jeshi's suspicions were confirmed.

'Sir.'

'Can we have *bhaiya* live with us?' asked Sibi. She was awed by what Vihan had done.

When Jeshi found out that Vihan was new to the place, with nowhere to stay, he invited him to be with him. 'Come stay with me till we find something suitable for you. We will always remain grateful to you for what you did for us today.'

'Do not even mention that, sir.'

To favour is to invest in the future. Jeshi obliged anyone or repaid an obligation only if he hoped to get something out of it later. His mind, chiselled at the grinding stone of self-interest, was sharp enough to capture any idea that was going to be a good investment. By then he had realized that Vihan deserved investment. He appeared intelligent, decent, undemanding and strong. He could be a useful pawn to further his consolidations and could also be used as his bodyguard.

'You are so simple,' humoured Jeshi. People have this great weakness of melting if they are termed simple by someone. This is one good adjective to extract favour from anyone.

'What is simple, sir?' asked Vihan. His folks were established in goodness, so they did not know the meaning of complicated.

'He! He!'

Sibi clapped in joy of having Vihan with her. She then pointed at the TV screaming about the attack. According to the detractors, the attack was choreographed by Mr Jeshi himself, who was very good at such things to stay in the limelight. An onlooker thanked God that the bullets had missed the unknown gentleman who seemed to be some kind of a martial arts man.

'These TV *wallahs*! They say anything, hehe! You are not a martial arts man, are you?'

'No sir. I don't even know what that is.'

Jeshi bundled Sibi and Vihan into the car and moved towards his place.

'Excuse me, sir? How does this move?' asked Vihan in curiosity.

'Diesel, of course! What else would you expect it to run a car on? By mere wish!'

'Sorry, sir.'

Vihan thought of his twin, Vihan MM that ran on mind power. He wondered how it must be faring without him. As for himself, he missed his company, particularly in this claustrophobic contraption that they called car.

The streets seemed so crowded, with shops on both sides appearing inviting, but in fact trying to encroach upon the public space and private purse. It was all new for Vihan, who looked this side and that side out of the car to take in everything.

Jeshi laughed at the inquisitiveness of the naive, 'I am sure your village does not have such sights.'

'No, sir.'

It was evening. Shouts and honking indicated that the busy were heading for rest, the rested one were getting busy, and the rest were out to laze around. Soon the infinite variety of the city would be sucked into the void of darkness. The patches of light here and there would remind of what it was and what it will be, but for the present it was all going to be one. Nature slowed itself down, preparing to take rest. Strands of music floated out the window from electronic sound system and at times from the practising hands on some musical instrument.

'*Ta thai thai tat, aa thai thai tat,*' responded the steps of dance of Usha, an unknown young lady of Devpuri to the melody of the approaching evening.

She was the same girl from the times when Kratu's story began thousands of years ago.

# 9

# NATARAJ

Karma, the force of nature that moves a person from sphere to sphere and birth to birth according to one's inner disposition, gets reflected in one's being and doings. God does not dictate the actions of anyone, anywhere. It is the divine cosmic order – known variously as God's will, Law, dharma, karma, and chance – that keeps animate and inanimate things drowning and flowing in the river of existence.

Lamentations and expectations of a person are useless before the all-giving and all-taking Karma. There is no injustice in the universe; one gets what one's karma has been in the past and the present. Karma makes one enjoy and it makes others poor. Wisdom, skill, capability, connections, pedigree: nothing is a measure for success or failure. Karma is the great ruler; it is the great regulator. Whatever one may do, its result will reach him sooner or later, in this or that birth.

This was true of Usha too.

Usha had died with Kratu and Aswin when Kratu had jumped in the Sindhu. Since then, Karma had flowed through her soul, taking her through experiences – good, bad and vicious – to make her what she was today: the daughter of a simple family.

Her love for dance remained constant, while gyrating through the cycle of birth-death. She did not remember any of her past births, but the mould of her mind minus the memory, reflected in her gait, which was that of a skilled dancer. There was a grace about her movement and a smile that reflected inner art, unknown even to her. The accumulated learning showed through every limb of hers. She moved around the house dancing: *Ta thai thai tat, aa thai thai tat.*

Unfortunately, her parents were dance blind. 'You want to be a *nachaniya*?' Her mom scolded her whenever she saw her break into dance amidst the chaos that surrounded them.

'Na, mom. I don't want to be a *nachaniya* or anything. I dance because I love it,' Usha would reply smilingly. 'Lucky is the person who can do what she wants. Isn't it, Ma? Now tell me, did you ever love doing something?'

Ma had no reply to that. She would grunt, 'Huh!'

Papa loved Usha the way only a father can. He would console Ma with, 'Character is everything, dear. Who can dare touch my precious if she has nobility within her?'

'Character! Pooh! Just see how girls these days dance before the public on television and in cinema. I would rather die than expose myself like that.'

'They are not you. Nor are they dancers. True dancers do not show their body to hide their incompetence. I believe that body exposure is directly proportional to the level of incompetence in any profession. What do you say, *beta*?'

'How do you know so much, papa?' saying so, Usha would embrace papa, which seemed so heavenly for him. He would let go of any slip of his daughter if he could get that much of love from her.

'Lucky is the man who has a loving daughter!' he would say to himself.

*'Ta thai thai tat, aa thai thai tat'*, would respond an unconcerned Usha.

She never had a teacher for dance. The little she saw on the television and internet was enough to awaken her inner calling. Her parents often watched her passionate dancing in awe when she danced all night, forgetting the world and herself, with only rhythm, bordering the divine, remaining all around her.

'She must be a cursed *apsara*,' thought Usha's father.

Usha was no *apsara*, she was just a soul wending its way to perfection through rhythm.

Rhythm – Kratu had learnt its importance in *gandharvaloka*, the sphere that has the souls who are dedicated to rhythm.

During one of the gestation periods after death, Kratu had presented himself before Yamaraj, as is the rule. Yama sent him to the *devaloka*, the heaven, which is the sphere of never ending enjoyments, luxury and long life for those who reach there after leading a noble, religious life.

Kratu moved around the heaven, tasting this, nibbling that. He also observed the inhabitants there who had a heightened desire for indulgence, resulting in greed, jealousy and anxiety. 'Best for me!' was the unspoken agenda of the land, which sickened the sensitive mind of Kratu. 'They call themselves gods and yet they are always on lookout for the weak for things that they can snatch from them. What a selfish bunch!'

By virtue of his unfading memory, he went back to the God of Death with, 'Noble Lord! I find it shocking that people live a righteous life, suffer pains of austerities and perform rigours of *yajna* on the Earth only to enjoy luxuries! The heaven appears to me like the extension of the Earth, with heightened feel for enjoyment as also with greater fear of losing what they have achieved with difficulty. And yet, they do lose that after a time. Why all the hard labour and struggle then on the Earth sphere? Just think my Lord! People abstain from enjoyment on Earth only to indulge in sensuality here? Why this hypocrisy?'

'That is the individual's choice,' said Yama. 'The unholy alliance of the mind with the senses makes one seek pleasure even in the heaven.'

'Forgive my impertinence, sir. Is my *acharya*, Angi, also enjoying all this dancing and drinking?'

The idea that Angi, the great sage, might have landed in one of these heavens after leading an austere and religious life was repulsive to Kratu.

Yamaraj laughed uproariously, 'May be. May be not. I cannot tell you what you are not capable of knowing yourself.'

After meeting Paras, Kratu had travelled through subtler spheres where the pure in heart went. The souls there enjoyed the uninterrupted contemplation on the divine. The *Saptarashi* – the seven sages – were the highest among such sages. Angi might have gone there. Or, may be not.

'Sir, without meaning to sound arrogant, I wish to state that I am a man of integrity. I do not want to be good only to give up goodness when goodness is no more good.'

'I appreciate that.'

'Truly sir, why indulge in morality when it would end in endless dancing and drinking? Allow me to go to a lower sphere where this kind of hypocrisy is not there.'

Kratu had not yet acquired the knowledge of self that

could make him free from this coming-going, nor did he have the power of Narada to visit any sphere whenever he wanted. Yamaraj advised him to go to the *gandharvaloka*, the world of dance-drama-music. 'You might learn something noble there,' said Yama.

The next moment Kratu found himself in the presence of Chitrarath, the king of *gandharvaloka*.

After the customary bowing by Kratu, Chitrarath said, 'We are not as powerful or respectable as the gods, but we are the chosen people of God.'

'Must be,' bowed Kratu.

The ups and downs of life had taught him not to prick the pride of megalomaniacs who drew their relevance from their insane ego. There was no sphere where these pompous maniacs could not be found. Whenever before them, Kratu tried to satiate the child in them that demanded constant pampering.

'You are lucky to be born here.'

'I am sure, O provider of the poor!'

The *gandharvas* are not spiritually exalted, so Chitrarath did not know the truth about Kratu and his indelible memory. For him, he was one of them, dedicated to their way of life.

'Do you know how God creates?' asked Chitrarath.

'I have no idea what you wish to say, my Lord.'

'Yes, how would you know,' said the pleased king. He then continued, 'Rhythm is creation. God creates the rhythm of the universe by His will when He wants to create and stops it when He wants to dissolve it. This rhythm of creation reflects in music and dance too. Poetry is a distant relative of music in matters of rhythm.'

'Yes, O master of rhythm.'

'To be wise is to know that rhythm is in everything. The

simplest action has a rhythm about it, although people fail to recognize that. Eating, bathing, cleaning, reading – everything has a rhythm about it, which when practised, makes one perfect in that act, and may even lead the practitioner to God.'

Kratu remembered Isan, the woodcutter, who had a perfect rhythm of wielding his axe that kept him and his axe fit. It was difficult to know if he had reached God through that, but surely he was not ordinary.

'We do not go for all that philosophy, son. Here we focus only on the rhythm of dance and music to be perfect in the art. Rest is in the hands of God.'

Kratu bowed humbly and thought deeply about the implications of what the king was telling. Chitrarath may not have been a yogi, but he surely knew a thing or two about yoga.

'Do you remember my saying that we are the chosen ones of God?'

'Yes, Lord!'

'Neither the gods nor the humans have mastered the art of creating rhythm; only we have succeeded in doing that. We can be one with the rhythm in matters of steps and voice, and we can also create new dance steps and new forms of music. That is why we are the best. Best of the best.'

'I feel proud, your majesty.'

'Everything in the universe is the physical form of an idea, and every idea comes from God. When you learn a dance, try to think how God must have thought of that dance, and then try to reach that state of perfection. If you cannot imagine that, then visualize God dancing a particular form. If He, the perfect, danced, then how that would have been? Visualize that and train yourself to dance like that.'

'It is humbling, Lord!'

'As with dance so with music. Imagine how God would have sung a particular music. What we sing here is a copy of that. Our goal is to reach that perfection in singing which would be one with God's music.'

Kratu remembered how sage Angi stressed on the importance of correct pronunciation, 'Children! Pronounce the words of the Vedas correctly. The correctness of pronunciation indicates your oneness with the idea that the word represents. This way you can make the corresponding object appear, for that is how God creates.'

Kratu had been thinking when Chitrarath interrupted, 'Are you thinking something?'

'Yes, my lord! I am overwhelmed by the immensity of your thinking.'

'It is not my thinking. It is the truth.'

'Yes, yes. Greatness is your name, Lord! If my master be pleased with me, may I ask if someone amongst us has become one with God through music and dance?'

The king laughed with searing pride, 'Many have done so. We are the land of liberty through rhythm. Those who master the rhythm in music or dance, become indifferent from the affairs of the world. They then shut themselves up in their own world and dance the steps of God for Him only. That is freedom. I myself have seen quite a few among us reach that state.'

'How if we all do that,' ventured Kratu.

'Spirituality is not for the masses. Even if you have a key to the treasures, you cannot get it until you have overcome all the obstacles that separate you from it. We have not succeeded in removing all the obstacles from our minds that separate us from God. So, we have to dance before the gods, since we don't have their power.'

Kratu had seen some extraordinary dance and songs in *devaloka*. He mentioned that much casually to the king.

'*Arre,* that is not so bad after all,' said Chitrarath. 'I have heard that the brahmins on Earth go singing the Vedas before the kings. The powerful will be powerful. We, however, take pride in the fact that these powerful can at best be the connoisseurs of what we produce, while we are the true masters of rhythm. No god can ever attain freedom, but we can. Rhythm is our way of life. We can be one with rhythm and can be one with God.'

'We are indeed privileged, your highness.'

'You have the zing in you. Your humility shows that one day you will be one of the greats of this land. I have fixed a teacher for you. Learn the art, master it and be blessed.'

'I will do as you wish, Lord.'

Kratu bowed out from the king's presence to be with his teacher, who took him around to show the world of performing art.

It was the world of rhythm indeed where dance and music seemed to roam around in physical bodies. Nothing was out of note, not a beat was missed. What he had discovered under the mango tree in the form of music, was not even a straw of what he experienced there.

*'Ta thai thai tat, aa thai thai tat,'* thus began his training.

When the quota of his karma to be with the *gandharvas* was over, he, like a loose balloon in a tempest, was blown away from there. After some time, he was back on Earth.

Kratu now saw rhythm in everything. The chirping of birds, humming of bees, mooing of cows, prattle of a baby, swaying of grass in the wind, life pulsating through different forms, the dusk and dawn, sun and rain, summer and spring: everything had a rhythm. The sound all around, howsoever cacophonous, was a descendant of the art that had its origin in the Lord.

Everything in the world was a worship of the divine: the flowering trees were the offering of a bouquet at the altar of the Lord, every sound was an offering of music to Him, and every motion was a dance step performed to honour the Lord. It depended on an individual to make his offering as perfect as he wished to.

At the cosmic level, the Lord seemed to be dancing, which appeared as the universe. This dance was the energy that pulsated through the universe, making life possible. The Lord was the creator, sustainer and destroyer of everything. He was the compassionate and also the terrible. It was His power that enveloped the universe as ignorance from knowing its true nature, and it was His grace to grant one freedom from this ignorance.

The Lord's rhythm. Creation – Existence – Destruction.

Rhythm requires expression through symbols like stories, songs, music, dance and sculpture. But how to express the Lord's rhythm, depicting all that the Lord stood for in relation to the world? Kratu thought deeply.

India preferred symbolism through poetry. The Vedas, ultimate expression of God through words, were in poetry. However, that was inadequate and confined in the hands of the brahmins. There was a need for a new symbol for the cosmic rhythm.

Art is integral to human nature. Starting from rudimentary sketches of cave paintings to immortal music and paintings by the masters, human beings have left footprints of their progress in aesthetics quite visibly. In India, art found its expression through various mediums. Most womenfolk have been good at indoor painting, while some male members took up art to earn a pittance or simply as a hobby.

In those days, artists usually painted or sketched what they had seen, but there was an unusual artist, Rishikant, who could draw and design by hearing a description of what one wanted to be sketched. People often demanded his service to brighten their earthen pots or homes.

When Kratu came to know about him, he walked miles to meet the talent.

Rishikant was a devotee of Lord Shiva, whom he worshipped as a *lingam* in his home. The practice in ancient times was to erect a pillar to mark the place for a *yajna* that was to be performed in the public. Following that, the devotees of Shiva had come up with their own version of symbol of worship, *Shivalingam*, which had certain characteristics marks. There were stones with other kind of marks which were used as *Shaligram sila,* the symbol for Vishnu.

Shiva was a popular God, particularly with the ordinary folks who loved the stories of his great deeds, and also his care and concern for Parvati. To them, he seemed so near and yet so far. He was Maheshwara, the great Lord who was the creator, sustainer and destroyer of the universe. He was unconquerable by any but could be won over easily by devotees. He was married first to Sati and then to Parvati and yet was the ideal of the monks. He dwelled in the mountains but was worshipped all over the land. He lived a frugal life but was bestower of great goods to anyone who worshipped him. He was beyond cause and effect and yet had thousands of stories of adventures centring around him. He was omnipresent but rode Nandi, the bull. He held Ganga in his matted hair when she had descended from the heaven, and could press down Mount Kailash with his mere thumb. And, he had held the poison of the universe in his throat to save the universe.

According to a traditional story, Shiva married Sati against the wishes of her father. Once, she went to attend a *yajna* of her father where her father talked ill of her husband in his absence. Pained, she gave up her body by her yogic powers.

Hearing about the death of his dear consort, Lord Shiva came there, took up her body on his shoulders and in the fury of the lost, he started his dance of destruction.

He danced and danced. The air, crushed under the Lord's ferocious feet boomed; the *damru* in his hands sounded the rhythm of destruction; his hair flailing all around made Ganga, who lived in his matted hair, run wild and destroy everything in her wake; the *trishul* in his fiery hand spewed thunderous lightning; his third eye closed and shut, preparing to burn down the universe; the hand that was used to give boons, now carried the cosmic blaze. This was the *tandava* dance of the Lord.

Fear.

Quaking fear.

The universe trembled at the imminent destruction.

Something had to be done.

The gods hurriedly hatched plans to calm down the Lord. Lord Vishnu, wielding his powerful *chakra,* cut the body of Sati into fifty-one pieces and threw them all over the continent. Wherever a body part fell became a place of pilgrimage.

The dead had been disposed. The universe now hoped that with the object of pain gone from his sight, the angry Lord would calm down. Yes, Lord Shiva calmed down and went deep in the Himalayas to contemplate on His own nature, which is infinite.

When Kratu went to meet Rishikant, he was engrossed in worship of the *Shivalingam*. He poured Ganga water and offered *bel* leaves with the Vedic mantra *Tryambakaṃ yajamahe*: 'May I be saved by Lord Shiva from the cycle of birth and death.'

Sitting outside the place of worship, Kratu mused over the story of Shiva and wondered if it was a story or a symbol of what he himself had been contemplating upon. Did this story depict the cosmic dance that permeated the micro and macro? Probably. But there was no harm in trying to use this story as model to portray the dance of the infinite.

Puja over, Kratu made the humble approach, 'You are such a great artist. Will you please agree to draw the *tandava* dance of the Lord?'

'Sir, what you demand is so abstract. I do not think that it can be put in a single figure.'

'You are a master artist and it is about your *Ishta*. Just think what a great service you will be doing to your brother devotees. The fusion of art and dance requires talent, which only you have.'

'I feel humbled by your words, sir, nevertheless, I am not sure if I can do that.'

'Rishikant ji, give it a try. Think on it. Meditate on it. Be one with it. Let us see what comes out of all that then.'

Rishikant stayed silent. Kratu went on his way.

Rishikant gave himself to contemplating upon the story of Lord Shiva's *tandava* day and night.

His work, even though ordinary, suffered. His beard grew long; he did not know when he ate or what. His wife, extremely caring that she was, managed to push a morsel or two into his unwilling mouth to keep him alive. The look in his eyes seemed to say to his wife that he was gone somewhere deep, a place from where one can return only with gems or perish.

Silence.

Shiva dancing.

The dance was not important. The rhythm of creation had to be captured; the essence of God had to be portrayed. Was that possible?

How does one attain anything in life, whether knowledge, wealth, love, attention or anything else? The usual understanding is that one makes an effort and, as a consequence, one gets the desired result. But the fact is not that.

Success comes as a favour from the giver. When the favour from the giver is in superabundance, then alone one becomes an achiever. A suitor can keep chasing someone and may even apply force. But to get the desired result, the favour has to come from the other one. No one ever gets anything by effort. Effort merely creates the platform where success may descend if the giver wishes so. God's grace is like that. It descends on a platform that has been made ready through prayers and worship by the devotee to catch it.

Rishikant meditated on Lord Shiva as the cosmic dancer to get His grace.

The rhythm flowing out from the cosmic order now made his mind resonate in the same phase.

More silence.

With eyes closed or open, he thought and thought only of Shiva. Slowly, he started feeling the dance of Shiva. The Lord was dancing everywhere, the way Kratu had felt. The feeling peaked one night when, in a semi-dream state, he saw Lord Shiva dancing around his bed, with the *damru* in his hand.

The Lord had four hands in three of which he held fire, the *damaru,* a snake; with the fourth he pointed downwards. His bent legs in while dancing seemed to burst with energy, and his whirling hair – spread into a fan behind his head – indicated the ecstasy of his dance. There was a ring of flames amidst which he stood on a lotus pedestal with his left leg trampling upon primeval ignorance, *apasmara*. The Lord was smiling the smile of the free amidst the din of turmoil. There was rhythm amidst chaos, creative design amidst the unpatterned, serenity amidst the wails, and life smiling amidst death.

Rishikant got up from the bed, shouted to his wife to light the lamp and excitedly sat down to make the first sketch of the Lord, a figure which was to be known as Nataraj. The cosmic dance of the infinite in the finite universe had finally been captured.

Rishikant never drew anything ever after that. He was fulfilled; one with his *ishta,* Nataraja.

'*Ta thai thai tat,*' danced Nataraja, the God of all dances and Lord of all creation. Rishikant kept beat.

'*Ta thai thai tat,*' danced Usha, not knowing about the events that went into making the dance that she had been practising.

Her steps were the descendants of divine dance forms brought down by Kratu from the land of the gods, and sculpted by Rishikant. If Chitrarath, the king of *gandharvas*, had known the truth about Kratu, he would never have allowed him to take the art out of his land to Earth.

Usha often danced the whole night. Exhausted, when she fell asleep, dreaming of many more dance forms, someone played, at the other end of Devpuri, *raag* Sohini on the flute.

It was Aswin, the friend of Kratu from the time that he had invented music.

Going through the cycles of birth and death, he too had landed in Devpuri in this birth. He had journeyed in this story along with Kratu. However, unlike Kratu he did not remember anything about his past. That way he was like Usha, and just like her, he too had perfected his art over births and was dedicated to it.

Aswin had graduated from a reputed university with honours. Betting on his talents in studies and music, someone asked for him as a partner to his daughter. Unfortunately, like most bets do, the bets in this case failed. Aswin checked the job profiles that would suit him. Finally he settled on being a guard to a housing society. He was sure that he would not be asked to work beyond the duty hours. That would leave him with ample space beyond his profession for his passion: music.

His family and friends argued with him, but he had the arrogance of the simple; he did not budge.

His wife loved him for sure but lack of money in the house turned her bitter. She soon started bickering and haranguing.

'Why can't you be like others?'

'Come on dear, we are born unique and die unique. So, should not we aspire to be unique in life too? Be not a factory product, but rather strive to be handmade; special.'

His wife, well-meaning though she was, could not bear

the pain of poverty. Slowly, she started complaining about his music too.

Then onwards, Aswin went out of his home every evening to sit on the riverbank with his flute playing Raag Sree to Raag Sohini, playing from early evening to early morning. That was his way of life. That was also his window to emotional freedom.

'Jio Raja!' would say the *charasis* sitting on the banks in the evening when he started his music, perfected through births.

'Jai ho!' would say the first bathers, when he was coming down from the clouds of freedom to the reality of belly and body.

*Charasis* and early bather were his only true audience and admirers.

When Aswin stopped his flute, the Sun yawned lazily in his bed to get up and cover the distance for the day. On way to the west, it watched everyday how Aswin faced the volley of his wife for being so worthless. 'Lady, if only you knew what he is!' mused the Sun. But it was not for him to interfere in the affairs of the mortals.

Aswin did not need much sleep, nor did Vihan.

Sleep is the time when the mind brings order to its house. More garbage means that a person would require more hours of sleep to clean up the mess. The active ones create a lot of garbage from the outside world, while the passive ones create a lot of internal garbage through wild thinking. The noble ones, dedicated to one purpose, do not need much sleep. Such persons are known as *sattvik*.

Vihan was a *sattvik* person.

He also had a clear purpose of stay in this land and time – he had to experience the life first-hand. To do that, he often left Jeshi's home and roamed the streets at daytime and also at night.

It was during one of his morning visits that he heard Aswin. 'What melody!' he thought.

When back home, he mentioned it to Jeshi, who said, '*Arre bhai, ye kya*? You should know about the flute of Sri Krishna, the divine flute player. Devotees say that his flute is still creating music which pervades the universe. You should go to Krishna temple today itself.'

The political compulsions of Jeshi demanded that he be seen visiting places of worship. Even if he could not go regularly, he sent Sibi with someone to be seen among the devotees. The event managers always tipped the press to cover the event.

'Will we have to pay something to enter the temple?'

'What do you mean?'

'I find that one has to pay for everything here. Talking, walking, eating, drinking, smoking, listening; everything costs here. Clever businessmen have entered the bedrooms too. So, I wondered if we have to pay for the temple visit too.'

'Not here at Devpuri.'

The next morning, he sent Sibi with Vihan to Krishna temple where Bhaktidas, an elderly devotee of Sri Krishna, sat singing, '*Maiya mori, main nahi makhan khayo.*'

The media was already present there.

# 10

# MANU BURNS

Hinduism is a living religion. Like a living organism, it keeps taking in new things, while keeping its fundamentals intact. It was through this dynamic nature that the people of India came up with the concept of temples, which replaced the need for a place for community *yajna*. Later socio-economic compulsions added value to the temples but its basic character as the centre for religion continued. The Sri Krishna temple at Devpuri belonged to that tradition.

When Vihan reached there with Sibi, two media persons rushed at them with, 'How do you feel to be in a temple, young lady?'

The other one recognized Vihan from his encounter with the Peace Party. She asked, 'Excuse me, sir, have you come here as a penance for hitting people in the marketplace?'

Ignoring the barbs, Vihan led Sibi to where the saint of the locality, Bhaktidas, sat, absorbed in divine communion with his Lord through his singing. At that time he was singing a song by Surdas, which was sung all over the land and was appreciated even by the spiritually challenged.

Surdas, along with many other saint-poets filled India with the melody of devotion at a time when blood, flowing from the swords of the cruel, was drenching the country. The Indian sword, rusted greatly by the ideas of non-violence preached by two great religions of the world, Buddhism and Jainism, was unable to defend its dependents. The brave died fighting while the public died of poverty. It was time to seek shelter in the love and care of God, the way a child runs to her mom when hit by the world.

In the days when *yajna* by the householders and contemplation by the likes of Ritam were the usual ways to connect with the divine, there were sages who loved to sing and dance in the ecstatic love of God.

*Draw thy Friend to Thee / Like a cow to milking*
*O Singer, wake up God the Lover!*

Thus sang a sage, out of fullness for God during Vedic times. To a sage, God is the ultimate of love: he is *rasa*, the ocean of joy. Wherever there is love, it is a direct presence of God. A cow suckling its calf, a lioness feeding its cubs, a mother caring for her baby, friends enjoying company are all expressions of love, which is God.

Paras, the fisherman-sage had explained to Kratu, 'Love means to be wise about existence. A child is loved by her mom but not by everyone else, a person is loved mostly by his dear ones the way a poem is loved the most by its poet. Why so? Because one loves what one feels to be oneself: wife, children, wealth, achievement and creativity are loved by those who feel that to be their self. If these had any objective reality, then everyone would have loved the same object; the same lady would have been chased by all men. That being not the case, self alone is the object of love for all. In the same way, a lover of God loves God as one's self. For the same reason, you should not expect everyone to love God, for few consider God as their self.'

Kratu could not agree more. The philosophy behind devotion was clear in those lines.

When Kratu had reached the wall of the infinite, he had realized what it meant to love God, the infinite. Love was when the mind had no thought other than that of God. The finite could be loved along with others too, but the infinite demanded complete attention. Since then, he had seen how God played the game of world variously. God, in his majesty, gave wisdom to some but kept them poor, and gave wealth to some without giving them virtue.

Why do the devotees of God have to suffer? Why is there injustice in the world? Why do the cruel have the run of the world? Kratu often heard these lamentations. He rarely answered these, knowing the truth: 'He is the Lord and master. Why would he be dictated by what you want or do not want? Tied to your puny little existence, you think that you alone have the right to all the fun in the world simply because He has given you a particular quality?'

Kratu was a cosmic citizen and sphere traveller, so he was born on this Earth only once in a while. Whenever here, he waited till he grew to adulthood and then left home on some pretext, moved around doing good and listening to good, and then moved on. He had no favourite sphere or city.

Once he was born in Varanasi, the city of Lord Shiva. The devotees of Shiva feel the Lord's living presence all the time there, but the mornings are extra special. To feel this, many take bath in Ganga before sunrise and go to worship Shiva, who is established in that city as Viswanath.

Kratu's family in that birth was flower vendors.

Following the family tradition, Kratu sat near the temple, selling flowers to the visitors. Sitting there, he once heard of Shankaracharya, who preached that Atman alone exists. Atman is pure consciousness and infinite, something that Kratu had known for a long time but not achieved because of his love and search for Aswin.

He also heard the popular story of Shankara (Shankaracharya) meeting Shankara (Lord Shiva), according to which Lord Shiva wanted to give lessons in practical Vedanta to Shankaracharya. Accordingly, Lord Shiva, through his power of *maya*, was a Chandala carrying a load of meat when Shankaracharya met him. The Acharya was annoyed at the sight and asked him to move away. Lord, in the form of the Chandala, said, 'If I am all-pervading consciousness, where can I move to? And if I am a body, composed of matter, then how can I move?' Shankaracharya, the great spiritual power that he was, realized the greatness before him. He fell at the feet of the Lord.

Kratu was eager to meet this great teacher who was soon going to unify India under the banner of Practical Vedanta, which came to be named as Hinduism. To meet him, Kratu moved his basket of merchandise to the ghat of Ganga where the Acharya came regularly.

One day Kratu saw the Acharya, walking with his disciples, and chanting, '*Chidananda rupah Shivoham Shivaham*': 'I am the ever pure, ever free.'

Kratu asked for a minute with the Acharya, who having learnt his lessons at the hands of a *Chandala,* smiled at the flower boy and gave him all the time he wanted. A person established in the non-dual state of existence has no duty left and hence he does not have to hurry for anything. Time stops having any relevance for him. It was true for Acharya Shankar too.

The exchange of a few words made the Acharya realize that Kratu was no ordinary flower boy. He looked intently in his eyes to see the power of the infinite shining through a thin veil in him.

'You are such a fit candidate for Advaita. Why are you fooling around like this?'

Kratu was impressed by the power of the great master. He narrated his story in brief.

'I can take away the curse that hangs heavy on you.'

Kratu remembered the words of Ritam who had offered to do the same. He politely declined out of respect for his teacher and also to save his friend.

'Do you want to continue like this, moving up and down in the giant wheel of *samsara*? Don't you get sick of this life and birth?' Saying this, the Acharya chanted:

> *Punarapi jananam punarapi maranam, Punarapi janani jathare shayanam*
>
> – Again and again one is born, and again and again one dies. And again and again one lies in the mother's womb. O Lord! Help me cross this difficult ocean of life.

'I can't let Aswin suffer in this world. He once died for me.'

The Acharya thought for a while and then said, 'In that case, you can opt to stay immersed in *samadhi*. You will then not be constantly on the move, nor will you have to be born repeatedly.'

Kratu bowed his head in acceptance. He stayed in Varanasi till the Acharya was there. Later he left his home and went to a secluded place to stay merged in the contemplation of the Divine.

Many centuries passed before he was brought down from the higher reaches of the mind to the mundane of the world.

India at that time was coloured crimson with the blood of the innocent. God in its impersonal form was of no use to the common man who wanted safety of life and security of livelihood. It was time for the Bhakti-idea of the ideosphere to come down and get physical bodies to show the majesty of its character.

The Bhakti-idea had not got many bodies to play around with, despite its colourful portrayal in the Vedas and philosophical presentation in the Upanishads. Now that the likes of Surdas, Mirabai, Tulasidas were around, Bhakti-idea had a free field to make merry in the pure hearts that were ready to bloom. The land of Advaita now sang and danced to the rhythm of bhakti.

Kratu met Surdas, the blind poet, who composed soulful songs, describing child Krishna and sang in front of a few idle listeners. Mostly, he sang all alone. Meeting Surdas was easy. He was in Vrindavan in those days. The devotees of Krishna had many spiritual tales to relate, centring on His stay in Vrindavan, the most famous of which was his letting out the note of '*kleem*' on his flute that filled people with mad love for the Lord.

Surdas welcomed Kratu. While talking about his Lord, he said, 'Do you know how creation takes place?'

'I would love to hear that from you.'

'God and his creative power are same. This power manifests in the world as seed of everything that you find here. Valour, love, knowledge, affluence – literally everything comes from the respective seed, which is power of God. The seed for desire fulfilment is '*kleem*' whose divine form is Lord Krishna.'

'Ohh!'

'When the Lord let out that note on his flute, the desire to love God reached its ecstatic height. If you listen carefully and silently, you can hear that note every night here, particularly in Nidhuvan.'

Surdas described many playful stories of the Lord, who as a child had stayed in that land, playing pranks and destroying evil in whatever form it appeared. His frolics with the maidens of the land, although symbolic of love between a devotee and God, had become folklore.

Kratu found the description and stories overwhelming. Jokingly, he asked, 'Bhagat ji, why don't you request Lord Krishna to alleviate the pain of the masses?' He knew well that God never intervened in these affairs. Life was His, so was death. Keeping a thing in one pocket or the other is same for the owner.

'My God is such a baby. What can he do, my poor baby! I have to take care of him all day and night. I bathe him, feed him and put him in bed. What can he do for me? I have to do everything for him,' smiled the sage, and then brought out the *ashtadhatu* image of baby Krishna.

'What about your poverty, Bhagat ji? Shouldn't the Lord think to alleviate it?'

'What He does is His concern, what I expect is my concern. A kid, when hit by the world runs to his mom. But when that kid is chastised by mom, where would he go? He then holds on to mom more tightly. For me, my miseries are to take me deeper in God.'

Kratu was moved to tears. 'With devotees like this around, India need not fear the sword.'

Kratu touched the feet of Surdas, the sage poet and left for Varanasi, where Kabir, a weaver, was believed to be blooming into a sage.

Kratu had been in Varanasi as a flower seller during the time of Shankaracharaya. He moved around the city to see the changes that might have taken place. Na, nothing had changed. If change is the eternal law of the world, then Varanasi had to be beyond the world.

Finding Kabir too was not difficult. Varanasi, the abode of Lord Shiva on the banks of Ganga, was also famous for its cloth merchandise. People came from all over the country to worship Lord Shiva and purchased Varanasi sarees to take back home. Kabir was one of those weavers. His weft-shuttle moved effortlessly all day over the warp, the way waves move over the ocean, while he sang self-composed couplets that talked about Advaita, Devotion and daily life.

After the preliminary greetings, Kratu asked, 'Master, many say that you belong to the tradition of Shankaracharya, while others say that you belong to the tradition of Surdas. Which one is correct?'

Kabir answered:

*Not of Shankar, Not of Sur*
*I am Shankar, And am Sur*

Kratu laughed. He realized that Kabir was established in the highest realms of Advaita, the non-dual state, from where he could identify himself with all. The distinction of high-low, wise-ignorant, living-dead, good-bad, virtue-vice had ceased to exist for him.

Kabir commented, 'It is all one, *bhai*. So, why compartmentalise?'

Mind is finite and the brain has limited capacity. So, to keep the unlimited variety of the world, the brain wants to keep things in a pattern, even if they do not fit. A child, with underdeveloped brain-mind, takes things in a mass, while a developed mind distinguishes objects. The super-developed mind, after having tasted the infinite, sees everything as a single mass. For such a mind, the waves of the ocean cease to exist. What remains is the vastness of the ocean. The darkest of ignorance and brightest of wisdom have this one thing in common: they both see everything as unified; the ignorant see all as mass of matter, and the wise see them as mass of consciousness.

Kratu suggested, 'Do you see how worshippers of different faiths are at the throats of each other. You are respected by all. Why don't you do something about it?'

*Fight over the basket whose flowers are gone*
*Blood spills only he, who knows not one.*

'*Bhai*, when the world is parched of true spirituality, then only people fight. God is there to show the light and he is there to take people through various paths to perfection. What can we do in that? I am like a water vendor who sits by the roadside to offer free water. But who wants that? In the rush of life, people do not want rest but is ok blood.'

Kabir then recited some of his couplets that portrayed the hollowness of the religious. 'People fight not for religion but for their selfishness. What role we have there? Prophets will come and go; there will be a temporary respite, and then people will be back to their viciousness.'

'Even then, saints do have a duty, master.'

'Saints never have any duty towards the world. Their only duty is to realize God. Be free. That is the mantra. Impressed by the saint's life, people flock to them on their own. Bees come when flowers bloom and flies swarm when a wound festers. The world is like a festering wound. No one can stop the flies of the world from dancing around it.'

'Hmm.'

After some more exchanges, Kratu bowed and took his leave.

Bhaktidas, the singer at the Krishna temple at Devpuri, belonged to the tradition of Surdas but he was also into singing *bhajans* of Kabir and hymns of Shankaracharya. Depending on the hour of the day, he sang in his own joy the songs composed by the masters. In the evenings, he sang one last song to his dear Lord and then went to his shack to meditate the whole night. His food habits were simple, and his clothes were simpler still. Saved from posing before society, and above pampering his belly, he could afford to put his entire psychic energy into the pursuit of a single goal: the love of God.

Vihan wanted to meet Bhaktidas but Sibi was getting fidgety, 'Bhiaya, *chalo na*.'

To calm her down, Vihan promised to get her a new computer game that very day.

Vihan was a fast learner, so picking up the tricks of computers was simple for him. Within a short period, he was tinkering with the hardware and software of the computer, which felt like a cheap toy to him. It took him mere minutes to create exciting games for Sibi whenever she wanted. The talent of Vihan had surprised Jeshi who never failed to ask him, '*Arre bhai*, why did you then study history? You could have been a computer engineer.'

'You promise that none of my friends will have that game?' demanded Sibi.

'How can anyone else have the game that I will make for you?'

'You are so good!'

Sibi then agreed to wait patiently while Vihan talked to the singer. Their words were boring to her, but the anticipation of a new game kept her calm.

Vihan was charmed by the words of Bhaktidas, who explained that Krishna was everything for him. Krishna was his Lord and master, saying so, he pointed at baby Krishna who sat smiling in his metallic form as an idol.

'What do you do the whole day, sir? And how does that benefit you?' asked Vihan.

'Do you know how God creates?'

Philosophy was not Vihan's strong point. He said so.

'God alone is true. When He wishes to create, He Himself becomes many. Whatever you see here or in the heavens, is God Himself. But we do not see the reality because we are so self-centred, so exclusive. Confined to our "I" ness, we refuse to see that there is no "I" but only "Thou". Everything belongs to God, and God is everything. The goal of my life and everyone else's life is to realize this fact and get established in inclusiveness.'

'Noble thoughts for Devpuri, sir. What I am seeing here is opposite of what you say.'

'God is everything; He is the noble, He is the evil. Whom to praise then and whom to condemn? I need to gain strength to break the shackles that tie me down to exclusiveness. My temperament allows prayers as the means to attain that, so I am at it the whole day and night.'

Sibi was getting impatient.

Bhaktidas continued with a twinkle in his eyes, 'People think that one can get devotion by singing and praying once or twice daily. But it is not so, *bhai*. Bhakti is a full-time affair. You have to earn devotion the way you earn wealth and college degrees. That way, God is far more demanding than a mistress.'

Vihan made mental notes carefully.

'*Chalo na*,' said Sibi. Vihan had to get up now. If possible, he would visit the simple sage again. He was happy to learn something meaningful. Once back to his land and place, he would be able to contribute a lot to the history of the ancient.

The conversation with Bhaktidas had taken time. Vihan hurried home. He had to create a game in which Sibi had to be the winner all the time. He smiled to himself. His world did not allow this kind of indulgence. Affection was best kept to oneself.

On the way, there was a roadblock. There was a bonfire and students were chanting, 'Down with Manu!' Manu was the great law giver of India.

A substantial crowd had gathered in the streets to burn the ancient laws. These were the students who belonged to the

Truth gang, whose only motto was to oppose everything that the public approved of.

'Down with Manu! Burn Manu!' the crowd shouted.

Vihan and Sibi were stuck on the road. Jeshi was informed, who hurried there in another car to rescue the duo.

There was a bonfire where some copies of Manusmriti were set ablaze. To make the fire look impressive, the Truth gang had put old newspapers too in the fire. The gang faced the camera of media and chanted, 'Down with Manu!'

The *tamasha* was organized by 'Truth Forum' which was the youth wing of Peace Party. College students, propelled by their youthful exuberance passing off as idealism, were easy prey for the wily. Politicians, idealists, and the shrewd applied their tact to guide the bubbling energy of the youth to their advantage. No politician worth his salt ever grew without riding the waves of youthful misguidance.

The Truth Forum, goaded by the Peace Party, opposed everything that did not suit their agenda. They were into raising slogans against any book, law, judgement, system and beliefs. Soon, Devpuri was used to hearing, '*nahi chalega, nahi chalega,*' to something and then the same slogan for its opposite.

Anvi was one of the active members of the 'Truth Forum', and so joined her college friends whenever they had to sit on some *morcha* or *dharna*. It was so exciting for her to gather the attention of the onlookers and at times of the media.

She had stood shouting 'Save the constitution!' in a *morcha*, and had also taken part in the march that had been taken out by the party claiming '*Ye azadi jhoothi ha*; this freedom is false'. Her parents violently opposed her participation in these undigested outbursts, but Kratu supported her.

'How can you expect Anvi to grow up unless she burns her hand in the wrong flames?'

To keep her safe, Kratu tried to be near her during the protests. Learning or no learning, he would not allow any harm to befall his sister.

'If she burns further, she will be left with stumps only for hands,' said an angry Ma.

Anvi's papa rarely took part in these arguments, but he also once said, 'Look at the great youth leaders of the past. They have all ended up with plush jobs. This *azadi* is not *jhoothi*, but the slogans are.'

Anvi would throw tantrums at that.

On that day too, she was at the protest site, shouting 'Down with Manu'. Kratu sat at a distance on the steps of a nearby shop and watched the *nautanki*.

Laws, imposed or evolved, are the sign of growth from 'might is right' to 'right is might' for any society. Hammurabi of Mesopotamia based his laws on the idea of justice with 'an eye for an eye' and 'an arm for an arm'. Moses based his laws as commands from God, while Christ suggested his followers to be perfect through love for God.

Indian laws did not follow any of these lines. For Indians, laws were a necessary evil to go beyond when one became truly spiritual. Till then, one had to frame a common code of conduct that would protect society and also help the individual to grow on his path to perfection.

The loose nature of laws gave rise to more and more laws till it reached the point of precipitation. That is when Manu came on the scene to frame a suitable code of conduct that would be acceptable to every Hindu. This happened thousands of years ago. In that birth Kratu happened to be his disciple.

Manu was not authoritarian, nor was he an idle reformer. He felt the need to codify habits that were going to be beneficial to all. For that he had to first know how the cultured lived all over Indian subcontinent and what they practised by way of *achara* (rites), *vyavahara* (dealings) and *prayscitta* (penance).

He tasked Kratu with collecting material on the subject. He instructed, 'Take a bagful of palm leaves to note down important things, Kratu.'

'I will manage, Acharya.'

'You may forget something. Memory can be tricky.'

'I won't let you down, Acharya. My good memory, by your blessings, is far superior to the best of stylus marks on palm leaf, master. A mischievous writer can create havoc with these marks, creating embarrassment for you.'

'As you wish, son. Take care of yourself during the journey. It may take years for you to cover the land under Aryan dominion.'

'Who would harm a poor learner, Acharya!'

Manu then chanted some mantras of protection for his dear disciple and then waited for his return.

Travelling all over the continent, Kratu found that Sanskrit and the Vedas were the only thread that ran through the land mass that stretched from the borders of Iran in the west to Indonesia in the east. Nothing else was common. He observed, analysed, classified and catalogued the practices, but these were simply too unwieldy. What was considered correct in one locality was a taboo barely a hundred miles away. Food, dress, custom, prayers, marriage, habit: everything that makes a person man, differed as one moved.

Kratu had been through these diversities in his various births. But now that he was studying them, he could feel their stark character. Initially, he felt sad at the looseness of the system. Then he realized how variety was a sign of the living and sameness was the flag of death. Sameness, he noted, implied death or the footfalls of death.

On his return, Kratu narrated to Manu what he had seen and observed. He hoped that being a perceptive person, he would find a way out of the morass.

'This is sad, Kratu. We should do something to organize the way of life. Freedom is good for growth but beyond a point it dissipates life.'

'Who will listen to us, master? People are so haughty.'

'God gives and God takes away. For us, it is important that we do not get weighed down by a sense of unfulfilled responsibility. If you feel that you must do something for the welfare of others, then do that and be free of the burden. Let the rest be with God.'

'I admire your outlook, Acharya.'

Manu was overwhelmed at the material that Kratu had collected. There was no key to converting the unpatterned into pattern. He was, as if, drowning in the ocean of social laws, with nothing to hold on to. The situation was growing hopeless as the days passed.

One day Manu was with Kratu in a marketplace when he saw a juggler making a bear perform tricks. *Madari*, the jugglers, were experts at training birds and animals to perform what they could do best. The monkeys were good at performing tricks, while bears were considered slow.

The juggler sounded his *damaru* to attract the attention of the passing public. The curious and idlers assembled to watch the performer copy humans.

'Is your name Yatibahu?' asked the juggler to the bear who had a ring round his nose. This helped the juggler control his pet.

'Grrrm,' responded the bear.

'Can you dance?'

'Grrrm.'

'Do you ever fall sick?'

'Grrm.'

'Grrm' implied that the bear was answering in the affirmative. To say 'no', it shook his head.

'The spectators here want to see what happens when Yatibahu falls sick. Show it to them, son.' The juggler then sounded his *damru* with force.

At the command, the bear fell down on the paved road, threw his arms and legs around and then went still. The crowd applauded.

'*Jio beta!* See how you got so many admirers today. They will surely reward us well. Now tell the crowd that you need medicine to get cured.'

'Grrm.'

It was time for the free-fun-lovers to make a move. The concept of high-priced tickets for entertainment, secular or religious, was not there in those days. The crowd thinned. The juggler moved his plate around with hope in his heart and a prayer on his lips. Small change changed hands.

'These are miserly people, son. With this money to get you medicine, you will have to remain sick for a long time. So get up and get well. Get up, *babu*.'

The bear got up, shook his body free of dust and looked around at the appreciative crowd.

'Now loosen your purse, sirs, for the greatest performance that you have seen in life.'

The crowd had thinned further.

Kratu tugged at Manu's elbow who was lost in thought. His stare was fixed as if he was seeing something at a distance.

'Acharya,' reminded Kratu.

'Oh, ahh. How much money we have, Kratu?'

'A few silver rupees.'

'Give them all to this juggler.'

'As you say master.'

The juggler was taken aback to see so much money. That was more than what he earned in a whole year. 'Bow, son, before this great giver,' commanded the juggler. The bear obliged.

On their way back, Kratu remained silent. A big part of their savings was gone. Was that going to be of any purpose? He had no idea.

Once back at their place, Manu said, 'We paid the juggler very little. He and his bear have solved the great riddle of life for us.'

'Acharya.'

Manu talked to Kratu the whole night about the discovery that he had made about life, existence and law.

'The nature, both internal and external, is untamed like the wild bear. Look wherever you will, there is the nature in its wild fury destroying everything that comes in its way. The rains, sun, wind, fire, all these may be gods, but as nature, these are wild and untamed for us. It is life that tames them to make them useful. Plants and trees grow by making use of Sun, wind and rains, while cooking is done by taming the fire in the oven.'

'Yes, master.'

'This taming is like taming the wild bear. But laws must not make human beings like the tamed bear, for we are not animals. We humans are destined for higher things. Our goal is perfection. Our goal is to be one with God.'

'No doubt, master.'

'There has to be a precise and clear philosophy of life – individual and social – behind our code of conduct, which we should call *Smriti* to distinguish them from the Vedas.'

What objection could Kratu have? It was Manu's work. He could do anything with his work.

'Just see how the universe is like a canvas of moving pictures in which different life forms present a perfect collage. Human beings stand out in this collage as the prime picture, because they can evolve culturally by mere will while others cannot.'

Kratu admired the fact that Manu could perceive that much, although he neither had the exposure nor the memory of Kratu. He said, 'You will be remembered for a long time for this, Acharya.'

'Do I care who remembers me after I am gone? Son, I do not care if people do not respect me even now.'

Kratu stayed silent.

'The code has to be about evolution from lower to the higher till one becomes one with the One. That is the state of equality. We must find ways to take inequality to the heights of oneness.'

'Master, every hierarchy is a pyramid. How do you plan to structure it?'

'People should not become like a dancing bear in the hands of the juggler. The soul is free by nature. When it acquires a body, it appears to be in bondage. Our goal should be to help a person get out of the idea that he is a mere body. For that, desires need to be curbed and every act must be consecrated.'

Interaction with the ordinary leads to loss of respect over time, but the great keep one close even after intimacy. Manu was great. Kratu's admiration for him increased every day.

'The freedom of man is reflected in the fact that he is born alone, dies alone, and enjoys the fruits of one's deeds alone. Father, mother, wife, children and friends do not come to one's help in the other world; only one's good deeds propel him higher.'

'How correct!' Kratu had no reason to doubt that.

'The acts that make a person unselfish are noble acts. This is dharma; this is the boat to cross the river of life and death, *vaitarani*. Let this law book, known as *Manusmriti*, revolve around unselfishness and inclusiveness. The goal of society should be to lead the lower to the higher and make the higher attain freedom. This is whole of religion and this has to be the purpose of this law book.'

Even if one has seen the whole universe, one will always be surprised to see the reach of human mind. The empire of mind is vast. Just too vast. No one can ever claim to know the whole of it or to have found a master key to understanding its realm. Manu's sweep of mind amazed Kratu.

Manu continued, 'You have seen how we have literally thousands of loose practices based on family and profession. We will organize them into four classes to make things easy.'

'It sounds so much like a symphony.'

'What is a symphony?'

Manu did not know the nuances of music. Kratu realized his folly and so not wanting to saddle his master with unnecessary information, he asked, 'How will one suffer if one commits transgressions to the laws set by you?' Kratu had his own quota of transgressions.

'Each soul is free. So, what can make it impure? Transgressions are like roadblocks that can be overcome by penances. Have you seen how the flow of water changes its course when it meets obstruction? If it does not succeed in that, as in the case of a dam, then it increases its volume to flow over the bounds.'

'How imaginative!'

'Keep doing noble acts and that will keep you free of whatever you consider evil.'

There was nothing more to discuss. Manu concluded with, 'Principles alone are important, the details are secondary. With time, a law has to be outgrown, and a time should come when human society would not need any laws. A person's own mind, purified in the river of unselfishness, would tell him what was right and what was wrong.'

'Acharya!'

When the work was complete, Manu recited it to his disciples who tried to popularize the work but there were not many takers. With time, many more lawgivers came up with their works and thus India continued to have a huge number of law books, particular to different regions.

'Down with Manu!' shouted the crowd.

Vihan was from the land and time that had outgrown the need for social laws. The mind of everyone was pure enough to know what was right and what was wrong. But in Devpuri, life was different. People wanted to do away with social laws without having the character to outgrow it.

Political correctness is the key to peace. Vihan had good qualities but he did not know how to be politically correct. He was appalled to know the details of what was happening there. Here he was, coming down from future to know the past, and these semi-literates of the present were out to burn their past.

He cornered an active member, 'How can you burn down your history?'

'We, the members of Truth Party, are progressive opposition. We believe in progress through equality, freedom and justice. That is the way to future. For that we oppose if we have to.'

'How can you have equality where there is freedom? Equality presupposes restriction in growth. You can either have freedom or equality. Bonsai look equal because their freedom is taken away. Trees grow in their own majesty when they have the freedom of forest.'

Another burner came forward to explain, 'We are progressive opposition. We believe in opposing whatever we do not believe in.'

Vihan was unaware of the ideology of the progressive. So, he continued, 'You can outgrow your past, but why burn it?'

'Don't do *lecturbaazi,* ok? Join us in burning the book.'

'If you burn your history today, you will then burn your future tomorrow.'

'Which college you are from? Don't you know that present is the gateway to the future, by steamrolling the past?'

'I know the future better than you can imagine.'

The book burner shouted to his friends, 'Leave what you are doing and come here. This fellow has to be taught lessons about the present.'

By then Jeshi had reached the spot. He whispered to Vihan, 'Run, Vihan! Run!'

The future slipped through the fingers of the present.

Jeshi knew well that the Peace Party was behind these protests, but being an astute politician, he could convert any adversity into opportunity. He now stood before the crowd and addressed, 'My soulmates! Piece of my heart! It is in the fitness of things that we burn down anything that reminds us of the past. Every monument is a grave that hides the skeletons from the past and it is the duty of you, the future, to get rid of them. If blood has to be spilled for that, may it be so. Down with Manu!'

Someone shouted, 'Right words!'

The crowd cheered.

Anvi did not like Jeshi or his methods. Once he started his address, she went back to where Kratu sat silent with moist eyes. One teardrop struggled to leave its nest. Anvi had never seen her brother like this. She threw her arms round her neck with, '*Bhaiya,* if you do not want me to be a member of "Truth Forum", I will leave it right away. I can't see you like this. Please.'

Kratu smiled the smile of the heartbroken.

Once home, Vihan asked Jeshi if he had read the book that was being burnt.

Jeshi laughed, 'You are so simple, Vihan. Why should I read something when I know that a crowd is waiting to be converted into votes for me?'

What to say of *Manusmriti*, Jeshi had hardly read any book outside his syllabus during his days of failure in college. He would tell his followers, 'Gold is everything. Next in the ladder is the gun. But learning! Pooh!! What is there in learning? Look at the history of India: Did the brahmins even have enough to feed their children? They slept hungry and made their family sleep hungry. Just see how Drona, the great brahmin of his time, did not even have milk to give to his son, so the kid had to drink flour mixed with water thinking that to be milk. Do you want your kids to drink that?' Drona was a famous brahmin warrior-teacher during the Mahabharata period.

'Never, sir! You are so brutally honest!' was the response of the satellites.

'An empty head is better than an empty purse,' was his favourite saying. 'Keep your purse full, and your head will never feel empty. He, he!'

Vihan was not satisfied with what Jeshi said.

'Why live a lie, sir?'

'Lie? What lie? He, he! How can there be a lie in the creation of God? God is true and so everything in his universe is true. What you call a lie is mere difference of perception. I speak as I perceive things. What is wrong with that? He, he!'

'Lies are lies, sir.'

Emotions, the eternal enemy of success, had been an orphan in Jeshi's personality. Whenever cornered, he summoned the crown prince of his inner self, the cold calculative craftiness.

Without getting annoyed, he said, 'How true! How true! I admire your perception.'

# 11

# VYASA BHARATI

Kratu was now old enough to leave home. The restlessness of a possible escapee showed in his face while his words and acts signalled of soon-to-leave. Two things troubled him. The first was his words to his grandpa that he would be there on his deathbed, and secondly that he had not yet come across anything substantial to justify his present birth.

Anvi felt uncomfortable after the incident of burning the book. She held herself responsible for the sad look in the eyes of her brother. She told that to Kratu, who stoutly refuted her conclusions.

'I swear that I will never again be joining any protest, *bhaiya*.'

'That is your choice, Anvi. I have nothing to do with that.'

'Then why do you have the distant look in your eyes.'

'You have nothing to do with that,' smiled Kratu.

With the pastime of revolution gone from her daily agenda, Anvi now gave more attention to her future. Every now and then she expressed her desire to be this and to become that. Kratu had difficulty keeping up with her ideal and aspirations but the indulgent brother that he was he bore with her megaplans.

Once when the Nobel Prize for literature was announced, she got the idea that she could easily become a writer. Earlier, she had also toyed with the ideas of becoming a model, singer, actor and economist.

'*Bhaiya*, you remember the story you used to tell me when I was young?'

'You are still young.'

'Say, *na*!'

'Of course, I do remember. But why?'

'I want to organize the story and write it down. To flavour it, I will sprinkle the spices of love, separation, pain and revenge. I am sure that it will be a major hit. I may even win an award!'

'That is an interesting thing about India. Its holy book is the *Gita* that preaches that you should work without any motive, but here people focus on motive without even working for it. No wonder we are in such a mess as a nation.'

The *Gita*, in seven hundred verses, is the essence of Indian religion, philosophy and spirituality.

'How can you work without motive?'

'You might have heard of the latest fad "yoga". Even Ma tried that for some days without much success. Yoga is much more than breathing or posture. It is the state when your whole personality goes into it. Writing too has to be yoga. Put your whole into it. Derive joy from writing and not by expecting to earn money or win a prize.'

'Who has ever done like that?'

'Why? Every mom does that. A mother tends her newborn without any compulsion or motive. Consequently, the joy of a mother after feeding her baby is next only to the joy of realising God. Try this outlook in anything that you do, and I assure you success.'

'Leave it, *na*. Just tell me something to start the story with: a bit of philosophy and insights. Not too heavy, I would suggest. Heavy stuff puts off GenNext.'

'Write for eternity, and not for this or that gen.'

Kratu then explained the idea of literature and story to Anvi.

'What is there in a story? It is about climbing a peak or sliding down into a pit. Depending on how well the journey up or the fall is described, the story gets it fame or failure. If a story has many such fall and climbs, as in the *Mahabharata*, then the story becomes immortal,' said Kratu.

'Where do you get these ideas from, *bhaiya*? You are the most wonderful brother in the world.'

'It is the power of your affection that makes me bloom,' Kratu said with deadpan humour.

'Ok, ok. Now tell me.'

'Everything in the universe has a rhythm. We are all wobbling and dancing in a particular rhythm in the ocean of existence, without even realising that.'

'That is a good one,' said a beaming Anvi. 'I think I will use it as the opening line of my work.'

'Rhythm expresses itself in acts, words and thought. When a person's rhythm does not match the phase in which he is wobbling, as is the case with nearly all, success eludes him. When one learns to resonate with the rhythm of life, he becomes great. This rhythm is the language of a person. Prose, poetry, drama, essay, algebra, geometry, equations, sketches, paintings, music: the infinite permutations of these form an infinite number of languages, which is unique to a person. The knife of a surgeon, the spade of a farmer, the pen of a poet, the *ghunghroo* of a dancer are all ways to express one's unique language.

'It is getting heavy, *bhaiya*.'

'The goal of life is to perfect one's language. Get the rhythm of your life, express yourself in that rhythm, and fame would come running to embrace you. People chase dreams and fame without realising that success is an orphan looking for a parent. Be capable, and success will cry to be taken up into your arms.'

'You make success appear so simple.'

'Where is the complexity in life, sis? We fail to rise above ordinariness only because we do not want to be in our rhythm, in our language. To be a wave, you need to first rise above the surface of the ocean. Find your rhythm and you will be great. That is the mantra.'

Anvi listened to her brother, which was quite unusual for a teenager.

Kratu explained the dynamics of creativity to Anvi, but his mind went back to the days when he had heard the philosophy of story making from Vyasa, the greatest poet of the world.

Thousands of years ago, Vyasa had made a name for himself as a great sage. Riding on his fame, he took the liberty of organizing the Vedas, which were floating loose in different traditions, as it was with Angi when Kratu was with him. The families maintained their tradition but fear of loss through running out of tradition was always there. The step taken by Vyasa in preserving the great knowledge was unique.

When Kratu, then a cobbler by birth, heard about the great achievement, he came to meet the sage-poet, who gladly accepted him in his ashram. Vyasa's father was a great sage while his mother was a fisherwoman. This gave Vyasa space to master the Vedas and also do away with caste prejudices typical of the brahmins. This reflected in his later works.

Vyasa had ashrams at many places. When Kratu came to meet him, he was living in Kurukshetra, where the famous war between the Pandavas and the Kauravas was to take place soon. But at that time, the place was famous for being holy because many sages had performed *tapasya* there. Indians believe that the planetary sin during solar eclipse does not touch those who are in Kurukshetra.

Many years passed like that. And then the epic war took place that saw the annihilation of major warriors and armies of the country. The story of the war, its cause and consequences, needed to be recorded for the future generations.

Vyasa became silent, going deep into the subject of his creation, as one would expect a great poet to do.

Kratu served the sage with diligence. Once in a while, he asked questions to know what was going on in the mind of the elderly sage.

Vyasa one day said, 'See this mango fruit? It is just a mango. But if you can take out its seed, which is the essence of its existence, and then plant it, it will then stay in solitude for a long time and then burst forth as a tree to give birth to many more mangoes.'

'How true!'

'One has to decide whether one wants only a mango fruit, or wants a mango tree to get many more mangoes.'

'Yes, master.'

'Persons are like fruits. If you go to one's essence, his personality is revealed, which is like the pulp of the mango. If you persist, then you will reach the seed, which is the principle whose product is the mango fruit.

Kratu was impressed.

'Person – Personality – Principle. That is the sequence. Once you reach the principle, you can create any number of personalities, and thereon you can have an infinite number of characters. This is how creativity takes place.'

'How do you differentiate between these three, master?'

'Person is one who is one with the collective, and you cannot distinguish one from the other. Personality is when a person's qualities and values become marked. He then has an individuality, well above the collective. Principle is when a person becomes one with a quality. His name then becomes an adjective instead of a noun.'

'Ohh.'

'You must surely know of Durvasa. It is the name of a sage. But it also signifies anger. Durvasa is less of a noun and more of an adjective. He is now one with the principle, although not commendable.'

No wonder that Vyasa was a poet, a worshipper of ideas through silence.

'The story of the *Mahabharata* is moving in my head. I will create the characters through this method only. Who cares how Arjuna was or Duryodhan was? People want to identify with characters in the plays and stories. For that, character must depict principle properly.'

Kratu had left the sage by the time he sat down to compose the epic, Mahabharata.

Kratu explained this to Anvi in simple words. 'See, sis. If you want to be a writer, you need to focus on the principles and then go into silence to allow its germination.'

'Is it my age to go silent?'

'Then don't hope to be a writer. You can at best be an arranger of words but not a writer. People will give a glance at your work and then cast it aside forever.'

Kratu did not know that there was a poet just like that in his city. He was Vyasa Bharati.

God creates by mere will and is knower of all that is there – animate and inanimate – in their complete existence. So, the Vedas address God as Kavi, the poet, from whose breath all words and thoughts emanate that become the basis of all creation. Being the eternal knower, God, the Kavi, knows the past, present and future simultaneously.

People, on the other hand, create with what they have. They think, plan, organize and then execute.

Great poets are different from a common man and also from God in matters of creation. They create spontaneously by going into the depths of silence. Poetry is thus neither effortless, nor a product of planning. True poets do not have to make efforts with words nor do they tinker with the thoughts. Consequently, great poetry is not limited in time or locality.

To honour this special power of the poets, Indians addressed the great sages as Kavi, a poet, for they were seen to be the true creators on this Earth, in the same way that God created this Earth. In later times, poets of lesser calibre misappropriated the adjective for themselves and made that a noun to bring self-importance to their own creation, howsoever ordinary.

Bharati, the poet from Devpuri, belonged to this second group of ordinariness. He called himself a *kavi*, although his poetry was neither spontaneous, nor unbound. Just like his personality, which had no existence beyond the circle of his own, his creation too was confined within his known.

Vyasa, whom Kratu had met and whose philosophy of creation he had explained to Anvi, had created such a huge volume of literary works that his name became synonymous with literary creation. While ordinary people talk about bringing glory to their name, the names of the truly great become adjectives. That is what Vyasa ultimately became – an adjective from a noun. Many later poets were thus called Vyasa, and many passed off their crude creations in his name with the hope that they would continue to live through their creation even after the garbage of their body had been assigned to the all-purifying fire. Many succeeded.

Inspired by this fact, Bharati, the poet of no consequence, took up the name Vyasa for himself. He felt that, being a poet, although no one read his poetry, it was in the rightness of things to name himself Vyasa. He also hoped that someday he would overshadow the original Vyasa, so he retained his name Bharati to the name that he had taken up. He thus became Vyasa Bharati.

Unfortunately, fame eluded his creations in spite of great branding.

Vyasa Bharati squarely blamed materialism for his failure, 'Do you realize, you bumpkins, how civilization has crawled forward holding the walkers offered by the poets in the past. Think you bunch of ignoramuses, think! What would you all have been without my ancestors there to guide you out of your wormholes to the light of knowledge?'

By his ancestors, Vyasa Bharati meant the poets of the world.

His verbosity was of no consequence to the discerning. People stayed away from his poetry.

Even the worst of creators find their luck turning some day, even if that be for a short while. Bharati's luck favoured him when he was invited to read his poetry during the *Ramleela* that year.

Devpuri had a strong cultural life in which art, dance, drama, speeches and religion got a free share of display.

During *Dussehra* – a lively festival observed throughout the country in various forms – a dance drama based on the Ramayana was performed in evenings at the Ramleela ground for ten days, in which the stage, story, actors and audience were the same year after year, without boring anyone. This is the speciality of great works; people do not get tired of these.

The Ramayana was composed by the great sage Valmiki who predated Vyasa by many centuries. The first epic of the world, based on the life and deeds Sri Rama, was later adopted by other poets in various formats to suit the local need. Devpuri followed *Ramacharitmanas* by Tulasidas.

The occasion was also used to present before the city folks the bevy of talents whose achievements had not yet matched their aspirations.

Someone with a stocky sense of humour amongst the organizers suggested that Vyasa Bharati be given a chance to recite his composition. 'After all, he is one of us. Some day if he becomes famous, we may even have to install a statue of him. So, why not start practising now what we may have to do in future.'

Not many in the committee got the joke and so Vyasa Bharati was given a chance. He was to present his creation on the sixth day of *Navaratra*. By then, the crowd had started getting thicker. The tenth day was to be last day of the festival when the great fight between Sri Rama and Ravan was to be enacted.

Kratu's family, liberals that they were, attended the *Ramleela* every year with the same enthusiasm as they attended seminars against religion.

The programme began with kids showing their tantrums more than their talent. To goad them on, their parents cheered more than the crowd.

After a few items, it was the turn of Vyasa Bharati to open his treasures to the public. The announcer did not know Bharati, so he sang paeans of his present hits and future glory. Ignorance can be hidden well in pomposity.

Bharati folded his hands in humility.

He then got up, checked the microphone, cleared his voice and began with his latest creation which he said he had written for the occasion.

I am
I am, I
Not me, mine but
I, only I

All said and done
What will remain
When all is gone
I, only I.

Look for I
Search for I
Wait for I
I, only I.

Clap all, clap
I, only I
Chant all, chant
I, only I

The ground broke into laughter. The announcer, embarrassed at the stupendous stupidity, signalled the audio-man to switch off the sound system.

A dejected Bharati left the stage. Unfortunately for him, his downslide to nothingness continued more and more. Soon he was to hit rock bottom, with no earnings and no recognition.

Kratu watched the wasted talent of Vyasa Bharati leaving the stage. 'No one knows how many talents asphyxiate in the absence of the right prick,' he muttered in silence. He then went back in time when he had met the mega poet, Valmiki. That was centuries before he had met Vyasa.

Journeying in the choppy ocean of birth and death, Kratu had reached the shores of life in the family of a boatman. His family took immense pride in what they did. 'You know, son, when a person dies, he has to cross the *Vaitarani* to reach the shores of the next life.'

Kratu knew that well.

'Noble deeds and inclusiveness are the ways to earn passage on the boat that takes one across the deadly river. We represent that ferrying. People may take pride in what they do in their life and may even practise exclusiveness, but when it comes to crossing a river, particularly the huge ones like Ganga, all passengers become one, with a single purpose and a single mode. We, like good karma, do not discriminate between high and low, rich and poor. We do our duty without any favour or fear.'

'Yes, father. We are great.'

'No doubt in that, son. No other profession represents life the way ours does. Life is like a river in spate, and we, like a saviour, are the ones to take the troubled across.'

'What a privilege for us. I will stay true to our profession, father.'

Kratu rowed the family boat in the river Tamasha, a tributary of Ganga. He was single, with the sole responsibility to feed his parents, which he did well. His limited needs and ambitions gave him ample space to be himself. The rhythmic motion of the boat, when he was ferrying, added to his serenity.

Valmiki was a respected sage who had his *ashram* near the river Tamasa. The great sage was suffering from inner urges to express himself, but he did not know the what, how and why of his want.

Many sages and their disciples came to take bath in the river, but no one impressed Kratu more than Valmiki. He longed to meet the sage, who seemed to him as a potential world mover, but occupational compulsions did not allow the meeting.

Once, Valmiki had to travel by the river with two of his disciples to join some *yajna*. Kratu was available with his boat for the journey. Finally, he could be near the sage who seemed ready to let out his juice of creativity. A large honeycomb may be heavy with honey, but one needs to prick it to get the juice drip down. Valmiki needed such a motivation.

While walking from his ashram, Valmiki had begun a discourse on creation to his disciples, which he continued during the journey.

'Oh no! Another theory of creation! Not again!'

'Creation comes from word, *sphota*, word, which permeates the universe. In the beginning there was God. When He wanted to create the universe, He breathed out word, which came to be known as the Vedas. Words are *Vak*, the goddess of learning, the foundation of creation, truth and bliss.'

The disciples nodded.

'Know that, every word, spoken or silent is an attempt at describing the Divine. *Satyameva jayate na anritam*: Truth alone prevails, for falsehood does not describe the Divine. So, you noble ones, always be gentle with your words and be true to them.'

'Yes, Acharya.'

Do you remember the lines from the hymn?

*I am the Queen, first of those who merit worship.*
*I make the man I love mighty, a sage, and a brahmin.*

The disciples chanted the mantra from the Rigveda with him.

Kratu wanted to say a word of appreciation, but realizing that he was not supposed to be a knower of the Vedas, he checked himself.

Hearing the word *Vak*, he remembered how he had once met the *rishika,* a sage-poetess Vak Chanvi who was the daughter of the sage Ambhrina. She had come up with the great hymn that was being chanted by Valmiki and his disciples. The mantra showed how a person in the depths of oneness could identify oneself with God.

'Words, when used in order, make a language. A refined language, polished neat by the use of chiselled words, becomes as soothing as music or a work of art. *Prakrit*, the unsophisticated, are not at all good with their words, and that shows in their behaviour.'

Sanskrit was adored by the masses as the language of the gods. The need for hard work to maintain the perfection of the language made people opt for the less troublesome local dialects, in which they could twist and turn words according to their whims and needs. Children and the less cultured could easily manipulate the dialects to come up with new words and expressions, which gave them freedom of expansion. But like any unbridled freedom, the dialects had a fear of dying out. And that is what happened with all those dialects later, while Sanskrit continues to be there as it was thousands of years ago.

Valmiki was talking in Sanskrit, never imagining that the young boatman was a master of that. 'Look at this wretch of a boatman. Do you think he or his tribe will ever climb the social ladder without first refining language?'

'No, Acharya.'

Kratu turned away his head smilingly at the philosophically correct but politically wrong statement.

'What a person thinks, he speaks and then he acts on that.' Later, the sage was to use this idea in his famous creation, *Ramayana*. A mischievous person first thinks of a nefarious activity, then starts talking aloud about it and finally commits that. A person desirous of being noble must cut one of the links of the chain.

'Words and acts are non-different that way. So, how a person acts is actually his language.'

Kratu was startled to hear this. He had never heard or thought that way. Indeed, there was no limit for human minds to explore. 'Wonderful sage! You are a world mover.'

'When you do something, you actually liberate an idea through that act, which otherwise would have remained in potential form inside you. In the same way, a language too liberates ideas from the captivity of the mind.'

Kratu could appreciate what he was hearing, but he had doubts about the disciples' understanding. 'O dear young disciples, you are great simply because you have Valmiki as a teacher!' He listened to the words intently and was convinced that the sage himself was a caged talent, seeking liberation without knowing that.

Kratu rowed and thought. The rhythm of the oars and the soothing words of the sage made his thoughts go deep. Finally he broke out in a soft humming:

O dear sage great!
What a pity is your sight
With not your language right.

Why fritter wisdom thou
For that which be not thine
Break away from ceiling tight
To be one with calling right.

Kratu meant to say that Valmiki should devote himself to creativity instead of being a mere teacher. The group in the boat, on the other hand, thought that the illiterate boatman was bored with their talks and hence he had started humming.

When they reached destination, the sage wanted to pay Kratu but he humbly requested with, 'May your grace be on the world!' Valmiki gave a surprised look at Kratu. There was something familiar about the boatman, the sage thought, without able to conclude what that was.

After the return, Kratu made a plan to put his conclusions about Valmiki to test. It was a kind of scheming but acceptable.

Every city, village or locality is like a cluster of islands where people of the same mentality and status dwell. Rich, poor, gangsters, thieves, beggars: they all live together in unseen islands. One can easily build links to find out a person, without knowing his address, even in the largest city if one knows the status of that person. One only has to move on the right ladder.

Kratu was low in the hierarchy of his locality. This helped him coalesce with people of lower strata, one of whom was a hunter, Veer. He was good with arrows and also with harpoon. Kratu was a good friend of his and took him in his boat for free to see his fishing skills with the harpoon.

Yes, Veer was the perfect choice for his plan, thought Kratu.

One day, he lured Veer to shoot at a frolicking pair of birds who were exchanging words of endearment during mating season. Remembering his lessons from the story of Homa, Kratu wanted to see what came out of the sage when he was in unspeakable agony. 'What comes out of a person when he is crushed is his strength,' Isan, the woodcutter had told him. The strength of a person was his language, Kratu had concluded.

It was early morning; time for the sage and his disciples to bathe in the river. Indians consider rivers to be living beings, so they don't bathe at night. Intrusion of any kind is unacceptable in India.

Valmiki walked with his disciples towards the river, lost in the oneness of nature.

Indian forest.

Deep.

Green.

With flora and fauna.

Life teeming with life.

Cruelty an exception.

There, up in the sky, was a pair of birds cooing at each other the little endearments of courtship. The sweetness was intoxicating for any.

Sound – Creation – God. The sage walked in the depths of stillness thinking of *sphota* as the source and sustenance of creation.

'Now, now,' hissed Kratu at Veer, who could not understand the exigency in the words.

'What is the hurry?' he whispered back. 'The bird is as good as in my hands, friend. But tell me, why you are so eager to shoot it down? Are you having some special dinner tonight? Do invite me.'

'Shut up and shoot.'

'Ok, *baba*.'

The stage was set, the die was cast. Kratu could do nothing more than what he had done to see his plans fructify. Like crystallization, success had to wrap itself around the noble thought and deed done by him.

'HUSSSSHHH,' was the sound of arrow cutting through air.

'KIIIII', was the response from the sky. One of the pair had fallen dead.

The plaintive cry of the separated filled the sky, whose broken strands of misery, hit the sage. His serenity, pierced by the pain of the lonely, let out a wail of words:

*Ma Nishada Pratistham Tvam agamah sasvati Sama*
*Yat Kraunchamithunadekam Avadhi Kama mohitam –*

– May you never have peace in your endless births, o hunter,
whose cruel hand has killed one of this gentle pair!

Valmiki was surprised at his own utterance, which was poetry, unknown till then in the world. The Vedas were considered divine and hence these were not treated as poetry, which required the intervention of human mind.

'Whoaaa!' cried out Kratu. It was the expression of success that he had learnt from Paras, the fisherman-sage. Instead of the fish running away with the bait leaving the hook, this time the fish here had taken the hook, as Kratu had wanted.

Veer was shocked into silence, 'What wrong have I committed to deserve such a curse from a venerated sage? I am a fowler and it is within my duty and rights to capture or kill all that run, fly, or swim. Why the curse then? Oh sage! Why you have love for the flying but not for the grounded?' He shed tears of agony.

Kratu paid no heed to the tears of Veer. Poetry had been liberated from the confines of the mind. Sacrifice of one or two lives was nothing at the altar of liberation. Every edifice requires tonnes of burial before it can be visible on the ground.

Veer felt that Kratu had something to do with the curse on him, 'What will I do now with this curse on my head? I will be born again and again with the pain of the curse. I have a feeling that this was part of some scheme. I am not as smart as you are, but I can understand what has hit me.'

Kratu laughed, 'You will not be alone in this type of curse. Moreover, you will become immortal because of what you did. The sage is going to hit it big, and whenever his story of creativity will be narrated, your presence will be a must. Not many are lucky that way.'

'What will I do with that kind of name which has infamy attached with it? I tell you, if I had powers, I would have cursed you.'

'One curse more or less makes no difference to the eternally cursed. Now come, I will take you to a better target.'

Veer did not understand the reason for Kratu's enthusiasm. Nor did he want to follow Kratu or be with him ever again.

With time, Valmiki's work became immortal. Sri Rama along with other characters, their deeds and relation, came to be seen as the measuring rod of values in India.

At the *Ramleela* that day, the play was about the friendship between Rama and Sugreeva. It was beautifully rendered with the help of music, narration and acting. When Sri Rama said, 'The Vedas say that nothing pains a person more than a foolish attendant, infidelity in the family, a miserly boss and an insincere friend,' Kratu felt tears welling up and streaming down his tears. 'Aswin, Aswin! Where you might be? I have a duty to fulfil towards you, I remember.'

The *Ramleela* was coming to an end for the evening. Kratu's mom had enjoyed the friendship part thoroughly, 'You know

Kratu, with the idea of single child catching up in India, the next generation will forget what it means to have a brother or a sister, and then they will forget uncle, aunt and *maasi*. But friendship will remain. Whenever people will think of friendship between two unequal, they will turn to Rama-Sugreeva.'

'Yes, Ma,' said Kratu with a little emotion. He was in no position to explain his own friendship to the family.

Ma being Ma, she caught the slight quivering in the voice. Tenderly she asked, 'You alright, *babu*?'

Kratu had composed himself. 'Yes, Ma.' He then turned his mind away from emotions and instead thought of the journey of poetry from Valmiki to Vyasa Bharati. 'Is it evolution or downfall?'

Sanskrit language had become so calcified that only scholars knew it. The vitality of language had vanished, making writers and poets use clever tricks of the language to cover the bankruptcy of their ideas. Momentary appreciation ate up creativity.

'Just look at the Western literature. How many ideal characters they have to measure personalities with? A few. Worse, the characters in the West are mostly magical. But look at Ramayana and Mahabharata, and you will find hundreds of characters roaming around in daily language, without any shade or even tinge of magic in them. And then look at the later literature – nothing to show!' thought Kratu sadly.

The vengeance of history was now on India.

Tired of the complexity of the sacred language, people now indulged in claiming dialects to be languages, and came up with words which had no root with 'principle – idea-words-objects'. Words were mere words, signifying hollowness, unless one belonged to the ilk of the users.

The price of exclusiveness, created by the learned of the land, was now being repaid at a high cost: the culture was in decay which showed in rot of ideas that were pissed out by the poets. The poetry of Vyasa Bharati belonged to that class.

Society also had a role to play in the decadence.

Creativity comes from the depths of silence and not from the din of words. When a culture permits its thinkers the silence that they require by providing the basics of their physical needs then alone come the majesty of creation that gives sustenance to culture.

Kratu had reached home. The delight of having seen a great performance was missing from his face.

## 12

# THE DANCE

Elections were approaching in Devpuri.

Being a politician, Jeshi was also supposed to be a patron of art and culture. What he lost in time and patience doing that, he gained by looting as a culture mafia in a dignified mask. The rich wanted the tickets to feel themselves cultured, and the artists vied for his attention to earn a handful. The hunger of others was meat for Jeshi.

For the autumn festival, he was advised to get Shivansh to perform, which he did. The media lapped up the news and made the city go wild with excitement. The crumbs from Jeshi's plate filled the belly of many.

Shivansh had earned international fame in dance.

He was from a poor family of dancers that lived in one of the villages that dot the Indian landscape like stars in the sky. His ancestors had been into performing art since Vedic times, which they treated not as a means to livelihood but as a way of life.

The sense of righteousness attached with their art provided the family with barely a morsel to their mouths but gave hope for a better next life, which was very important to them.

Things were changing now, and the members focussed more on livelihood and so moved away from the art.

In earlier times, whenever there was a festival, the family went to perform, sometimes to please the gods and sometimes only to entertain the crowd. A kind brahmin had once taught Shivansh's ancestors a prayer from the Rigveda:

> *Clad in a vesture, beautiful as heaven to look on,*
> *Thou hast been as an active dancer.*

Since then, the family recited this prayer before every performance. The idea that God was the divine dancer, gave the family pride in their dharma, the way of their life. Following *Varnashrama dharma* – the code of life – popularized by the great law chronicler Manu, the young ones of the family learnt dance, the adults performed, the elderly taught it, and the old ones contemplated on the divine as the divine dancer.

The strength born of *svadharma* helped them withstand the vagaries of life in the form of death, disease, drought and deluge. 'Adversity is only the gateway to opportunity, son,' said the seniors. The learners nodded their head in obedience.

Good conduct is no guarantee for a good life. Shivansh's family, as also his ancestors, suffered from perpetual wants. But when the whole country lived a frugal life, there was no reason to complain. '*Dha dhin dhin dha*', streamed the beats from the dancing feet, morning to morning, unconcerned with the wants of the belly.

Even the best of talented families sometimes gets an unexpected prodigy, who is a natural talent, who surpasses all performers from recent memory, and who brings honour to his family name. Shivansh was that. His steps had a spark of genius that left even his masterly grandpa charmed.

'Believe me, he is the lost soul of some *gandharva*,' said grandpa.

'That would be our karma,' said grandma.

Shivansh's ma took secret pride in these exchanges. She basked in the praise of her son, so she wanted to hear more of it. 'How do you say that sasu-ma? Such-and-such a person is a great performer.'

'You are such a fool. I wonder how my husband chose you for our family. Just wait till Shivansh proves your stupid belief wrong.'

Shivansh's ma soaked in the warmth of pride.

Once, a great master of dance from Varanasi came to Shivansh's village to meet a relative. This master never performed in public and not many knew about him. A chance meeting with Shivansh made him see the natural talents, so he took the child with him. The family did not object. It was customary to allow children to go for higher training with a master as Kratu had done with Angi.

'God is love, *rasa*,' said the master. 'The Vedas describe God as *raso vai sah*: He is love personified. To love something, it has to exist and then it has to be known by you. You cannot love something that does not exist or about which you have no knowledge. The sages and saints realized and continue to realize in their pure hearts that God alone exists. That being so, God alone is the known, and He alone is the object of all love.'

Shivansh listened to the philosophy behind dance with devotion. His grandpa used to say, 'Ordinary minds learn the how, mediocre learn the why, and the great minds apply why to how.' So, the talk on philosophy of performance by the master was value addition.

'The goal of every dancer, I don't mean the *nachaniyas* who sell themselves for money, is to reach that oneness from which multiplicity has emerged,' said the master. 'To be one with God is our only goal. For that, you have to be first in rhythm, then *rasa*, and finally be one with it. When the dancer, dance, and deity to which dance is offered, merge into one, then alone true *rasa* is created. That is how you become one with God.'

Shivansh nodded with understanding.

'If you want to be one with Rama, Krishna, Vishnu, Shiva, Durga or any other form of God, then you have to first feel His presence within and outside you, and then create one of the six *rasa*. There are six *rasa*, while some others claim the number to be eight, but I prefer only four of them: *shringar* – love, *raudra* – fury, *veer* – heroic, and *adbhut* – wonder.'

Shivansh had learnt the basics of *rasa* in the family tradition.

'My ideal is Lord Shiva. So I love to offer what He gave to the world: *tandava* and *lasya* as two major forms of dance. You focus on these two. Of course, to be a maestro, you will have to master every other form and every *rasa*.'

The master taught Shivansh what he had learnt in the *guru-shishya-parampara,* whose origin no one remembered.

It is easy to get a teacher, but it is difficult to get a good disciple. Shivansh was a prize find for the master, who felt blessed to have a disciple like him. '*Nritya Vidya*, the sacred tradition of dance, will not get lost now,' he told himself.

Shivansh lived up to the expectation of his teacher by putting his whole being into becoming one with the art. Guru poured out all that he had till his last heartbeat. As his end approached, the master withdrew himself more and more, and then before moving on, he whispered to Shivansh, 'The beat must never die.'

Shivansh shed copious tears on the death of his master, who was nothing less than a sage. He had attained through dance what sages achieved through meditation. The master had not married, so Shivansh performed his last rites. The day it was all over, he danced all night in honour of the departed.

With the skills that he had acquired, he went out in the world to make a way for himself. One thing led to another. He soon proved his class over the greats in no time. When in a competition or with other dancers, he showed how easy it was for him to perform what the other had done, and then he performed what other could not.

The step to the West was easy for the talented, so he was soon in demand there too. The famed Western dancers met the same fate as the Indian dancers. He outstepped them.

This, of course, did not make him roll in wealth. The culturally challenged preferred shriekers and screechers on whom they poured their wealth, leaving only crumbs for the great.

Whenever not in public performance, he danced his heart out before *Nataraj,* the god of dance.

Social network is the web where every spider is a potential prey. People meet, weigh and then make plans to suck the juice out of the other. One cannot let go of the web nor can one be inattentive on it.

Jeshi reached the auditorium with Vihan and Sibi well before time to be with the grease and wheels of the society. The powerful have to make small sacrifices to suck big.

Kratu and his family also came to watch the performance.

The programme started.

After the customary mutual admiration by the organizer and the performer, Shivansh announced that he would perform the *tandav* dance of Shiva on the hymn composed by Ravan.

The mythologies describe Ravan to be a great devotee of Lord Shiva. He once went to Mount Kailash on which the Lord lived with his consort, Parvati, and tried to lift the mountain to bring it to his land with the Lord. When the mountain shook, everyone was terrified. Seeing that, the Lord smiled and pressed his seat with his toe, which now carried the weight of the universe with it. Ravan's arm was crushed under the mountain.

Crying out in pain and realizing that only Lord could now save him, he broke out in the hymn:

*Jata tavi galajjala pravaha pavitasthale*
*Galevalambya lambitam bhujanga tunga malikam*
*Damad damad damad dama ninada vad damarvayam*
*Chakar chand tandavam tanotu nah shivah shivam*

To create the mood of the audience, the sound system started to play the hymn in its original tune.

Time for show.

Shivansh appeared on the stage, bowed with folded hands before the invisible Lord and then bowed before the audience. To an artist, the audience is one with God. Performance is for God, which is present in the hall as audience.

He started with short narration on how Lord Shiva had gone into *tandava* mode when he wanted to destroy the universe after the death of Sati, his wife. He then began the preliminaries with various poses of hands, face, feet and legs on the accompaniment of percussions to create the mood in the mind of the audience. After that he showed some moves, from where he started flowing out into the dance. The untrained eyes could not make out when the basics had turned into the real, with Shivansh's steps and poses becoming faster.

The beats on the percussions became more audible and faster. The sound system had vacated its place to the accompanying artists who sang out the lines:

*Dhaga-dhaga-dhaga jjvala lalata patta pavake*
*Kishor chandra shekhare ratih pratikshanam mama*

Shivansh was enacting how the Lord danced with ferocity: His matted tresses loose and flying out like a fan behind his head, legs moving aggressively, *damaru* trying vigorously to keep the beat, the *trishul* spewing cosmic fire to burn down the universe.

The gods and sages trembled with fear, the worlds faced earthquakes, dark clouds and deadly storms tormented the Earth, people were convinced that *pralay* had come, the wild animals hid in caves, birds clutched the branches, snakes coiled themselves around whatever they could get, crocodiles bored through the mud, fishes dived into the water bed, trees and huts swung wildly. Life was going to be dead, with death dancing alive.

Those who could pray, prayed for peace to return, children cried and hung on to the legs of their moms while moms got strength from the nearness of their children, cows and buffaloes mooed to be released from the ropes around their necks, but their owners did not dare venture out. Fear rocked everyone's confidence. No one knew what was happening and why.

The beats were now vigorous:

*Smarachchidam purachchhidam bhavachchidam makhachchidam*
*Gajachchidandhaka chidam tamantaka chchidam bhaje*

Shivansh created alive the Lord's dance of looming destruction.

There was something more in his dance that day, which no one knew the reason for. There was an unknown presence somewhere near, that freed Shivansh's dance forever. Shivansh had been a great dancer. He was a maestro. But for no known reason, he appeared as a force of nature, a blessed of God. Some invisible, unknown presence had pushed his dance to ultimate freedom.

The vigour of his dance was now difficult to keep pace with.

The accompanying artists were used to the genius of Shivansh, but that day they felt their hands go wild on the percussions to stay in phase with the furious steps. The tabla and mridangam sounded fearsome. The footwork and the hand movements of Shivansh were too fast to be distinguishable and yet they were conveying exactly what they intended to. Had Lord Shiva Himself taken over?

Time, the measure of events, stopped.

Vihan was sitting with Sibi and Jeshi. He wondered if the motion of subatomic particles in the ocean of energy was something like this: wild and yet coordinated.

'*Achha nachate hain, nahi*?' whispered Jeshi to Vihan. 'Good.'

Vihan startled violently. He could have killed Jeshi for the intrusion.

The dance continued at:

*Dhimid dhimid dhimidhvanan mridanga tunga mangala*
*Dhvani karma pravartita prachanda tandavah shivah*

It described the figure of the Lord, dancing with lightning speed, holding the great fire on his head to the beat of *dhimid, dhimid* from his *damaru*.

The stage was afire. Rhythm now danced on rhythm, fury matched fury, step embraced steps, wave stormed on waves.

The ocean of the collective minds let the rhythm of dance have a free play on it. Even the most untamed minds in the audience resonated with the contours of the dance. All had gone numb with bated breath.

It seemed as if Shiva, descended on the stage, would indeed burn down the creation. Devpuri had not seen anything like that.

Ever.

The invisible presence, pushing Shivansh's dance to way beyond freedom, was Usha. But even she was not aware of it. It is often that one influences other powerfully, without either of them knowing about it. Company has its advantage.

Usha had pleaded with her parents to get tickets for the show of Shivansh even if the family had to sacrifice on some other expense. Mom was not willing.

'The whole day you are swinging your hips. Now you want to see others doing that,' said an angry mother.

The doting father persuaded ma to allow Usha to go for the performance. 'Our *bitiya* will soon be going away to some other family. Let us fulfil all her wishes, *na*.'

Getting tickets was going to be difficult, but India, the land of jugaad, can get one anything, provided a person can build the bridge with right connections. Usha's father used his skeletal connections and succeeded in getting seats in the back rows of the auditorium.

Shivansh was gyrating at unbelievable speed when Usha got up from her seat.

'Sit down,' hissed her mom, 'what will people think of us!'

'Wait here,' whispered back Usha.

She walked to the exit, reached the green room, put on some make up hurriedly, and then tiptoed on to the stage. The attendants were all absorbed in the dance, and so no one noticed Usha doing all that till she was on the stage.

The crowd thought that it was a part of the performance. The music team was surprised at the intrusion while Shivansh got the shock of his life. However, masters that they were, they did not let the beats and rhythm suffer a break.

Usha's mom nudged her husband, 'See how we are going to lose our face forever because of your *bitiya rani*, as you always call her. See the result of your pampering. Who will marry her after the ridicule she is going to face? Please do something. Please.'

Papa remained silent. Something inside him told that he was going to be proud for life. Even otherwise, what could he do? He patted his wife's hand soothingly.

Maintaining the rhythm of Shivansh, Usha slid into the dance like milk into water.

She started performing *lasya* to soothe Shivansh's *tandava*. Her expressions and movements indicated that it was Parvati, calming down the fury of the Lord, who was out to burn down the universe. Being the mother of the universe, Parvati was not going to let the universe be destroyed even by God. Calamity is expected and acceptable in the universe, but annihilation is a strict no-no.

Shiva is the destroyer of desires. When Kamadeva, the god of union, wanted to disturb the Lord by arousing amorous emotions in him, he burned him down with his third eye, the eye of wisdom that can send any passion to the farthest black hole. How can such a God be ever tamed by the goddess?

Parvati is not just any female. She is the essence of Lord Shiva, and is also his kinetic form. Calmness comes when a person is face to face with oneself. Anger, pain, hatred, greed, obsession, and pride are expressed only with someone who is not considered to be oneself. Tenderness and whispers are signs of nearness while shouting and screaming signals distance. One calls out a person loudly when separated by physical or emotional distance only.

Parvati is Shiva. They are one. Inseparable. Lord, howsoever furious, has to be calm when with himself, He has to be calm before Parvati.

Usha's dance was to soothe the frayed. Shivansh, even in the rapidity of his movement, was surprised at the steps of the young lady who seemed to be taking away the wild energy of the Lord into herself.

'Whosoever she is, she is great. She is the big thing,' thought Shivansh amidst his master performance.

Energy. Intense. Calm.

Usha's dance was a harmony of wild forces in nature. Starting from the heights of fury, she was leading the Lord down to the realm of calmness. That is how Mother Nature takes the soul to freedom by showing it the majesty of creation and then leading it out of the maze.

Usha's movements were passionate and fluid with grace and splendour. She was into circular, spiral and swirling movements, taking Shivansh along with her. The colossal masculine power of God seemed to get channelled in the tenderness and sublimity of Mother Nature, resulting in different *rasa* of love, wonder, laughter and ecstasy. This is what Shivansh had learnt at the feet of his master, but he never had the opportunity to perform with a partner like this.

Parvati is not only the wife, but she is also the mother of Shiva. The infinite appears as finite only because Shakti, the feminine power is there. It is her duty to keep the Lord tamed when He gets wild.

What to say of Devpuri, even Shivansh had not imagined a performance like this. It was in the nature of his dance to end at crescendo, but Usha brought the steps and music to a soft, floating stop.

Shiva embraced Parvati. The tumultuous clap from the audience tore through the roof. The screen dropped but the clapping continued. Like the life of the greats: they get claps well after they are gone. These are the stories that are told and retold in every home by every generation.

Anvi muttered, 'I want to be like her.'

Kratu was too absorbed to hear what Anvi was telling. Her uncountable life experiences had not prepared him for what he saw at the stage. Who was she? Someone he knew from the past?

'Who are you?' asked Shivansh.

Usha smiled and then without saying a word, she touched Shivansh's feet in *pranam*, got up, folded her hands again in a final *pranam* and then left the stage to vanish in the tumult.

Forever.

When the time for paying Shivansh came, he refused payment and instead asked for the name and address of the girl. Unfortunately, no one knew who she was or wherefrom she had come. The fruitless search went on for many days. There was no photograph or any detail of the young lady through which she could be traced.

Shivansh waited fruitlessly in the city in the hope of getting the girl as her protégé.

On their way back, Vihan said, 'What a refined culture you have, sir.'

'Why do you keep saying "you-your" all the time? Where are you from? Heaven? He, he!' commented Jeshi.

'No, no. I am not from Heaven but my folks do not have this art.' The advanced civilization had let go of many good things along with the bad.

'We should try to get this girl for you to get married. You can take her to your folks, wherever they might be living. She will awaken the culture in you.'

'Marry? What is that, sir?'

This was too much for Jeshi to digest. What kind of society Vihan was from that did not mate through marriage?

'A savage he must be,' concluded Jeshi.

The future was savage for the present.

The papers next day carried large news item about the dance and also ads to locate the girl. But she had vanished from the public eyes. Usha prohibited her parents to talk about her to any, who anyway did not want to make their life public.

In the evening her footwork continued to sound, *'ta, ta. thai, thai.'*

Aswin did not know of all this. He continued playing on his flute all night on the bank of the river.

# PART THREE

# 13

# DADDU DIES

Kratu's grandpa was getting ready to bid farewell to those who were with him in this life. He knew well that death is not an end but only the portal to a new life. To express this feeling of his, he was often found singing a self-composed song:

Joy of the Dying, ah! joy of the dying

*With play mine over, and wares all sold*
*Duty all done and burden all rolled*
*No debt to pay, nor pay to take*
*No fear to lose, no gain to make.*

*Gyrated by fate was lot mine cracked*
*Now I sit with lot my packed.*
*No one to hurt me, nor fear more*
*Look for I life lies that 'fore.*

*Joy of the Dying, ah! joy of the dying*

Last days had come, everyone guessed.

Grandpa now expressed the wish to be taken to his village so that he could die amidst the familiarity of the innocence of his childhood, away from the intrusion of injections and oxygen of the old age.

'Fresh air, earth, sky, water and fire – this is what we had when I was growing. I wish to feel the loving earth, open sky and free flowing water of the river once again. Chasing the mirage of gold, we lost connect with the five fundamental elements. Please take me back,' said grandpa.

'Father, we can afford to keep you here and bear medical expenses,' said Kratu's Pa.

'What will people say, papa?' said Kratu's Ma with tears in her eyes. She loved and adored her father-in-law. From the time that Grandma had died, she had looked after Grandpa as his daughter would have cared for him. In addition, there was this problem of whisper-mongers who would badmouth her.

'Daughter, this is my one wish. I have stayed away from seeking favours or avoiding your wishes, so allow me this one luxury for the first time, which will actually be the last.'

The moving words moved Ma to tears.

He then turned to his son, 'We have forgotten the dignity of death, son. India mastered the wisdom concerning death a long time ago and taught it to the world. Now we ourselves seem to be forgetting it. Spare me the pain of letting this wisdom slip from me through the ventilator and ICCU. If you do this much for me which I cannot do myself, I will feel that you have repaid your *pitri rin,* the debt due to your father.'

The family agreed tearfully.

Accordingly, Kratu was sent to their ancestral village to arrange for basic amenities for the stay of all.

Kratu had been to his village when he was a small boy. Anyone else would have forgotten the stay such a long time ago, but Kratu, with his cursed memory, remembered everything. It was going to be easy for him to build relations and organize things.

He purchased the lowest class ticket to feel the mind of the present India.

Indian trains. The machine and mechanism that had united India and had broken down caste and religious barriers had now created isolations of class. Those who could, started their journey, went through it and reached destination in the cocoon of their privacy. The interactions and exchanges – the two positives of a journey – were replaced by the insulations of private space in the form of compartments and e-gadgets that seemed to pull the heads of the owners down to stay glued to the screen. Travellers stayed in their encasements and were transported to new encasements through the capsules of higher-class travel and reservations.

'Travelling on a magic carpet or a broom would be more exciting than this kind of journey,' pitied Kratu. 'If life is about gaining exposure and experience, then these people are surely travelling back in time.'

The lower classes of Indian trains often provide freelance talkers. Jagadev was one such whom Kratu met in the train. He had his opinion about everything under the sky; he could comment on the Vedas and also on quantum physics.

During his talk on this and that, he said, 'Isn't it amazing that our sages knew everything about quantum physics? They had mastered the making of aeroplanes, rockets and atomic bombs.'

Kratu started violently with, 'What! What!'

'Ha, ha. *Bhai*, you are from the newgen; you won't know about the Vedas. Even then you should know something about Indian traditions and our spiritual heritage.'

'Are you serious?' asked Kratu.

'I pity you, the young. The whole world knows this, only our Indian youth do not know what is theirs. *Bhai,* how can we hope to have future for our great nation?'

'What is great about it when you yourself are not established in any of the virtues that our ancestors had mastered? Have you mastered any of the scriptures, art or even language of the ancestors? Do you ever feel like the proverbial snake that carries a gem on its head but eats frogs all its life?'

'So, what should a frog eat?' mocked Jagadev.

'Exactly. Then why talk about the gem on the head? Secondly, examples are made to drive a point and not for literal use. This is where we have descended sir. We argue endlessly without trying to reach a conclusion.'

'*Arre bhai,* we converse to stay engaged during the journey time.'

'We can also utilize this time in exchanging meaningful ideas.'

'*Haan.*'

'As for the future of India, I must say it is brilliant. But for that to happen, the cultured have to come down from their high pedestals. Brahmins ruined the flow of culture to the masses by being exclusive. Now the same mistake is being duplicated by the present generation. The cultured have to be responsible towards the society, but see how the neo-rich are interested only in accumulating power and wealth for themselves. By becoming exclusive, they are harming the society, which will collapse again. Once the bright ones realize this and get down to rebuilding India, things will surely change forever.'

'*Yaar*, you talk very well. Where do you study?'

Kratu ignored the compliment and continued, 'Do we ever

realize that we have a responsibility towards the world? Are we ever conscious that we are the land of sages, the land where once the likes of Valmiki and Vyasa, Buddha and Mahavir walked and talked? No, we don't.'

Kratu's passionate talk brought some freelance listeners who nodded their head in agreement.

'It is time to get up, gird our loins and achieve the best to serve the world.'

'Ahh, our station is approaching. We indeed have to get up, *bhai*.'

Kratu introduced himself to the villagers, who very eagerly reminisced about his last visit. In turn, they were surprised to see how he remembered them so well.

'Isn't it surprising that you remember us so well although you met us when you were just a kid!'

Kratu laughed, 'You are so important to me that I cannot let the memory fade.'

A village is not just a mishmash of houses as one sees in cities. It is a large family where every one cares for everyone else, in spite of their squabbles and occasional *lathibaji*. The young ones of the village organized everything for Kratu before the family arrived.

When Baba was brought there, things were in shape. No one complained. Once they were settled, Kratu informed, 'I wish to perform all the last rituals of Baba once he gives up his body.'

Ma gave a worried look, 'We are not brahmins. People will object. Be reasonable in matters of religion, *beta*.'

'Ma, we are all brahmins now. From the day that India became independent, we are all brahmins. *Staya Yuga* has begun now. There is only one caste and only one way of life – it is to be true to be what one does and stay unselfish while doing that.'

'What has the last rites to do with what you are saying? And who will listen to you?'

'India will have to listen to me, or it will perish. But it can't perish. India is the land of God where every child knows what it means to be one with God. So, God won't let India perish, rather He will finish off people and occupations who tend to be exclusive.'

'Are you really my son?'

'You gave birth to me, you know the best,' said Kratu and then continued, 'Do not worry about the priests for the funeral. We will invite learned ones from Varanasi. After all, they too have to survive. But rituals will be performed only by me. If you have any doubts about my capabilities, I assure that I will check for the correctness from the internet.'

Of course, he had no need for internet to do that.

Papa was not amused, 'Son, you want to start e-*shraddha*?'

Kratu was adamant.

Baba gave up solid food the day he reached the village, and then he gave up liquid food too. Death was not going to drag him away like a hunted animal, but was going to bow in the honour of someone who knows the eventuality and dignity of the event.

Realising that the end was imminent, Ma put Ganga water and *tulsi* leaves in his mouth. That was the last intake that Baba took from the world that had fed him and nurtured him for so long, starting from the moment that he sucked the first mouthful of milk from his mother.

'Fortunate to have you, daughter, and Kratu with me,' whispered Baba for the last time to the family. He then tried to raise his hands in *pranam* and took the names of God in a dying voice, 'Narayan, Krishna, Shiva, Narayan...' and then shut his lips forever.

Ma cried softly but inconsolably. Loud tears are the sign of the uncultured; the brave rarely show them.

People from the village came running. Some of them sat around the cot and started reciting Gita, the sacred book that is recited daily and is read out as the final bye. Kratu went near his grandpa and recited softly from the *Yajurveda*, '*Aum! Krato smnar, krato smar.*' 'O mind! Remember all noble deeds that we performed, remember, o mind!'

When the chants from *Gita* reached the verse that said, 'As a person changes his dress, so does the soul changes its body,' Baba was gone. His vital breaths, working within his body since his birth, now merged with the universal air. Sanskrit word for the living is *prani*: one who breathes. Baba was no more a *prani*.

Kratu looked up to see Baba's *jiva*, the subtle body of a person, hovering free in the room. It is *jiva* that travels from sphere to sphere. The true self, *Atman*, is ever present and everywhere present; it knows no birth no death. Baba was waving at all, but no one could see him, excepting Kratu. He waved back. The villagers thought that Kratu was getting emotional. They wiped their tears.

The body was carried to the local Shiva temple for one last blessing from the great Lord of life and death, and from there the funeral procession walked towards the village cremation ground where pyre had been readied.

Fire was lit. Kratu chanted from the *Yajurveda*: '*agne nay supatha raye asman*: Agni, O Priest of gods! Lead us to blessedness by the good path. O Lord! Thou knowest all our deeds, remove all evil and delusion from us. To Thee we offer our prostrations and prayers again and again.'

There was a soothing rhythm in Kratu's voice and gravity in the intonation. The village priest, who knew the mantra and chanted it well, was surprised to hear the chants. He had not heard this melody even from his teachers at Varanasi.

Dignity in death. Dignity in departure.

A tear drop.

Kratu shed a tear, only a tear in memory of his grandpa. 'Such a fine man! We will not get to interact anymore.'

*Tilanjali*, the offering of water with sesame seeds was meant to indicate politely to the departed to move on to the next level of existence. Physically, Baba was now gone. *Asthi*, the charred remains, were collected along with the ashes which would be immersed in flowing water. Kratu's Papa had decided to keep a part of the ashes to immerse in Ganga at Haridwar. It was a sacred act at a sacred place in sacred waters.

The act of immersion signified the inner aspiration of the race to move from the individual to merge with the universal, symbolized through the rhythmic flow of the waters liberated from the matted hairs of Lord Shiva to the infinity of the ocean. The individual had to merge with the universal; this idea needed a reminder every now and then, throughout one's life. Even death and the rituals associated with it required that reminder.

Life is not important, the philosophy of life is. Death is not the end, nor it is a beginning; it is only a link in the continuum of existence.

Attachment to affection is a strong bond. Glued to one's body and near ones, a dead person often feels disoriented. He seems confused as to why he is not able to communicate with those whom he can see clearly. Worse, they sometimes do crazy things to draw the attention of those who still have their body intact. Kratu had experienced that intensely when he had died in Sindhu.

Baba was different. He had a clear mind about death and had been victorious over it. So, he hovered around the place where he was cremated and the house from where his body had been taken up to wait for the completion of the rituals, which would release him from the last bonds, howsoever tender.

Seeing Baba hover like that, he remembered the great sage Kapil who had a discussion on creation with him. Later, he went on to formalize that in his philosophy which came to be known as Samkhya.

Kapil was a born sage, with wisdom ingrained him, since his birth. His mother, Devhuti, was a gross materialist who revelled only in the pleasures of the world. Pleasures titillate the senses but do not last. The senses, like a demanding kid, want more and more of novelty while enjoying the spread of the objects in the universe. Kapil, great sage that he was, made his mother realize this fact and explained to her the dynamics of creation to make her rationalize her acts to be free. 'Joy comes in being one with your nature and not in chasing what you are not.'

The power of words that Kapil carried with him because of his spiritual eminence convinced her of the fact and she gave up worldliness.

When Kratu met the great sage, Kapil had grown old. After a little this and that the sage asked, 'Do you know how creation takes place?'

'I will prefer to hear that from you, O great Sage!'

'Consciousness and energy run like parallel streams eternally. Whenever they come near each other, there is creation. I call this energy Prakriti, which is composed of three qualities of inertness, kinetic and stability. When there is no conjunction between Purusha – the conscious – and Prakriti – the energy – the three qualities remain in balance. This balance is disturbed when Purusha comes near Prakriti. This results in creation. Creation does not take place magically, nor it is spontaneous; it evolves through a set process, which takes into account the evolutes and Prakriti.'

Kratu knew the structure but did not know the details, which, of course, varied from sages to sages.

'Energy is unconscious, obviously. It is beyond the cosmic energy to create life or even to have a mind of its own. When Purusha, the consciousness, comes near it, energy acquires the light of consciousness and then appears sentient. This is why some people, mistakenly, consider energy to be the ultimate source of creation.'

'Yes, Sage.'

'The cosmic mind is the first evolution of the consciousness-energy junction. Once mind is there, everything else follows in its wake. The first of the lot is the cosmic ego, from which come the five subtle elements that carry the property of five perceptions of touch, smell etc. These five subtle elements combine and recombine to give birth to five gross elements that you are aware of through your sense organs.'

Kratu was impressed at the rationality of the process proposed by the sage.

'The bodies that are composed of the five subtle elements are the subtle bodies that move from sphere to sphere, while the bodies made of five gross elements stay stuck to the Earth. At the time of death, the subtle body gives up the body made of gross elements and moves on.'

Kratu could now understand why his experiences had been different in various spheres.

'As with bodies, so with objects; the objects that you see all around, have subtle and gross properties. A subtle body, as of a dead person, can experience only the world of subtle elements.'

'Yes, Acharya.' That, of course, he knew.

'Our goal is to go beyond the subtle body and subtle world. We need to go beyond the realm of mind and cosmic energy and be one with what we are: Purusha, pure consciousness. This requires giving up of all that is not us through a massive will power, built by the power of meditation.'

Kratu stayed silent. He knew that he could not be free because his mind carried the thought of helping his friend.

'Freedom is the goal, young man. Be free. That is the greatest service that you can do to yourself and to the world. Be what you are. Do not chase what you are not.'

*Pindadan*, the offering of rice balls in honour of the departed, continued till the tenth day. Baba accepted the food with equanimity. To an onlooker, the rice balls remained as those were, but Kratu saw how Baba was taking the subtle part of the food.

The norms set by the sages demanded that the son perform the *shraddha karma,* the last rites. Kratu's Papa, in spite of his being a high official used to ordering people around, now obeyed every wish and command of the priest. The power over the dead was the exclusive domain of the priests.

Pundits from Varanasi had come to perform the thirteen-day ceremony. Kratu firmly told them that he would superintend the entire ritual process. Initially, the pundits objected to this, but when they heard him chant the mantras and observed his *mudra*, the hand movements, they condescended.

'Kratu ji, we find it unbelievable that someone who has not been brought up in brahminical traditions can have such clean movements. You are cleaner than professionals.'

'This is not my profession, so it appears charming to you, sir!'

'No, honestly. Internet *mein ye sab bhi milta hai kya?*'

'Honourable, sirs! Who knows? This may be the beginning of Satya Yuga. This may be a sign from God to you to give up your exclusiveness and see how religion flows out free.'

'*Aap abhi bacche hain*! You are such a kid!' They laughed.

Eleventh day of the departed.

It was time for purification of the house. Howsoever great one may have been in life, once dead, the body is impure, and the place where it was kept becomes spiritually impure. It needs cleansing through rites and rituals.

Kratu supervised through all the rituals, making sure that the gifts were made properly and the departed had been honoured to the fullest. Baba must not start his journey to the next world with a sense of unfulfilment, which would hurt his happiness and wellbeing in the next birth.

The village priest recited from the *Garuda Purana* on all those days, to which the family listened with respect. The Puranas, ancient stories current in modern times, are more of symbolism than actual truth. Kratu knew this from his own experience, but he never said a word. If people loved to think of damning hells, and if fear could keep them righteous, they were free to have any number of hells and heaven.

The twelfth day had arrived. It was time for Baba to become a *pitri*, the manes. He now had absolutely no right over what he had left behind. The brahmin priests indicated the final push from their side, and the assembled villagers cried out in memory of Baba. He was no more theirs.

As described by the great sage Kapil, Kratu's grandpa was becoming more and more subtle in his composition. It was like a balloon going up when filled with light gases. The law of levitation and gravitation holds in the next world as much as it holds here, the outcome depending on what one did here and what one's mental state had been.

Baba waved a final goodbye, which again only Kratu could see. He waved back vigorously to his Baba, whom he would never meet again, both on their separate journey on different pathways.

Seeing the vigorous waving of Kratu at the invisible, his Ma got worried and whispered to Papa, 'Do you think that Kratu has become unhinged by all these rituals and the loss of Grandpa?'

'He unhinges others, dear. Don't you worry about him.'

The thirteenth day marked the transition of the family from the gloom of death to the light of continuing life. The villagers were invited for a sumptuous meal, although the great law giver Manu was not in favour of this kind of extravaganza.

The rituals, signifying the dignity for the departed was over. Life, dedicated to nobler ideals, had to restart. For the purpose, puja and *kirtan* had to be performed the next day to signify that everything had become normal for the family and the community.

The morning next day was spent in puja and in the evening, there was a gathering of the locals to sing *bhajan–kirtan* in the Shiva temple. Lord Shiva was the local deity of the village. The first produce of fruits, vegetables, grains, milk and everything else was offered to the Lord and then distributed in the village.

Indian villages had changed over the years.

Most youths had left villages, preferring the hovel sack of cities over the open air of community. Losing their roots, identity, language, culture, they ended up being a mere number in the statistics of the government. The responsibility of carrying the culture, passed on to them for thousands of generations, was no longer important to them. If perchance their children were to ask for their cultural inheritance, what would they have to offer?

'When Buddha was asked by Rahul, his son, for his inheritance, the Lord had given him the begging bowl of the monks. It was a royal inheritance of a different kind. But what will these people give their children? Cultural poverty and spiritual bankruptcy?' thought Kratu looking at the plight of the village.

The loss was evident when people gathered at the temple in the evening. *Kirtan* – which is a devotee's connect with God through songs – had degenerated into *manoranjan*, religious entertainment.

Shallowness had hollowed the way of religion too. The land of Surdas and Mirabai, now heard self-composed songs by the local youth, if those wordings could be called songs, set to the tunes of popular movie songs. What to say of arousing devotion, the wordings, which were mere arrangements of rhyming words, were not fit enough to arouse even admiration. The God-fearing among the assembled swayed their heads in appreciation, with their eyes closed deliberately and hearts closed permanently.

Kratu came with Anvi. The villagers were surprised to see how Kratu was not the least hesitant to move around with his grown-up sister, whereas they felt embarrassed at any such possibility.

Kratu had become close to everyone in the village by then. The youths assembled there, requested him to sing something, '*Sunayia, sunaiya. Ek ho jaye.*'

Anvi, overcome with the charged atmosphere of requests, too urged him to sing one song. She had heard him hum but had never heard him sing.

'Forgive me if you do not like my singing,' said Kratu. He was singing in honour of his departed grandpa and not to keep the requests.

'*Arre, Wah! Wah*! Please *bhai*. We will love anything from you, the city man.'

To create the ambiance, he first took the *mridangam* and closed his eyes. The first stroke of his hand on the percussion sounded like a thunderbolt. Everyone was surprised. He then started playing on it, weaving the magic of waves coming out from the enslaved air inside the *mridangam*. He played and played, creating waves and more waves.

Bholen, an elderly villager, had been a master of *mridangam* but had stopped playing from the time of *kirtan*s based on film songs. The first stroke by Kratu woke up his sleeping art and he hurried to see who was weaving the magic of waves.

Anvi stared at her brother. Was he really her Kratu? She wanted to run and inform her parents, but her feet seemed rooted to the floor.

Once the mood had been created, Kratu kept the instrument down.

Anvi's trance broke. She ran to her parents to inform them of what was happening at the temple.

Kratu now began with *"a re ne na, té te re ne na"*. This was the *alap* used in Dhrupad genre of songs, which is the oldest surviving form of songs in India. The *alap* was derived from Vedic mantras. It started with a slow, deliberate development which gradually rose to an accelerating, rhythmic pulse. Bholen, the *mridangam* master had never heard such a deep voice that seemed bursting forth from the navel region.

Every sound has four layers *Vaikhari, Madhyama, Pashyanti* and *Para*. Of these, *Vaikhari* is the uttered, audible sound, whereas the remaining three are subtler. The mother of all sound is *Para*. The great masters of music try to emulate *Para* by generating sound from deep down that seems to come resonating from a deep, very deep well.

Bholen's presence surprised all. He took up the *mridangam* and tried to match the sound from Kratu, whose voice was booming far deeper than what the *mridangam* could produce.

Kratu's parents came hurriedly to watch what was happening.

With the preliminaries over, Kratu took up the song, composed by Swami Vivekananda, *'Ta Thaiya Ta Thiya nache Bhola'*: 'Lord Shiva is dancing *"ta thai"*.'

The beats increased and syllables were sung out at a very rapid pace.

*'ri re re ne na, te ne toom ne.'*

The villagers who rarely visited the temple for these *kirtan*, came running to listen to the singing that seemed to have descended from the heavens. The flute of Lord Krishna had drawn the *gopis* like this with the magical *'kleem'* on his divine flute.

The singing went in praise of the Lord, who seemed to have come down from Mount Kailash to listen to his devotee sing his praise. People listened transfixed; their breathing entered the *kumbhak* state, when the breath is held back by the yogis. What remained there was the deep magical voice, letting out the notes, and the sound of the heavy percussion keeping rhythm.

Bholen played the *mridangam* as one liberated. He instinctively knew he would not play this instrument ever again, nor would he ever need to do so. His lifetime ambition of playing with a maestro was finally fulfilled by the grace of Lord Shiva. He could now look forward to death with dignified indifference.

Kratu slowly brought the music down from the heights of Mount Kailash, as if, to the temple of the village. The singing was over. He folded his hands before the *Shivalinga*. Bholen too bowed down his head in reverence.

The audience breathed free.

On the way back home, Ma whispered, 'Did you learn all this from internet, *babu*? I can't believe it.'

Kratu laughed, 'Just check it on the web and you will find it for yourself.'

Ma knew that if Kratu did not want to reveal something, nothing could make him.

The next day the family was to depart. The entire village came to say bye. Many were crying. They were not sure if they would ever see Kratu and others again.

By staying near the deathbed of his Baba, Kratu had fulfilled his promise. The price to be paid for being born and taken care of had been paid. He was now ready to leave his home yet again. If God had brought him down for some purpose, then He himself would take him there, he thought.

One can enjoy a thing only without getting attached to it emotionally.

Kratu wanted to have one last look before he would be gone from the charms and harms of the present age. He had lost all hopes of finding Aswin a long time ago, so he would go back to his deep meditation to avoid going through the rigours of birth-death cycle till God, the Lord of all, pushed him back into this world to serve the society.

Often he moved around, looking at this and talking to that. He and the world would be centuries away from each other after this.

He also started hinting at his imminent departure to his family, but Anvi and Ma were not taking his suggestions seriously.

He wanted to tell them, 'It will be pitiable to see you cry if you do not prepare yourselves well for the separation.' But then he checked himself. 'The world goes on by holding on to that which will go away, and by ignoring that which will stay forever. Like a pendulum gaining maximum speed at its point of stability and staying at rest at the point of its maximum instability, the world enjoys peace in things that are unstable. Who can help these deliberate ignorant?'

## 14

# DIVI

The royal court of the idea world – the sphere in which ideas stay as individuals and from where they descend to take possession of beings to work themselves out – was in session. There Kratu had encountered many of his self.

The Prince of the idea world approached His Majesty with, 'I have been without a proper body for a long time now. If it continues like this, soon I will be a forgotten idea.'

The Prince had his full manifestation in the like of Ritam, Paras, Buddha and others. Every few decades, and sometime in centuries, he descended to get a human body. It had been a while since he came last, and so it was now time for him to play in a human body again.

The King smiled.

'Our commoners take possession of a body even before a baby is born. When these babies grow up, they spend their life running after life and livelihood only. Your Majesty! This is disappointing.'

The Prince was the favourite of the King, but His Majesty would show no partiality. A true King treats everyone as equal.

The favourite only gets more of his time to interact with. He replied humorously, 'You never like to share space with others.'

'Forgive me for my impertinence, but since when has the royalty started sharing space with commoners, Your Majesty?'

'You have a point there, Prince.' The King then thought for a moment and then whispered 'Divi' in the ears of the Prince and then said aloud, 'Proceed, Prince.'

The Prince sped through the spheres and was in Devpuri in a wink. There, he roamed around as a butterfly, watching over Divi.

The seed comes when the field is ready; greatness comes when the mind is ready. Unknown to Divi, her mind, washed pure in the waters of unselfishness, was ready to receive the Prince.

It was afternoon; time for Divi to go to the park, the place that Divi felt to be her real extension, much more than her home, where she could be her true self.

She tiptoed inside her grandpa's room and banged shut the book that he was reading, with, 'Now tell me what you were reading, and I will tell you how good your mind is!' This was her revenge on her Daddu who always advised her to have a great mind. 'Great mind, huh! Who else has a great mind as I have?' She used to assert.

A startled Daddu overcame the suddenness and said with a smile, 'Ummm... Well, you will not understand it, dear.'

'Why do you read silly fat books which no one understands? Look at me. I already know all that is to be known, and what I do not know is not worth knowing. Why then you have to read?' The books of her grandpa appeared to her as 'silly fat books'.

'It takes a lot of learning to know that you know nothing.'

'Silly.'

'I will always be silly before you,' Daddu smiled.

'So, what were you reading?'

'*Yo vai bhuma tat sukham*. Joy lies in the infinite.'

'What is infinite?'

Daddu did not know how to explain a concept that had no physical basis. He thought and then said, 'It means larger than the largest.'

'Huh! Even I know that I like two chocolates more than one. What is so special then in what you read? It is so silly!'

Daddu gave the indulgent smile.

Divi did not want to waste her time on this routine exchange. She let go the argument with, 'Time for you to take me to the park.'

'Yes, yes.' Daddu said, and got up to take her to the park where the busy of the city took a break and the lazy took a walk.

Partly running and partly walking, she reached the gate of the park where an old bull sat, musing on his life.

The frame of the bull spoke of his past majesty.

Now that he was old, he sat most of the time near the gate of the park, waiting for death and travelling in the thought world to encounter what was and what could have been. In old age, memory and failed aspirations weigh heavier than the body, unlike young age when ballooning ambitions make light of everything.

'What a burden now I am on myself! My strength, vigour and virility are all gone. I am now an unwanted one for the world and even for myself. My legs now cannot carry the weight of my body, so I have to sit here, hoping for some kind passer-by who may take pity on me and oblige me with some food. Even that is often snatched away from my mouth by the uncouth stray ones. No respect for the elders. When the decay began, fun went out of my life and now life is slipping away. I now pray that my life goes away to relieve me from the ache of an empty belly. The world is going on with its frolics, as it always does, while I sit here, living in my present misery and past glory.

'I was young then and I felt the world to be under my hooves when a leopard had entered the city with the thought of attacking the helpless.'

'Grrr,' it growled in satisfaction.

'Huuun,' snorted I in anger.

'You may not believe it, the cunning predator tried all its tricks, but I was the charging bull. I gored him to his flight. The coward! You can smell out a coward by his aggressiveness. The strong are never aggressive; it is the coward whom one has to fear. It is they who cause all damages in the world covertly or overtly, and not the brave ones. I was brave. But who will believe this story of mine today when even a child comes and kicks at me and I only try to move my tail in desperation!

'Those were the days when people needed my services for their cows. Most kine that you see in the city are my children. The milk supply in the city owes largely to me. Most people in this city have grown up on milk for which I was directly responsible. And see my plight today! Here I sit all day hungry for a morsel of grass, while no one cares if I am dead or alive.

'Have you seen the Shiva temple here at Devpuri? I loved going inside it and sitting there for hours in front of the statue of Nandi, which was designed by a sculptor using me as the model. I had the privilege of seeing my reflection in the waters of the pond in front of the temple. My broad shoulders and powerful horns mesmerized me. So, when I saw the statue modelled after me, I recognized who it was.

'I often sat in the temple to see people come to worship Lord Shiva and offer flowers at the feet of my statue too. They worship Nandi even today, but they have left me, the living one, all alone, neglected and uncared for. Why do people worship images but ignore the living? Hypocrite humans!

'Now I sit here all day, thinking of my perfect past and tense present. One who is nurtured in weakness does not mind a kick here or there, but the strong resent even a frown from the unworthy. So, what to do? What to do? I do not want to live. Release me from this misery, O God!

'Death is better than this life. It is the ultimate cowardice to hold on to life while quaking in fear of death. The brave do not hold on to life nor are they scared of death.'

Divi daily brought two *chapatis* for the bull, without knowing his past glory or present pain. Every day she offered those to him and entered the park where she and Daddu spent time in their own ways. That day too, she held the *chapatis* before him, which he took gratefully. She then patted his cheeks tenderly and entered the park.

Unseen to her, a butterfly had been hovering around and following her. 'Indeed a nice one,' thought the Prince of the idea world.

Kratu was walking near the park when he saw the sweet act of the young girl. Curious, he entered the park to see a little more of her. She seemed to be the symbol of gentle India.

Once inside the park, Divi parked Daddu on a bench, who lovingly called out, 'Do not get lost in the flowers, Precious!'

But Divi was not listening; she was already gone and was busy 'talking to flowers, chasing butterflies, and watching the birds sing,' as her friends taunted her at the school.

Kratu took in the scene with, 'There is something noble about her. Something should be done to take her higher.'

He approached her, introduced himself and then asked about her.

'My mom has asked me not to talk to strangers.'

'I am no stranger. Not to anyone, Miss,' laughed Kratu.

Divi found the words impressive enough to be used later. She made a mental note of novel words and ideas, which she used to her advantage, although not always. There were occasions when the usage had malfunctioned. After all, she was still tender in age.

Impressed by Kratu, she asked, 'Tell me, what do you want?'

'Nothing, Miss. I want nothing. Not from you, not from anyone. I only give.'

'I want nothing. Not from you, not from...' she wanted to say 'anyone', but then she realized that she was quite demanding from her family.

Kratu burst out laughing. It was cute. Too cute. He had to pass on something big to her. He thought for a moment and then put his palm on her head and said, 'May your best come to you.'

Divi's mind went light. Very light.

Feeling different, she moved towards the flowers, as she always did. Kratu left her at that, but watched from a distance.

Divi knew every plant and its offspring in the park and wondered how different they were from her, 'The plants and their children, flowers and fruits, stay together till one of them withers away. But here we are! Getting separated every day from the family to go to the school. My friends even have separate homes for father and mother. How sad! If only I could be one of these flowers! Better to be a flower than to be a schoolgirl.' She concluded with dejection.

A bud had blossomed overnight. Divi had been watching the journey of the closed bud to freedom for some days and so her heart lighted up with joy to see the little one unfolding its majesty.

Divi was admiring the baby flower and trying to talk to it when a magnificent butterfly came hovering above it. She had never seen such beauty in a butterfly, or in any other thing. The elemental colours seemed to have woven elaborate magic around the winged beauty. She was so awestruck by the sight that she went silent and in a moment was lost in the oneness of beauty. The park, tress, flowers: everything, every manifestation of beauty vanished from her consciousness. Beauty, simply beauty remained.

Beauty faces cruelty.

There in the park, cruelty came in the form of a bird that swooped on the butterfly. Divi's heart made a loud thud and she was brought back from the joy of oneness to the bounds of the fragmented. Her heart beat loudly, pulse raced furiously and she trembled all over.

The predator missed its chance. The poor hexapod was injured mildly and had fallen on the ground, where it fluttered its wings helplessly. Divi ran to save her from the evil bird, who was preparing for a second dive.

She lifted the helpless creature in her cupped hands and scolded her, 'Can't you be careful about your life, you silly beauty? If you have to show off, then at least learn self-protection. And, be thankful that I am a girl. Had you fallen in the hands of one of the boys, you would have lost your wings by now.'

Talking to it tenderly, she nursed it with her soft caress, warm love and words of affection. She also kept an eye on the bird who was circling above to make a second dive. However, seeing its victim in safe hands, it withdrew.

When the winged one had calmed down, it raised its head and said, 'Thank you'.

'Surprising! No flower has ever replied to my caring words. Who spoke now?'

'I, the butterfly, spoke that.'

Divi wondered if she had fallen asleep and was dreaming. Keeping the butterfly on the ground, she pinched herself. Yes, she felt pain.

'I will meet you again,' said the butterfly rising from the ground and flying away.

'I think I am hearing things. My friends will surely brand me crazy.'

With the butterfly gone, leaving her mind in a muddle, she lost interest in flowers and with slow steps she returned to where she had left her grandpa.

Daddu was surprised to see her return early. Usually he had to search for her and tear her away from the flowers. On their way back, he was further surprised to see that Divi was not her usual chirpy self. He asked, 'All well?'

'Yes, Daddu. What can be wrong?'

That meant something was wrong. But Daddu kept silent, knowing well that she would speak only when she wanted to. Unknown to him, Divi's mind was like a beehive, buzzing with too many thought – infinite, speaking butterfly, feeling of flying – what was all this?

They walked in silence when Divi asked, 'Tell me something. Can butterflies talk?'

'Yes, of course. One is talking to me right now.'

Divi kept quiet.

That night Divi went to her bed early without complaining. That was worrisome. Parents cannot understand tantrums nor can they stand no tantrums.

Morning. School Time. Protest time. 'Why must I go to school every day?'

'Because you have to become someone someday.'

'If I have to become somebody I would rather become a flower, butterfly, star or something like that. I don't have to go to school to become anyone of that.'

'Stop this and get ready for the school. No delaying tactics, Divi.'

'You send me to school to get rest and when our Madam wants rest, she sends us home. I know the tricks of you grown-ups.'

Routine does not attract attention. Mom ignored her words.

On way to school, she kept thinking, 'What a strange place our school is! It promises to bring out the best in us but ends up bringing out our tears only, as if that is the best that we have.'

When she reached the class, her classmates were absorbed in big discussions about their small world. Their voices rose high to express approval and higher to show contempt. Everything was important to them: every event was novel; the small was big; the imaginary was real; and the ordinary was great.

Seeing her enter, someone greeted with giggles, 'Hi, Two plus Two!'

She ignored the words. She loved her friends, but she did not like to be addressed as 'Two plus Two'. The story was that when the class was learning addition, she had claimed to see the faces of the numbers smiling when they were added and had seen them sad when there was subtraction. This had brought on the laughter of the class.

In turn, Divi wondered if her friends were actually dumb. How could they fail to see what she saw distinctly? And, why should one tease others for what she does not have herself?

Divi reached her seat and let herself into the world of her friends. She now grew big while talking and became small when she had to listen. She also joined her voice in welcoming the new entrants with their tease names, forgetting how she herself disliked being addressed so.

A sudden hush announced that Madam had entered the class.

Madam began the class with a smile, 'I have a surprise for you, kids. Today we will have our "Share a wonder" competition.'

'Huuuuu!' the class erupted in joy.

Divi and her friends loved this competition, held occasionally, in which they narrated their unusual experiences. The wonders to be shared were never in short supply. The participants were at an age when every event tastes novel and every word smells fresh.

Madam noted down the narration and then gave a book signed by her to the best story. Everyone wanted to win the prize. Competitions and prizes mattered a lot to them; it would be years before they would grow up to learn the value of cooperation and sacrifice in life.

Divi had never won the prize but that day she beamed, thinking of what she had seen the previous day.

The narration began. Secrets started tumbling out of the closets of innocence.

'Last week my mom cooked for us.'

'I finally came to believe that grandmas do exist. I even saw my grandma when she came to visit us for an hour.'

Clapping followed clapping.

The class bully came forward sheepishly with his secret, 'I had a fight and I was licked.' There was thunderous applause from the class.

Divi sent a chain-mail, 'Karma has finally caught up with you! Be ready for more.' She had recently learnt the word 'Karma' from her Daddu. Like most people, she did not understand it but felt it impressive to use.

Madam made furious notes which she would use to counsel the parents about their ward.

When Divi's turn came, she began, 'Yesterday I saw a butterfly...'

She could not complete her sentence because of the loud booing from the class. Even Madam raised her eyebrow. Everyone in the class knew that Divi went to the park every day, where she 'talked to the flowers, chased butterflies and watched the birds sing'. So where was the secret?

Upset at the behaviour of her friends, Divi sat down and cried softly. Her punctured sensitivity turned into torrents of tears that trickled down her cheeks. Looking at her, anyone would have concluded that she had brought the art of shedding tears to perfection.

'Sissy...Cry baby...Where is her tank for so much water?... Drama Queen.'

Even Madam did not like her frequent tears. She decided to send a note to her parents.

That day's winner was Parni, who told the class that she had read a book. Everyone agreed that Parni deserved the prize since she never read anything. Whenever she had time, she lost herself in the world of games and day-dreaming where she could be whatever she liked to be without labouring for that. The self-created world, the ultimate bane of humanity, was eating up the young mind.

Divi knew the truth that Parni had never read the book. She had heard the story from Divi a few days ago during the lunch break and was now parading fake knowledge as real achievement.

The injustice made Divi a fireball, 'Liars are winners and the truthful are laughed at! What a world! And, this is what we come here to learn!'

Determined to tell the truth, she got up but then remembered the words of her grandpa that anger never did any good to anyone. She paused and counted up to ten and breathed deep. This calmed her down. 'If Parni feels happy telling a lie, let her be happy. Karma will catch up with her.'

But she felt upset.

She was also angry that the butterfly, whoever she was, had cheated her.

That evening, Divi moved around the garden, hoping to see the butterfly again. Yes, there it was, maintaining the safety of distance.

Distance.

Divi's anger dissipated. She longed to meet the winged one, who kept eluding her. She returned home disappointed.

After the evening chores, Divi retired for the night. With her eyelids heavy with sleep, she was wading through dreams to reach the depth of sleep when the butterfly floated in through the window in the form of soft light, which filled her room. She jumped out of bed in excitement.

'I came to say thank you once again,' said the butterfly.

'How cute of you! But who are you?'

'You will not understand, Divi.'

'How do you know my name? And why you also talk like my Daddu, telling me that I will not understand.'

'Forget it, Divi. I am here to do you a favour. Tell me what you want?'

That reminded Divi of Kratu uncle who also wanted to do her a favour. Was this butterfly a part of that favour? She could not understand.

'I don't know what to ask for. I want nothing.'

'You complain every day that you want to be this and that. What about that? How about becoming one of that?'

'Ohh, that? Can you really make me one of those?'

'I can make you anything. It is all within you.'

Divi did not understand that but she did not want to show her ignorance, so, she said, 'I do not know anything about how the life is as flower or bird. I must first experience that.'

'Clever, right? It is fine. Follow me.' Saying so, the butterfly flew out the window. Divi followed it, without fearing that she might fall. Indeed, she did not fall. Instead, she found herself in the garden which she loved so much.

The park at night was so different from what it looked at daytime. Birds, squirrels, butterflies; they all seemed to have vanished. But Divi knew that they were only waiting for light to make their appearance. Light – darkness – light. What a powerful duo to make things appear – disappear – appear!

The flowers too looked different. All of them were emitting soft reddish light of various shades. This made their size and shape distinct. Although their dazzle of daytime was missing, they still looked grand.

'What beauty, ah!' she thought. Immediately she felt a change come over her. Lo! She was becoming a flower and she found herself sitting on a small branch, swaying softly with the wind.

'Finally! Finally!!' Divi exclaimed.

She was excited to become what she had always wanted to become. 'How wonderful! My prayers have been answered!'

She now wanted to know how she looked. She had seen her mama spending hours before a mirror whenever she put on a new dress, but Divi depended more on the words of others to know about herself. Why sit in front of a mirror when there are people eager to be mirrors for you? Even her mom had once told angrily about a friend of hers, 'People with no work become the mirror for others.'

Divi was not disappointed in her wish. Soon she heard a soft clearing of throat, 'Ahem! Welcome to the world of flowers. You look majestic.'

The words had come from a marigold. Under normal conditions this should have surprised Divi, but she was so happy with the praise that she stuttered politely, 'Thank you! You too look grand.'

'But you look majestic, Miss Divi.'

Divi blushed, 'Thank you again.'

Now that the novelty had passed off, the reality set in. She wondered how a flower could talk, so she asked cautiously, 'So you people do talk!'

'Yes. And we hear all that you speak to us. We also make replies, but as a human being your ears are too crude to pick up our words.'

'I am not taking it as a compliment.'

'Anger does not suit your beauty.'

This embarrassed her, so she turned her head in a different direction where she saw a caterpillar curled under a plant and snoring indifferently.

Divi went in a playful mood, 'Hello gentleman! With so many legs, how do you choose which one to put forward first?'

Mr Caterpillar woke up annoyed, 'Folks with no legs have to be jealous of a hundred legs, stupid flower. Now keep shut and do not disturb me in my sleep, or else...'

'Else what? Mr Lazy-bones, have you ever seen your speed? Just a little more than a snail.'

Saying so, she started a chat with a chrysanthemum about the world and the weather. When the conversation became repetitive, the chrysanthemum said, 'Isn't it sad that we will not hear of you after tomorrow. The gardener will note your beauty in the morning and then he will pluck you to put in a vase. That will be the end of you. We will miss you so much.'

The rose sobbed, 'I will shed extra tears for you. People will see many dew drops on my petals.'

Divi laughed, 'I may not be here till then.' But the thought of being placed in a vase was exciting for her. 'Supposing that I was placed in my mom's room, and when she came admiring me, I would politely say that it was me! And she would say...'

'Eeeeeeeek!' Divi screamed. Mr Caterpillar was climbing up Divi's plant and was about to reach her. It was so repulsive.

'I must get out of this flower business. Let them remain with their bees, butterflies, and... caterpillars. Run Divi, run.'

That is how she became a deer.

Divi felt happy to become a deer. She ran around the park merrily and looked at her legs and back with admiration. Soon she was back with the flowers where she had been a while ago. There she saw Mr Caterpillar busy looking for the vanished flower. This made her laugh and she said, 'Hello Mr Many Legs! Forgotten something?'

The joy born of belittling others made her break into a song,

*I got a flying friend*
*May be from a distant land*

She sang with all her lung power, but the deer voice was not the musical voice that Divi used to have. Instead, it was the bark of a deer.

This annoyed her. She was a young lady of taste; she could not stand such voice. 'This is the problem with package deals.

No wonder my mom always complains when she has to go for a package deal – most of it is useless. Huh!'

For a while she decided to keep quiet and be happy with her good looks. But the deer bark had drawn the attention of a dog who after the day's rest was in the restless mood of night. The sudden call of the deer was like an unexpected invitation for feast.

He barked the invitation to others, and soon many arrived.

A terrified Divi wanted to scream, but no sound came out of her throat. 'If only I could fly somehow,' she thought desperately.

No sooner had she thought thus that she became a bird. 'Ufff! Saved by seconds!'

The dogs were looking for the deer everywhere, but there was nothing to be seen or smelt. The dogs looked foolishly at each other and then started barking furiously at the dog who had invited them for the feast.

Divi had a grand view of the quarrelling dogs from high up the tree. She shouted at them with joy, 'I am the one you are looking for. Hahaha.'

The dogs did not understand what the silly bird was trying to say. Nor did they care to understand. They were too upset at their dashed hopes.

Too much of running as a deer had made Divi hungry. 'I can eat up a choco mountain.' But wishes are meant to be elusive. She got nothing. So, after a lot of thinking she politely woke up a bird for some food.

'Go below that tree, and you will find a good supply of worms. They are fresh and nutritious. They must be sleeping right now, so it will be easy for you to get a full belly easily.'

'Eeeeeeek! What! Eat those worms?'

'What else do you want to eat? A whole snake? For that you have to be born as an eagle.'

'Mommy....' Divi screamed in disgust. The next moment she found herself in the bed.

Her mom entered the room hurriedly with sleepy eyes, 'What happened, Divi? Thirsty?'

'No, not thirsty. Hungry.'

'That is what happens when you finish your food in a hurry and wake up at night.'

Divi wanted to tell mom what she had experienced but Mom was in no mood to listen to tall tales in the middle of night.

The Prince of the idea world came to meet Divi again after some days, asking her if she had decided to become something.

'To be honest, the garden was disappointing.'

'How about enjoying life as something small?'

'That would be wonderful. I can then buzz around all, without their knowing who I am.'

'That is fine.'

Divi now felt as if the walls and windows of her room were growing larger and farther. 'This is fun,' thought she. She also felt speed in her bones. 'Am I moving at the speed of light? That would be truly interesting.'

A spherical city loomed before her. She wanted to slow down but she could neither increase nor decrease her speed. Worse, she had to keep moving in a circle around anything to be near it. 'How annoying!' she thought.

She entered the city to see quite a few gentlemen with fiery bodies running around in circles, shouting, 'Move away, move away'.

Divi went near them and asked, 'Why, sir?'

'Your presence is taking away my energy and I am not able to maintain my path. A longer presence of you will make our world collapse. Move, move. Please.'

Divi changed her direction to find herself inside a royal court where the king and the queen sat together. Divi introduced herself as politely as she could.

'Ahh, you are from the land where people are born and die,' the king commented.

Divi felt insulted at the prick. She bowed with, 'I am sure no one dies here, Your Majesty!'

'How true you are. No one dies here,' smiled the king with the calm of the royalty. 'In fact nothing can take away our power. After all we are the original royalty of the universe.'

'Ohh,' commented Divi.

'Is it true that you folks eat animals and also keep them as pets?' asked the queen.

This hurt deep. Divi wanted to say something strong, but nothing came to her mind. To get out of the place, she asked, 'Is my presence taking away your energy also? Your guards seemed pretty threatened by my presence.'

'Now that you asked, I must say that although you are not taking away our energy, you are increasing it. Unfortunately that is also bad for our world. Your added strength will make our world unstable and then we will have to do quite a few things to stabilize it.'

'Do you mean to say that my mere presence can make your world collapse? I feel important.'

'Life is strange, Miss Divi. It collapses if a little extra is added or a little is taken away. A perfect balance alone makes life go well.'

'Thank you, your Majesty! I do not want to be in a world where my presence makes it collapse. I will prefer to be beyond nuisance. Thanks for your hospitality.' Divi had picked that statement from her Daddu who used to tell her not to be a nuisance to others.

On her way out, she had to face the fiery guards again. Knowing that the lady was on her way out, the guard gave her a big shove; a shove big enough to make her land in her bed.

Divi found herself wide awake in her bed.

Then onwards, Divi's demands to be this and that decreased. The family was surprised that she was not complaining as before.

Kratu kept visiting the park to watch Divi from a distance. 'Yes, the seed is germinating,' thought he with satisfaction. He had played his part and felt that he had completed the task for which he was here.

There was at least one person in Devpuri who now knew what it meant to 'be' instead to 'become'.

It was the day for the 'Share a wonder' competition in the class once again. As on earlier occasions, secrets kept popping up.

When Divi's turn came, she began, 'I saw a butterfly...'. But she could not complete her sentence. As on the previous occasion, this time too there was loud booing and catcalls in the class.

The class teacher was about to raise her eyebrow, when she was surprised to see that Divi was also clapping and laughing joyfully with the class.

It was beyond the teacher's understanding. 'Where have her tears gone? Isn't she the cry baby of the class? How is she laughing with her friends at herself?'

Madam did not realize that Divi was not laughing with them, but she was laughing at them.

Only Divi knew what she knew.

Divi had been taken over by the Prince of the idea world, who is responsible for making a person universal, as Kratu had learnt from Paras. In some years, there would be a major revolution within Divi.

But that is a different story.

# 15

# ASWIN

The election *yajna* was approaching.

Jeshi poured all available oblations in this great *yajna* so that he could continue with the power that appeared heavenly to him. One of those oblations was to invite all the friends of her daughter to a grand party so that the kids could talk about him in their homes. That would ensure some more votes. Invitations were sent in the name of Jeshi, father of Sibi.

Divi was among the invited.

As in the school, her friends greeted her with 'Hi two plus two!' To everyone's surprise, Divi smiled calmly.

The kids were in a shouting match in describing all that they had seen or heard recently; only Divi stayed composed, which attracted the attention of Vihan. He was not sure if she was reticent or indifferent.

The enjoyment was at peak when Jeshi appeared amidst them and announced that Vihan would entertain them with magical tricks.

To make Sibi smile, sometimes he used to show his powers, which were natural to him. Jeshi had seen that and had concluded that Vihan knew tricks and magic. 'These people from remote areas have their own share of magic and voodoo. He must be knowing those,' he had concluded.

Vihan felt offended at Jeshi's words. What was natural to him and his people was being described as magical, and he was paraded as some circus man. It was his affection for Sibi that was holding him back in this hell of noise and smell.

Vihan's irritation seeped into his mind, affecting his powers like poison. 'Emotions are the great enemy of mind power,' was taught to his folks from the first day of their learning. The situation here was such that the basics of life were flying away from him. 'No good,' he told himself.

'Show it na, *bhaiya*,' demanded Sibi. This was her great moment when she could show off what she had beyond the reach of any of her friends.

Grudgingly, Vihan took a pencil to convert it into chocolate. The order of molecules determines what object that would be. If someone could change that order, physically or mentally, the object would change. It was a common phenomenon in his land.

What should have taken seconds, took minutes for Vihan.

The kids shouted in joy at the magic. Or was it a miracle?

Vihan felt dejected at the diminishing strength of his mind. His emotions and irritations at the state of affairs were bleeding his powers. If things continued like that, it would be difficult for him to go back to his land. That was scary.

The kids clapped wildly. Only Divi remained unmoved. She gave an indulgent smile which smelt of, 'Yes, I know that.'

Vihan approached her with, 'You did not like what I did?'

'I liked it very much, sir.'

'But you did not appreciate?'

'It is so natural, isn't it?'

'May I request you to tell me what you know?'

Before Divi could tell anything, Sibi came to him and drew him away. 'She is crazy, and I do not like to share you with any.'

Vihan was annoyed but he controlled himself. He would have to find a way to meet Divi, he decided.

The party ended with Jeshi giving expensive gifts to all, about which there would be talk in the families all over the city.

The election demanded that Vihan travel to the deeper bowels of the society. What he saw there, was painful, to say the least.

'Sir, do you realize how much poverty exists all around us? And illiteracy?' said Vihan to Jeshi one day after his interactions proved too painful.

'He, he! You want all this to go away, young man? Poor are God to us. To worship God, we need to have poor. Look at the religious masters of the world: they have all promised heaven for the poor, while hell has been created for us, the wretches. Do you realize that we make sacrifices so that the passage to heaven is smooth for the poor? If you cannot appreciate my work, at least do not ridicule it. He, he... Do you know that God created the poor, and that we are just the product of the wild forces of the society? Probably you won't know that much. *Bhai*, we cannot let poor give up their poverty; poverty is a gift from God.'

'Hell. Yes, that is where your ilk should go,' thought Vihan.

Unknown to both of them, Viswakarma had already made extensions in the Cosmic Correction Centre to accommodate the pseudo-rationalists.

'On a lighter vein, who will elect us if there are no poor? What will the media do, what will the Truth Forum and Peace

Party do, what will the liberals and intellectuals do, what will the writers do if there is no inequality? I thought you are intelligent. Do you seriously mean to say that all these people should lose their jobs by removing poverty? So many bellies get food and rooms get light only because there are poor. Have you heard of Karl Marx?'

No, Vihan had not heard.

'The gentleman's theories on economy ruled the world some years ago. What was the theory all about? Alleviating poverty. Can you imagine no one would have heard of the gentleman if there were no poor, and half the world would have remained beyond the control of the Marxists if poverty had not been there. *Bhai,* have some sympathy for others too. He, he.'

'Parasites,' said Vihan under his breath.

'I can smell your anger Vihan. But why be angry? Sameness is death, inequality is life. When Marxists tried to bring sameness, do you know what happened? Their countries ended up producing a large number of capitalists. There is nothing called sameness, *bhai.* Here, in India, the poor get their share of privileges by demanding their rights, media gets its coverage, social workers get their engagement and we get our power. It is such a wonderful symbiotic relation. Why then destroy it? Everyone has to live, and everyone needs to have an engagement.'

'I cannot take it, sir.'

'You cannot take it because you are a kid. Philosophy, literature, art, religion, economy; everything thrives only because there is poverty and ignorance. Do not even think of tinkering with it, he, he!'

'Yes, sir.'

Vihan decided to leave this present for his own present. 'These perverts can justify anything. And why not? These are the people who once justified the killing of God and now they do the same not on the cross but by their pen.'

Vihan's mind was a complete muddle. Without his knowing it, he was losing the capital with which he had landed at Devpuri.

Jeshi won the elections handsomely. The opposition called it the murder of democracy.

'What do those buffoons mean by murder of democracy? Yes, I do have guns and gold. But how did I get them? From the general public. If this is not democracy, then what is? Public is God for us. Whatever I have is from God. The losers are losers in their logic too. No wonder they lose elections. Imagine what they would have done to the country if they had reached the higher steps of power in Delhi!'

'How correct, sir! The opposition has to *meow* to show that they are still alive. They don't realize that if you want, you can make them count their days instead of counting their votes,' said one stooge.

To put a seal on his victory, Jeshi ordered a 'Victory of Democracy' programme to be organized in the *Ramleela* ground. The crowd was mobilized with the persuasive power of the musclemen. 'A nice snack or a good smack. Choice is yours,' said the powerful.

It is stupid to be brave where cowardice is wisdom. Long centuries of oppression have taught India the basic line of survival. The world belongs to the living cowards than the dead brave. Devpuri came to the ground in large numbers.

Jeshi got up to the stage with folded hands. After the customary 'it is your victory', 'you are my God', and 'humble servant of the poor', he introduced Aswin to the waiting crowd for a star performance. 'Friends, here is a great artist before you whom no one recognized but me, your humble *sevak*. Give him a big hand!!'

Aswin, the flute player in solitude, had continued with his *sadhana* on the banks of the river. He neither knew his past nor did he care for the present. Indifferent to the victory or loss of any, he cared not if Jeshi had won.

Aswin's wife, tired of her poverty, had persuaded one of the henchmen of Jeshi to get the family some money through Aswin's performance. When Vihan heard the name, he strongly recommended to Jeshi that he be allowed to perform. A lot of emotional blackmail went into persuading Aswin to perform.

Aswin, looking fresh in clean clothes, came on the stage. His wife looked at him with pride and also trepidation, 'I hope he does not mess it up. This is one good chance for us to get rich. Let us see if his flute indeed has any capability.' She then prayed to all the gods and goddesses that she could remember.

Aswin looked at his wife lovingly and then looked at the faces in the crowd. 'How pathetic! How pathetic! Is this the land that once appreciated Tansen? Is this the land that gave the best in music to the world; traditions that have been running for thousands of years now? How I wish I were not here,' thought he but checked himself. He had promised his wife, towards whom he did feel a responsibility, that he would bring her honour and money.

Aswin asked the announcer what time it was. Seven pm. He decided to play *Suddha Kalyan*. Taking the microphone in his hand, he said, 'My *pranams* to Lord Krishna, who is the Lord of the flute as Shiva is the Lord of percussions. May the play of the notes through this flute arouse in your hearts love and devotion for your *ishta.*'

People responded with respect. They folded their hands.

'My *pranams* to you too. The crowd is the cosmic form of God on Earth. Now allow me to play *Suddha kalyan,* the raag suited for this time of the day. For us, music is the sound equivalent of rhythm that pervades the universe. Rhythm and raag are the manifestations of God. We, in India, use music more as the way to reach God than to entertain. My ancestors in music dedicated their life to find and feel the rhythm that envelops everyone, all the time. What they discovered through their *sadhana* was that time, season and occasion was related to the rhythm of music. An angry person cannot present his face as smiling. Just like that, every *raag* has a mood of its own which sets perfectly with the time, season and occasion, and hence there must not be a violation of that.'

Someone shouted, '*Shuru karo, bhai* – begin.'

Ignoring the words, Aswin continued, 'The medical sciences came to believe that music can heal maladies if sung properly, and many believe that by singing a *raag*, a good musician can create the external environment suited to that *raag*. Tansen was believed to light up lamps with *Deepak raag*, and he could summon clouds in a clear sky with *Malhar*. These may be stories, but we stick to the principle that only the *raag* that is suited for the time period should be played. Now allow me to proceed.'

'Who has been stopping you, moron?'

Aswin raised the flute to his lips and started blowing softly on its primary hole. He played the basics of the *Shuddha kalyan raag*, and then slowly, very slowly let out the notes – *Ga Re Ga, Re Sa.*

He continued.

And continued.

To keep the untrained ears tied to the pillar of culture requires tact. Aswin lacked that. He also lacked fame, persona, or the presentability of the famous. The crowd was not amused at what he was doing.

*Ni Dha Pa*

The crowd was getting restive.

Jeshi was a master at gauging the mood of the public. He was also culturally challenged. He called one of his men, '*Arre, ye pein-pein kitna chalega*? How long will we have to bear this pain? Do something.'

'Sure, sir.'

The announcer sent a slip to Aswin to wind up in five minutes. Five minutes! He would need at least an hour to bring the *raag* to completion. His lip quivered and the note lost its intensity for a micro-second – something that had never happened with him before. Tears streamed at the disrespect to music. He could bear anything against him, but music was God for him. He stopped his play and raised his head proudly to say bye to the unworthy. To his horror, he saw Jeshi munching peanuts.

His mind went blank.

In sheer pain, born of the greatest possible insult, he broke the flute into two and swore never to play in public again.

His wife looked dumbly at him from a distance. All her pleadings to him and prayers to God had ended up in a big zero.

Jeshi had Aswin called near him and said, 'He, he! *Lagta hai aap naraj hain*! Don't be upset. We will get you a new flute.'

Aswin was in tears born of violent emotions. 'Allow me to leave the place, sir,' said he.

'*Arre*, take some money.'

'Leave that sir. You can purchase salt for your peanuts with that, sir.'

'He, he. You are so humorous.'

Jeshi then turned towards one of his henchmen and signalled him with his eyes. The rustic had to be taught a lesson.

The crowd in the ground was baying for popular songs.

A singer-dancer whose voice was as bad as his dance steps was, came up to the stage and started with a popular bawdy song, '*Aara hile, chapra hile.*'

The crowd went wild.

The shock of the song brought Aswin back to his senses. 'Was I expecting respect from these people whose consciousness is rooted at such songs! Fie upon me!'

Wiping his tears, Aswin asked for forgiveness from Jeshi for being impolite and left the ground. His wife, angry herself, refused to follow him.

Once out, he was accosted by two of Jeshi's men with, 'Hello, singer! You seem to be in a hurry, leaving the place like this?'

There was nothing to answer.

'Where is your flute? We would like to shove it where it may hurt you. OH, we remember, you broke it, right? So, let us break you to show how the flute must have felt in your hands.'

Saying so, they kicked him, taking turns to make sure that he never again expressed anger before the mighty. 'No clothes to wear, no food to eat, and you dare share your pride, stupid fool!'

Once they left, Aswin got up. The emotional pain and insult shattered his sensitive body and ego. He sat down by the side of the road, shed tears and then mentally said goodbye to Devpuri and his wife towards whom he was responsible but whom he could never make happy. He had made sacrifices for music,

His God, and yet he had let down his God here in front of the vegetables.

'Serves me right. How I played false to my God and world both! I have been rightly served by the goons. No, I cannot live anymore. I prefer Death over such failure.'

With tears flowing freely from his eyes, he walked towards nothingness in the dark in the hope of seeing light beyond this life.

Vihan was not happy to see the plight of Aswin. 'What are you doing, India? Exchanging pearls for glass beads! Entertainment over class!'

The crass song was in full volume along with the untamed outbursts of the crowd when shots were heard. People thought that it was celebratory fire by the supporters. They cheered wildly.

Vihan looked around to see who was firing when he saw the same trio of the Peace Party whom he had beaten up when he had first arrived at Devpuri. They had been released on bail from the prison and were out to take revenge.

Some more shots and the crowd realized that it was not celebratory but an attack on celebration. Entertainment was now entrapment. People ran to save themselves.

Jeshi took Sibi with him and lay flat on the ground to save himself from the flying bullets.

Vihan stood up and tried to focus his mind to harden his body but failed. The long association with folks, who were way below his level, had cost him dearly. He had lost his powers. He felt like crying.

He was also scared.

Fear.

Vihan had never known fear. It was an alien emotion for people of his land. He now bathed in that emotion. Sweat flowed freely from his body.

There were police personnel to guard the ground. They opened fire at the gang, for whom life was nothing at the altar of peace.

As was his nature, Vihan raised his one hand as a sign of peace, but the gunners kept firing at him. He shouted, trying to get in a word, but the trio was in no mood for that.

One of the bullets fired by them hit Vihan's hand. He cried out in pain and sat down. A feeling he had never known before.

By then the police had overpowered the wicked.

Jeshi was upset that Vihan was not the superman he had thought him to be.

Sibi was crying piteously. She could not bear the blood of his dear *bhai*. She was taken home hurriedly.

The wound was superficial. After dressing the wound, the doctor released Vihan to go. Jeshi was informed.

Vihan thought during the whole operation. No, he did not want any more of this sty. He would go back. He had learnt enough of the present for the future. With firm steps, he walked away in darkness to contact his mind-machine. He had to get out of the place.

It was painful for him to leave all that had become part of him, in spite of the stupidity connected with them. He was like the snake charmer who comes to love his snakes.

Vihan's land did not allow harsh punishment, but even then he was worried by what awaited him back home. 'I will surely be shamed for my transgressions, but that would be a small price to get out of here. I may also be forgiven because of the knowledge that I have gained here.'

He walked deeper in darkness, thinking of future which was his real present.

'Better to be ashamed and punished to live amongst one's own than to live with pride amidst the aliens,' he thought.

His teacher had once told, 'Never be a big fish in a small pond, but always try to be a small fish in a big pond. A big fish in a small pond can be adored by the minions, but its growth stops there. To grow in life, which is the goal of human life, always strive to be among your peers or with the greats. You will not get adoration, but you will surely grow.'

Vihan was getting some adoration at Devpuri, but it had completely shut down his growth and had also taken away what had been natural to him.

He focussed on Vihan MM, his mind-machine twin, without succeeding in contacting it. He had been confident till then that reaching his machine-twin would be simple, but the world is not that simple. If he failed to get his machine, he was surely doomed to be among the folks who were like savages to him.

He focussed more but he failed.

Desperation.

Fear.

He tried harder. But there was no connect.

He let out a scream at the entrapment. He was trapped. Trapped. Completely trapped in the land and time which was not his.

'Save me!' he wailed.

There was no answer.

He cried for a long time. There was no way that he could go forward in the future, nor was he willing to go back to the past. His present had doomed him. Forever.

His eyes full of tears, he looked all around helplessly, when he saw a bull staggering towards someplace. In desperation, he followed it. It was the bull of the park, whom Divi fed *chapatis* daily.

Vihan followed it from a distance.

# 16

# THE ETERNITY

Mountains are so like humans: beautiful from a distance, but menacing, and even dangerous, when close.

My life and deeds have brought me to this mountain peak which has been the launchpad to eternity for those who find the burden of self too heavy to carry. Over the years, this peak has served the city silently by liberating many from that burden.

Here I am today to accept the services of this Karma Yogi whom many call 'The suicide point', but which actually is 'The Liberating Point'; the event horizon for the living.

Down below, flows the river that is partner to this peak in the great liberating act. The rivers are the arteries and veins, rolled into one, of the physical body of the country. These fulfil the want of the land and also take away the unwanted from it. Like the veins in the body, this river has carried away a lot of the dirt of humanity.

Intense life makes existence heavy. Unfortunate is the person who has not felt the burden of existence too heavy to carry, for it means that he has lived a superficial life of flitting from event to event and person to person. One problem with intense life, however, is that it craves novelty, and when it fails to get that, it sinks into insipidity, which can be killing, as has happened with me. Of course, I am not alone in that.

In recent times, the river has worked overtime. More people have been out here to hasten the ultimate of intensity-boredom duo. Poor river! The life-giving water that it carries to the plains also has to cleanse the pain of the failed.

I sat alone on that peak in the light dark night, regurgitating the events of my life which was not a waste, but also was not worth living all over again. The flow of my past in the present was quite rapid like the flowing waters of the river thousands feet below that has served as conveyor of the garbage that fell from the peak. However, unlike the river that serves people, my life was not of much use to any, in spite of its intensity and rapidity.

Entry and exit are of significance for those who matter, but my entry in life had been largely unnoticed. I am now here to set things right by making my exit a spectacular event – at least for myself. In anticipation of the great event I clapped, for there was no one within miles to boo or wow at my exit.

It was 10.10.10 of 10.10.

I had twenty-five seconds more to bear the burden of breathing. I had chosen this time to synchronize my departure with the clock timings that I had seen all my life in advertisements of all types of clock – cheap, expensive, light, heavy, indigenous and foreign. This particular time has the air of socialism that proffers not to discriminate. I would make my exit at the time chosen by ad-executives all over the world. That way, I will be one with a major success story.

I walked slowly the last few steps that separated me from my great achievement. Did I feel trepidation at the prospect of looming loss? No.

Since my childhood, I had watched nature with the pride of the owner, knowing that I was the master of it. The Earth turned round under my feet and the sky was a hemisphere centring around me. Whenever I walked, the centre above me moved, always keeping me as the focus, the way an umbrella keeps the head in the centre of a person walking with it. The feeling that I am the centre of the universe and that I stand on top of the globe, was intoxicating.

The reality hit me hard when a friend, curse be upon him, told me how he too saw the globe under his feet and the sky centring his head. I was devastated. But I moved on.

I found new persons, objects and events where I was the centre. I succeeded. One good thing about the education system is that it fills you with enough arrogance to make you feel the master of the universe when you are not even fit to be the slave of its slave.

My secure feelings about me being the centre of wherever I was or with whomsoever I was, was punctured now and then by the unintending cruel. Finally I was at the end of my egocentric world; there was nothing more left where I could feel myself to be the centre.

So, here I stand to make myself the centre of death. Finally I have the achievement from which no one can dislodge me.

How wrong I was!

Sound! Yes, there was this sound of footsteps. Rapid. Disturbed. Angry.

A mind can spontaneously recognize a similar mind, be that lustful or wise. I had read stories about great sages who could know by looking at the face of a prodigious disciple that he had acquired spiritual wisdom. I too could recognize the murderous intent, even though that was aimed at oneself, in the mind of the newcomer.

I shuddered when I looked at the new arrival. She was so young! So impressionable.

What might have brought her here? She was yet to experience the world and was yet to work out her karma. And here she was, at the place where no one with the least love for life ventures even at daytime.

I forgot that my moment of reckoning would pass within a few seconds. The one mega event of my life would become a mere hiss if I did not complete the job when I had intended to.

A man is a combination of cruelty and compassion towards all, including oneself. I was being cruel towards myself by deciding to end myself. On the other hand, I was filled with compassion towards this young lady whose motives were clearly not compassionate towards herself. I cried out, 'Hey sister! Stop. What are you up to? Mind your steps. Please!'

'I am not your sister, so don't dare address me like that. If you are keen to have a sister, then go and ask your Pa to father you one.'

God! What language!

I looked at my watch. My chosen moment of 10.10.35 had passed. I felt stupid. Even my death was not going to be spectacular, as I had so much wished for.

With my low camphored because of my loss, my compassion turned into anger. Human beings are strange in matters of emotion reversal too; you can never be sure when a person's emotions will turn into their opposite. To do so, one does not even have to be whimsical. I was now all fury towards this stupid specimen of humanity who had ruined the greatest event of my life. What an intrusion! They can't even let you die in glamour.

I wanted to hit her hard. I even thought of helping her do what she had come here for, by giving a kick at that part of the body that must not be mentioned in civilized society. I screamed at her mentally, 'You lost ET with a broken antenna!' My screams, however, did not come out. I remembered how I had screamed all my life at people without any favourable results for me.

Her verbal explosions continued first against me, then against the world, then God and finally settled on her mom. She plastered each of them with expressions rarely heard in cultured society, although she appeared to be from a dignified family. I felt sorry for her creative talent with words which she could have used for better purpose.

Life is so strange! Here I was waiting to end myself, and instead I got down to saving someone else. How worried her parents must be, I thought. Children can be so cruel towards their parents.

'We both will jump together, friend. But let us first share our stories. It is not a good idea to die prematurely without letting the world know the story of the great sacrifice,' said I. 'You must be lonely in life, but you can be now happy that you have company in your death.'

A person with a friend will not think of ending herself, I had expected.

'Be with yourself! What makes you think that you can have that privilege, you junk head?'

What temper! This was the result of present education and culture.

'It is not a good idea to die with words in your belly. Do share your story, and then we can jump together.'

Before the young lady could respond, probably more harshly, I saw a young man approaching the site. He introduced himself as Kratu.

Kratu had decided to leave the world behind and go back to his way of life: meditation. He had given enough hints to those who had been with him. It was not his fault if they missed to see what was coming in their life. Or, rather, what was going away.

'Having fresh air, I suppose?' asked Kratu in general.

'You can say that,' said she. Her resolve delayed for a while, she was calming down a bit. This is one thing that I have learnt in life that if one could delay the action-reaction time, a lot of garbage can be avoided from piling up.

He introduced himself. He was too full of cheer to have the same idea about life-death as I had just then. He was neither desperate nor despondent: the two triggers for the extreme.

Silence is the sign of maturity. Kratu seemed to have understood the situation, but he never said a word about it, unlike others who might have started sermonising or screaming like, 'Hey, what do you think you are doing, standing at the suicide point?' I started admiring him.

'Now tell me friends, do you want to narrate your stories, or you want to hear from me? I am comfortable with both,' said he smilingly. I wondered if anything could trouble him ever.

'You are a babbler, it seems.'

'If you say so, young lady. How about if we sit down and have a free pass at stories from our lives?'

His requests were like commands. We sat down and then he started narrating stories that seemed to entertain and also uplift the mood. The stories were new to me. The girl too seemed lost in the story.

My watch showed eleven when we saw a *babaji* walking up the hill.

'Is that you Bhu Baba?' laughed Kratu.

Bhu Baba was out from the jail after some years. Not being brave enough to face the public, with head hung in ignominy, he had decided to end his story.

'How do you know me?'

'You won't recognize me but you know me well: the boy who gave you the snake in return of the powers that he took away from you,' saying so, Kratu got up and touched the feet of Baba.

Let me tell you, now that I am narrating the story, I had found it very unusual that Kratu made *pranams* to Baba. Now, however, I feel that the gesture of Kratu speaks for Indian culture and also of his own values.

The Baba clenched his fist in anger, 'I lost everything that I valued after the incident. All these years I have prayed to God to send the worst on you, the imp. How I prayed that you end up as a worm in a gutter! Now I get some satisfaction at the thought that you are here on your way to eternity. Prayers do not go in vain.'

How quickly we conclude to our advantage!

Kratu laughed, 'Thank you *baba* for praying for me. I myself do not get much time to get connected with God. Even the Vedas have prescribed that if you have to be angry at someone then do it through *yajna*. At least you were connected.'

'You know about the Vedas also?'

Before Kratu could answer, the girl interrupted, 'Snake? What snake? Where it is?'

We were interested in hearing the story, to which the grumpy *baba* said, 'Leave it.'

'Why leave it *baba*? Here we are enjoying stories from the lives of each other,' laughed Kratu. He then told us the story in short. Forgive me, but even I could not stop laughing out loud. I think, the girl too smiled, but I am not sure.

One problem with suicide is that you cannot commit it in public unless your goal is to draw attention to some issue. We had come there with that idea in mind, but now it was difficult for any one of us to perform the act for which we were there. The situation appeared funny to me. It was like the stage was ready, actor and audience were there, but the act had to be abandoned. Pretty sad!

Before Baba could comment anything further, we were all surprised see an old bull staggering up the mountain, leading a young man behind it. It was evident that the bull was having difficulty in making the gradient.

The gentleman had his hand wrapped in bandage. I thought that the bull had gored him, so in anger he had brought it here to push it to eternity. The rage of human beings usually borders lunacy.

The sight made everyone laugh. 'We are having a suicide party here!' said Kratu with his infectious laughter. The girl too laughed. Baba, conscious of his age and state, stood serious.

'Who is taking whom and where?' asked Kratu to the bull and its companion.

'I am just following the bull. I don't intend to go anywhere,' said Vihan and then just mentioned his name. We were not sure if he had come to join us in the liberating act.

'Come, let us sit down and share our stories,' said Kratu. 'Let us light a fire. October can be quite chilly here.'

'I do not want prying ears on my private affairs,' said the girl.

'You are so correct philosophically! But we are now a family, bound by the common act of running away from the world. So treat us not as public, young lady.'

'Whatever! I am not going to say a word. I will do what I want.'

How do you treat a demanding kid? There is no clear answer to that. May be through discipline, or may be through indifference. Allowing space is the worst possible way to handle such people. The Second World War could have been avoided only if people had stopped the appeasement policy towards Hitler. And, what are these demanding kids other that a Hitler? Nothing. Hitler was a grown-up child and every child is a baby Hitler.

Kratu had seen the world, as I would know later. Ignoring her, he collected some twigs, I gave the lighter and a fire was lit. We tried to be as comfortable as we could. The girl too joined. Who would let go of privileges?

In hindsight, was it fair for us, the suicide party, to want comfort at the time of taking the extreme step? Why bother with the small luxuries when the comfort of liberation waits ahead? But we are we; we do the craziest of things most of the time.

'Oh no!' I screamed in delight at the approach of another gentleman. He was in kurta-pyjama; a casual dress, and at times of the failed philosophers and poets in India.

'Come on, the party is now a crowd! *Jai ho*!' shouted Kratu. 'Believe me friends, I have seen the world, but this is one of the funniest moments of my life.'

'What have you seen of life? You are hardly older to me,' said the girl.

'Looks are often deceptive, sister.'

To my surprise, the girl did not object being addressed like that. I wonder what Kratu, whose answers had an originality about them, might have said if the girl had burst out the way she had done with me.

The new one was Vyasa Bharati, the poet: a scribbler, or at the best a chance poet.

'What did you say your name was, sir?' asked Vihan, with disbelief dripping from his words and expressions.

'Vyasa Bharati, young man. I am a poet who is not valued by the world. So, I have come here with my collection to pour them down in the stream of infinity. Someday, somewhere, my thoughts will reach the right ears through the waves of the infinity. What do I care now? I may even let myself float with my creation. After all, creator and creation are not different. How does it matter if I leave or die once my creation is gone?'

'Are you sure that you are Vyasa Bharati, the poet?' asked Vihan again.

'Why do you doubt my identity, young man? People down below doubt my talent and up here you doubt my identity. Why this cruel joke?'

'It is not that, sir. You are great. That is what I meant.'

Kratu looked at Vihan with curiosity. 'Can we hear your story, Vihan?'

'There is nothing in my story. My present and past are dead.'

'Surely then you have a future. Do tell us.'

Before Kratu could say anything, there was interruption. This time the girl laughed out the loudest at the new arrival.

It was Aswin, the flute player. After his performance and getting licked by the unworthy he had walked around Devpuri for a while, and then had come up to this point, without knowing why or how of his act.

'Aswin ji! I was at your programme today. What a wonderful flautist you are!' cried out Vihan and ran towards him.

It was one in the morning.

Company is the panacea for dejection. Aswin, dejected though he was, seemed to feel good in the company of people, for no special reason. Probably, our common purpose had created the level of concentration of the place to such extent that it suited Aswin's basic requirement for performance.

'Welcome, brother, welcome!' It was Kratu.

Vihan narrated excitedly what had happened in the evening. Kratu listened intently to the description. Slowly a change started coming over him. The joviality left him to give its place to seriousness. I had not expected such a mood change in him.

'What did you say the name was?' asked he.

On hearing the name a second time, he got up and held the hands of Aswin. A strange seriousness overpowered all of us. It was the weight of a gestation ready to give birth to something big. We felt weighed down, squeezed and becoming small. This smallness was like the sand particles in front of the pyramids, one complementing the other. There was a sense of greatness in our smallness.

Aswin trembled, as if in a trance. Kratu whispered something in his ears, to which Aswin kept nodding his head. His acts seemed more and more to be controlled remotely. Probably by some power about which I was not aware. We watched in silence.

Exchange of whispers.

Finality.

Kratu left Aswin's hands, made him sit, and let out a sweet laughter, the like of which I have never heard. His smile seemed to be dancing all around in a physical form, and it seemed to refuse to go. Believe me, I have never seen that enchanting smile ever, and I can assure you that I have seen life.

Aswin was still trembling all over.

'Let me tell you a story,' began Kratu.

We all sat silently, waiting for the pregnant silence to bear words. And then he started, slowly, softly, with his usual laughter gone. The story continued for the rest of the night, in which he narrated the story of Aswin's death and how he had been searching for him through all these lives.

Honestly, it was a mesmerising story.

'You are such a great storyteller, sir,' said the girl after it was over. 'Do you think that, we, the cybergen, will believe the garbage that you have been dishing out to us?'

'Fast food, fast life. What else you, the whatever-gen folks know?' smiled Kratu with the strength of one who knows otherwise. He was not being derisive or contemptuous.

Others were not as doubting as the girl.

Aswin asked humbly, 'I am most willing to accept your story if you can tell me how to find Usha?'

Kratu laughed with a gentle laughter. He was debt free; free of the responsibility of his words to his friends. He said, 'That is your problem, friend. My responsibility, born of my words of affection to you, ends here. If you feel responsible for Usha, then go search her out.'

Unknown to them, Usha was absorbed in her, *'Ta ta thai thai.'*

'Going by your story, it may take thousands of years,' hazarded Aswin.

'What is a thousand years in the eternity of existence, brother? Caged in our bodies, we think that life begins with it and ends with it. A bird trapped in its cage thinks the space to be just that much, without ever realising what space truly means. Think beyond the cage and you will see the infinite space waiting for you.'

'Suggest something. You seem to know so much.'

'Go back to your place, brother, and dedicate your life to singing like a yogi. From the powers that you gain through your *sadhana*, you will find Usha the way I found you.'

Vihan was impressed. Genuinely. It showed on his face.

'Let me see what happened to your hand, Vihan.' Saying so, Kratu held his hand playfully, and then let out a pure and joyful laughter.

'Sorry, sir. Why are you laughing at his wound?' asked the girl.

'I know it, he knows it,' smiled Kratu with a strange joy.

Vihan stayed silent. 'Why invite trouble and ridicule?' thought he.

There was silence for a while, and then Kratu said, 'I am the past, these all are present and you are the future, Vihan. And see how we all are tensed in the present! What else can be funnier?'

None of us understood what Kratu was telling.

'Will someone explain what is happening here? Who is Vihan? And who is this bull? And what is this Cock and Bull story about? Or, should it be Vihan and bull story?'

'Wait, wait.'

Kratu sat silent for a while and then he began with a determination that one usually sees only with great warriors before a great fight. 'Allow me to say a few things to you all.'

'Only you have been talking, mister.' The young lady was truly unstoppable.

'Eternal separation alone is true on this Earth, everything else falls short. Death will come to each one of us, even if we do not want, so give life a chance.'

Another silence. He was addressing all of us.

'Death is not the end but a mere link in the chain. When you die, your story does not start afresh but continues the way it was. Life is the great chance, the great platform that allows one to improve and move ahead. Make use of this opportunity to walk on the road to greatness. Greatness is the goal. Nothing short of it will do for anyone of us. Each one has to be established in greatness. That is life.'

There was a power in Kratu's words that made our minds go plastic. Even the girl was not objecting.

'Bharati ji, go back to your poetry and dedicate yourself to *Kavya*, the art of poetry, without caring for fame and fortune. Merge in silence; complete silence. From there, emerge once in a while with gem of words that can last eternity. Go back and give up your struggle to arrange words to pass off as poetry.'

'You are insulting me, sir,' said Bharati.

'Vyasa Bharati ji, I have nothing to gain from this world, nor do I have anything to lose here. So, why should I insult you or even make fun of you? The chance meeting here, as always in the world, is an opportunity for you to open up your locked possibilities. Let this not go waste. You may have to wait for a very long time till such an encounter knocks at your psyche again.'

Kratu moved a step forward and touched the poet's hand. Bharati went silent. I felt that some kind of change came over the poet and he agreed to do what he was told to do.

He then turned to Vihan and whispered, 'Come with me to learn meditation. You have lost your present in our present. You can regain that through your mind power and then reconnect with your folks to go back.'

I was the lucky one to hear that and understand.

'Are you sure, sir?' asked Vihan.

'As sure as sun rises in the east. *Na anyah pantha vidyate*; no other path exists, brother. One achieves everything in life only through concentration. You too can regain your lost glory through that. For that, you have to come with me.'

Vihan had no other plans to work out, so he agreed.

The bull had been looking at Kratu with sad eyes. At least that is what I was imagining.

Kratu got up and sat by the side of the bull, patting it lovingly, 'You have been the great patriarch of the bovine family of Devpuri. Don't let your mind be swayed by your memories. You will then be at peace. Think of Nandi, your own image, as divine. Know that Lord Shiva will not ride anything ordinary. Think of your own image at the temple day and night, and you will be free of your pain. Here, I touch you with all my blessings.'

The bull seemed to understand him. He nodded his head. Kratu loving embraced his neck. I am not sure, but I felt that the bull had tears in his eyes.

Kratu then went to Bhu Baba. 'Baba, I offer my respects to the tradition to which you belong. For the same reason I made *pranams* to you too. Yes, you have suffered, no doubt. But know that every suffering is the conflagration that burns down the dross in one's personality.'

Baba stayed silent.

'Now find a suitable place and get established in *tyaga*; a complete giving up of everything for God, a complete surrender. Believe me, you are very much capable of doing that. It was to that purpose that I had taken away your magical powers. Now be devoted to your spiritual growth and help others on the path. Never again look back or else you will have to face worse.'

Baba stayed silent, but his face reflected his resolve to do that.

Kratu then looked at the girl and said, 'Suicide is not the gateway to peace but is the trapdoor to hell. Go back, build your strength by loving something or someone, without wanting, expecting or accepting. Want nothing, accept nothing. Believe me, you will become great.'

'Yes, I am the last one left for you to sermonise. Right?'

The darkness was becoming lighter. Devpuri, at distance below, was waking up to a slow start of the day. There was not much time left.

Kratu smiled and said, 'You are not convinced of what I said. Now let me show you something.'

Before the girl could know what was happening, Kratu touched her between her eyebrows. The girl went silent, with her eyes looking wild. That very instant she landed with Kratu in the spiritland, which was still ruled by Pret Vardhan. He was indeed serving a long time!

'Is that you, rascal?' said Pret Vardhan to Kratu. 'I told you not come here ever again, you worm of the living-dead sphere.'

Isn't it interesting in life that we remember negative things more clearly than all the positive things that might have happened to us? This rascal of a king enjoyed all the privileges of the land, and yet he had not forgotten the slight from Kratu.

'I have brought someone for you,' said Kratu in humour to Pret Vardhan, and pointed at the girl.

'I can see that. Is that another joke from you?'

'No, it is a future resident for your land.'

The girl looked around in terror. The filth and foul of Earth was there in hugely magnified forms. So was the negativity. Unknown to her, Viswakarma was also busy creating cells in the Cosmic Correction Centre for such demanding ones.

'How terrible this king, or whatever he is, looks!' whispered the girl, clutching tightly Kratu's hand. She trembled all over.

'Horrible too. I have been here in the past.'

'Please let us run back.'

'We can't as long as you are suicidal, dear.'

'What is she saying?' asked Pret Vardhan.

Suddenly he brightened up. 'Here is a deal. If you promise to leave this place silently, I will then make this girl my seven hundred and third wife. The ladies have always been in such short supply here. And if you don't agree to that, then....'

Before he could complete what he intended to say, the girl screamed in revulsion and terror.'

Before we could react, she ran down the mountain, 'MOMMY!!! Save me!'

I never met her again.

Kratu narrated the episode to us.

The bull had been sitting there, devoid of any energy. We wondered what would happen to it, in spite of Kratu's words. Kratu sat by its side, tapped its back, and said, 'Get up, O ride of Lord Shiva. May you have the strength to reach the park!' Miraculously, the bull got up. He was ready to walk back. His happy look seemed to be inviting. Anyone could join him in the journey back to Devpuri.

'What will you do, Kratu?' asked Aswin with genuine love and concern.

'My work is done. Now I will find a spot to be in the contemplation of the infinite. If the Lord wants, He will liberate me, or else He will send me to serve His creation. Either way it does not matter with me now. I am debt free. Now you go back.'

Kratu embraced Aswin. There were tears of meeting and separation.

The girl was coming back. At least that is what seemed to be. This time she was being led by a dog.

No, it was not the same girl. It was Anvi, as I was to know a little later.

Unlike her parents, Anvi had a premonition that something unpleasant was happening in her life, centring her dear brother. She had tried asking Kratu about it, but he had laughed it away. 'Why complicate matters?' was the general attitude of Kratu.

Around midnight on the day of this event taking place, when Kratu was well on his way to wherever he was going, Anvi got up with a jerk from a nightmarish dream in which she saw that her brother had left her. With trepidation, she went to have a word with Kratu, but to her horror, she found that Kratu was not in his room, even though he herself had said goodnight to him a while ago.

Deciding not to alarm her parents, she ran to a neighbour who was close to the family and asked for Jackie, their Alsatian dog with whom Kratu had been close.

'Please do not ask me anything. Just let me have Jackie for a while. Please.'

The good-natured uncle let her have the dog.

Alsatian dogs are such a fine breed in smelling out people. After the routine hints given to him, Jackie started moving in circles, confused at too much of Kratu's smell everywhere. Anvi held on to the leash and ran after him. If Jackie's movements were to be believed, Kratu seemed to be present throughout the city. And much more at the park where he had met Divi.

'Where all you have been, *bhaiya*?' cried Anvi in pain. 'And we never knew of all this!'

Jackie finally got the scent trail that led towards the suicide point. Initially, Anvi was a little scared, but then her love for brother overpowered her fear. She ran through the tunnel of streetlight amidst the overpowering mountains of darkness all around. When she reached where we were, the light was becoming bright.

On seeing Kratu, Jackie ran and jumped at him affectionately and barked furiously and licked at his face lovingly at the accomplishment. Kratu patted his head.

*'Bhaiyaaaa,'* shouted Anvi, running just behind the dog, and held Kratu in a tight embrace. There was something moving about the scene. Probably, it seemed to say that she was not going to leave him ever.

It took me some seconds to realize that they were brother and sister. 'Ah! Even God has feet of clay,' thought I. In these past hours, I had started seeing Kratu as God, who was beyond the affairs of the world. It did not occur to me that he too had a father, mother, sister.

Embarrassment for us.

What do you do at such moments which are awkward and yet not? When Jesus was informed that his mother and brothers waited outside where he was talking, he had famously replied, 'Who is my mother, and who are my brothers?' How might the crowd have reacted to that? Such was our plight.

Courtesy demanded that space be given to those who were with the master in his journey through life. We moved away to a little distance. We could see them but could not hear the words.

'You cannot do this, *bhaiya*. What crime, what sin, have we committed to deserve this?'

'I am not committing suicide, Anvi; I am only on my journey.'

'That I know. You are not a foolish passionate to do that. But it breaks my heart to think that you are leaving us for whatever reason.'

Silence.

Severe sobbing.

'Tell me, brother, every story that you had told me when I was a kid, was about you only, *na*?'

'You are still a kid.'

'Just tell me what I asked. This is one last favour that I ask for,' sobbed she uncontrollably.

'You are free to conclude, Anvi. Some questions are best left unanswered.'

Anvi was inconsolable. I wondered how my 'God' was going to break this bond of tears.

'Calm down, Anvi,' saying so, Kratu patted her head softly. She calmed down to the state of soft sobs.

He then said his final words, 'Be great in your own right, sis. Take up either dedication to knowledge, or creation of wealth for the society, or service to others, or give up all for the world. Take up one or more of these, and become blessed in life. We all have to do it, Anvi. Now compose yourself.'

Anvi continued sobbing.

We, the crowd of the unwanted, watched how Kratu was moving away with ease from those who wanted him, loved him.

Tears welled up in my eyes thinking of Anvi's searing pain. Was I getting soft?

Kratu again broke the spell. 'Hello, Vihan! Come, let us make a move.'

Bhu Baba also wanted to go with Kratu. He and Vihan then joined Kratu to go towards the depth of the mountain. We, the remaining, turned towards Devpuri. I led the bull back. We walked slowly, hoping to meet Anvi again on our way back.

Anvi stood on the spot, watching Kratu go away till her tears completely blurred her vision.

# ACKNOWLEDGEMENTS

It took me more than ten years of contemplative writing to complete *Kratu*. Some of the ideas incorporated in it came floating to me more than twenty years ago! To be fortunate enough to get those ideas and to put them together in a comprehensive manner would not have been possible without the very special grace of God. I bow my head to the Lord of all, in all humility, for being an instrument in His hands.

My heartfelt thanks to my great friends, monks, and non-monks, whose love and care for me can never be repaid! Their kind help and support over the years has resulted in my being able to serve the cause of Indian religious-literary culture.

My special and heartfelt thanks to Sri Ajay Nayak, IAS (retd.) who has been a great inspiration behind all my works. This work owes special thanks to him. He suggested many conceptual and structural changes in it and went through the manuscript at every stage of the creation of this book.

My excellent friends, Dr Hema, Sri Dibyajyoti Chatterjee, and Sri Rajshekhar have been pillars of support in my life. More than that, in spite of their hectic professional life, they helped me immensely by going through the manuscript at different stages of production and listening to my uninterrupted outpourings whenever I wanted.

Ms Shiwangi has been with me like a doting mother through my good and bad days. I, as also this work, owe massively to her. Thank you, Shiwangi for being there when no one seemed around. Her husband Sri Devmurty ji, a great friend of mine, too has been vocal in praise and support of my work.

Sri Avinash Singh has been the big pillar of support to me in every kind of need. Special thanks to him.

Sri D.N. Gautam, former Director General of Police, Bihar, has been a great well-wisher of mine and has helped me hugely in honing my skills at writing since my *Tiya* days. My gratitude to him for his unconditional support from the day that we first met.

Mrs Payal Garg has been a great fan of my work since my *Tiya* days. She has been untiringly trying to make my works popular. Thanks to her unselfish support.

I take this opportunity to express my gratitude to my noble friend Dr Rashmi Paraskar Sovani, from Nagpur, who is an eminent professor of English and also a master at dance. She tutored me in the basics of dance steps for this book and prodded me over the years to complete the book.

Sri Ajey Ranade, IPS, has been associated with this work for a long time. He loved the manuscript and encouraged me in various ways when I was working on this book.

Mr Shyam Anand Jha, from Muzaffarpur, who is associated with management teaching, has taken a lot of responsibilities that I was supposed to carry. Without his active support even my monastic life would not have been possible. Thank you, sir.

The manuscript of this book was read and re-read many times by a number of my good friends. Of them, the more involved ones were Sri Amit Ray Chowdhury, Sri K. Gopalakrishnan, Sri Biswanath Bose, Dr Gurmeet S. Narang, Sri Arpan Chakraborty, Mrs Piyali Datta, and Ms Priyanka Dutta. Thank you all for being and bearing with me on other fronts too. My creative pursuits owe a lot to your continued support. You all deserve individual thanks, but lack of space prevents me from doing it.

Every work of mine owes special thanks to Sri Abhayananda ji, former Director General of Police, Bihar, and his scholarly wife. They have been the fountainhead of support for me for more than three decades now. Soft spoken, the couple has inspired me by their saintliness and silent encouragement. Thank you.

My friends Sri G. Sreenivas, Sri Siddharth Baskhor, Sri Nabin Chandra Ghosh, Sri Amit Kumar Chatterjee, Sri Anibrata Sen, Sri Anupam Mukherjee, Ari Arup Kar, and Sri Buddhadev Das have been supporting me unflinchingly for years. Thanks to you all.

My good friends, Sri Rajdeep Mukherjee of Pan Macmillan India and Sri Prasun Chatterjee, publisher of the book, have been very kind to bear with me patiently during the formative stages of the book and also during its production. Thank you so much!